USA TO. _____ _____

DALE MAYER

Evidence in the Echinacea

Lovely Lethal Gardens 5

EVIDENCE IN THE ECHINACEA:
LOVELY LETHAL GARDENS, BOOK 5
Beverly Dale Mayer
Valley Publishing Ltd.

ISBN-13: 978-1-773361-49-9
Print Edition

Books in This Series:

Arsenic in the Azaleas, Book 1

Bones in the Begonias, Book 2

Corpse in the Carnations, Book 3

Daggers in the Dahlias, Book 4

Evidence in the Echinacea, Book 5

Footprints in the Ferns, Book 6

Gun in the Gardenias, Book 7

Handcuffs in the Heather, Book 8

Ice Pick in the Ivy, Book 9

Jewels in the Juniper, Book 10

Killer in the Kiwis, Book 11

Lifeless in the Lilies, Book 12

Murder in the Marigolds, Book 13

Nabbed in the Nasturtiums, Book 14

Offed in the Orchids, Book 15

Poison in the Pansies, Book 16

Quarry in the Quince, Book 17

Revenge in the Roses, Book 18

Silenced in the Sunflowers, Book 19

Toes in the Tulips, Book 20

Lovely Lethal Gardens, Books 1–2

Lovely Lethal Gardens, Books 3–4

Lovely Lethal Gardens, Books 5–6

Lovely Lethal Gardens, Books 7–8

Lovely Lethal Gardens, Books 9–10

About This Book

A new cozy mystery series from USA Today best-selling author Dale Mayer. Follow gardener and amateur sleuth Doreen Montgomery—and her amusing and mostly lovable cat, dog, and parrot—as they catch murderers and solve crimes in lovely Kelowna, British Columbia.

Riches to rags. ... Controlling to chaos. ... But murder ... well maybe ...

Doreen's success at solving murders has hit the news-wires across the country, but all Doreen wants is to be left alone. She has antiques to get to the auction house and a relationship with Corporal Mack Moreau to work out, not to mention a new friendship to nurture with Penny, Doreen's first friend in Kelowna, and Doreen doesn't want to ruin things.

But when a surprise accusation won't leave Doreen alone—about Penny's late husband George's death and made by one of the men Doreen helped put away—she thinks that maybe it can't hurt to just take a quick look into her new friend's past.

Before Doreen knows it, she's juggling a cold case, a closed case, and a possible mercy killing ... along with cultivating her relationships with Penny, Mack, and Doreen's pets: Mugs, the basset hound; Goliath, the Maine coon cat, and Thaddeus, the far-too-talkative African gray parrot. And while Mack should be used to Doreen's antics by now, when she dives into yet another of his cases it's becoming increasingly hard to take ...

Sign up to be notified of all Dale's releases here!
https://geni.us/DaleNews

Chapter 1

In the Mission, Kelowna, BC
Sunday Afternoon ... the same day she closed her last case

IT HAD BEEN such a rough day, and it wasn't over yet. Doreen groaned. At least her incident with Hornby was in the past. Although today was the same day of that Hornby incident, she felt like this was a whole new beginning. Then she'd said that many times since her soon-to-be-ex-husband had replaced her with his newest arm candy—her former divorce attorney no less.

Although it was hard to be upset about that now. If she'd stayed in her marriage with her controlling husband, she'd never have had all the wonderful experiences she'd had since moving to her new house, her grandmother's old house. And all the cases Doreen had solved since arriving in Kelowna, well, ... she'd helped bring closure to a lot of people.

And now maybe one more—Penny—although Doreen still struggled with Hornby's accusations that Penny might have killed her husband. Doreen could toss it off as sour grapes from a man heading to prison for the rest of his life, but what if there'd been a grain of truth to it?

Mack had finally gotten a hold of Penny, given her the official account as to her missing brother-in-law—now confirmed as murdered by Alan Hornby—and she'd come home from visiting a friend in Vernon. As soon as she'd hit town, she had walked to Doreen's place. When Doreen opened her front door, Penny threw her arms around her.

"Thank you so much for getting me answers," Penny cried out and hugged her again. After a moment, she stepped back and said, "I'm so sorry. I didn't mean to run out on you. But I didn't know what that horrible man meant to do. I couldn't stick around long enough to find out."

"It's okay," Doreen said. "Hornby can't hurt you again."

Needing to walk and talk, both of them still too keyed up to just sit inside, they strolled along Doreen's backyard as Doreen gave Penny all the details. When their questions and answers ran out, Penny noticed the large garden beds along the side fence. "This will be lovely," she said, motioning to a long stretch of Doreen's overgrown garden.

"I've got a long way to go to get it back to what it was when Nan lived here," Doreen said. "It's a lot of work."

"Understood. It's the same at my place," Penny said. "And not sure I want to now. Before Johnny disappeared, I loved gardening. Then it became a way to wear off the worry and tension over the years, but after George's death …"

"I'd leave it as is," Doreen said. "You're selling, and your yard doesn't look too bad."

"And yet, selling the house feels like a betrayal of George."

Doreen looked at Penny. "Were you happy with George?"

Penny beamed. "Very happy. He was a good provider, a good man, a good husband."

Doreen didn't know if she should ask about George's death. It was an uncomfortable topic. Just because Hornby had made some accusations, that didn't mean it wasn't true but also didn't mean Hornby wasn't just causing trouble. "How did George die again?"

"A heart attack," Penny said, her face stilling. She put a hand to her heart. "He went very quickly."

Penny walked toward the rear of the property, where a large bunch of echinacea stood. The blooms hadn't opened yet, but it looked to explode with flowers soon.

"I'm sorry for your loss," Doreen said. "That must have been very difficult."

"Oh, it was," she said. "It was, indeed."

Doreen looked at the low patch of echinacea and smiled. "I remember how your plants are much bigger than mine." She motioned at her echinacea, adding, "I have all kinds of plants crowding mine. Plus my garden is full of others I need to move, like foxglove, belladonna, nightshade ..." She slid her glance sideways, checking Penny's reaction to Doreen's list of poisonous plants but saw absolutely nothing untoward. Satisfied, Doreen linked her arm with Penny's and faced her new gardening friend. "I'm glad Mack got a hold of you before you heard it elsewhere."

"I'm sure I have you to thank you for that," Penny said. "I should get home now." She looked back at Doreen's gardens as they walked toward the creek. She pointed at another clump of echinacea. "You know what? Considering we found Johnny's dagger in the dahlias at my place and then Johnny's medallion in my front yard, I won't ever look at a big clump of plants again without wondering if more evidence is hiding in it."

Doreen's mind kicked in, repeating *evidence in the*

echinacea, evidence in the echinacea. But that was not today's case. That would wait for another day. With a smile she said, "Forget all about that for now. We can talk gardening and plants and evidence another day."

Penny chuckled. "Sounds good to me. At least we have something in common."

Doreen nodded. "We do, indeed. We plant things, all kinds of seeds, even ideas we weren't aware we were planting …" Her tone was cryptic.

Penny looked at her sideways, but Doreen just smiled and suggested, "Maybe you should set up a memorial garden for Johnny now." At Penny's startled look, Doreen explained further. "I know that came out of the blue. But I was thinking, you know, as I looked at that echinacea, how you have lost both Johnny and George, and both of them loved your home."

"But I'm selling it," Penny said. "Remember that?"

Doreen nodded. "Maybe that's a nice way to leave it then, as the home you all shared together," she said. "Creating a memorial garden before you move out would be a nice thing to do for them. If the new owners rip it out, well, all fair and good. You wouldn't have to do much. Just set up two rings of rocks and a little marker stone in the center of each ring and say some kind words over it. You'll get Johnny's medallion and his knife back at some point from the police. There is that little cross as well."

Penny looked thoughtful as she stared at the creek. "You're thinking about me getting closure, aren't you?"

"I am," Doreen said, but she was also thinking of something else that just wouldn't leave her alone. "For your own sake. Plus you don't know how long it'll take to sell your house," she said. "But, if you think about it, it could be a few months or even a year. You haven't put it on the market yet, have you?"

Penny shook her head. "I couldn't while you were investigating," she said starkly. "It seemed wrong to. Now that you're done, and we know what happened ..." She shook her head. "George spent most of his adult life searching for his brother, and to think he never found out, ... but, in just a few days, look what you accomplished?"

"I'm really sorry about the long passage of time without answers," Doreen said, her voice compassionate. "I think one of the hardest things for people is to never find out the truth."

"And you did it so fast," Penny said in amazement. "That's what really blows me away. I only talked to you like, what, last Tuesday, Wednesday? And then, all of a sudden, it's Sunday, and here you are with it already solved."

Doreen didn't know what to say. While she formulated an answer, Penny burst out, "Why couldn't the police have done that years ago?"

"Because years ago, people stayed mum for a lot of different reasons. Things were different back then. People kept secrets, likely out of fear," Doreen said slowly, thinking about what it had taken for the answers to come to the surface. "And I think Hornby stayed low and out of trouble, even leaving town as soon as he could. Now that so much time had passed, he thought he was safe to return to town."

Penny said, "It makes no sense. He killed all three of those boys, for nothing."

"Yes," Doreen said, speaking slowly. "It also helped Hornby keep his secret when Susan couldn't remember anything from the car accident. She was under the influence of drugs and still hungover, so it's no wonder the cops didn't take her seriously. Yet she's the one who kept saying a multicolored vehicle was involved, whereas Alan said it happened so fast he couldn't remember anything, other than a small car. Black, he thought, but he wasn't even sure of that. Could have been dark green or dark blue. Apparently he'd been fighting with Susan."

"And, of course, it was all make-believe anyway," Penny whispered. "It's just too incredible."

"It is," Doreen said, "but, honestly, often the truth is the simplest answer of all."

"They had no DNA back then that led to any suspects. They had no digital anything back then," Penny said, "like to see if Johnny showed up in another county or whatever."

Doreen nodded. "And, of course, Alan's father stuck up for Alan, gave him an alibi, believed his son was at home. And Mr. Hornby never saw a body in the trash truck's compactor. Julie's family wasn't any better. Nobody wanted to point the finger at Alan Hornby, though nobody liked him. Even Julie had no way of knowing that an argument or picking one man over another would cause this kind of a reaction."

"But to think it was a love triangle gone wrong," Penny said in bewilderment. "And for all of it to stay a secret over all these years ... We didn't even know about Johnny's relationship with Julie."

"It may have happened twenty-nine years ago, but Mother Earth gives up her secrets eventually," Doreen said. "Think about the dagger. Think about the medallion. Think about the cross."

"No chance Johnny's body could be found, is there?"

"I doubt it," Doreen said softly but firmly. "I'm afraid that idea has to be set aside. He was placed in the old landfill. Everything there was all mulched together and reclaimed, and now a whole new subdivision has been built on top of it. I think the community of Wilden is there now."

Penny looked at her. "All those new fancy big houses in Glenmore?"

"I think so," Doreen said. "If not that area, another one nearby." She watched her friend, still trying to take it all in, to make peace with it. "Come on. You're a bit shaken up, and I need a walk anyway. Let's get you home."

"Are you sure?" Penny asked, but she looked grateful nonetheless. "I admit I'm feeling pretty shaky. Knowing that it's over, that all this that haunted us—that haunted almost my entire marriage—is over. If only you had moved to Kelowna years ago," she joked, "then George would have known what happened before he died."

"The thing is, back then, I probably wouldn't have been involved in these cold cases like I am now."

"Why is that?"

"Because I'm a different person from who I was even a few years ago," Doreen said with half a smile. She called out, "Mugs, you want to go for a walk?"

Her basset hound—who'd long lost his pedigree and his good manners that her ex had tried to instill upon Mugs—appeared, jumped up, and twirled around on his back legs. She chuckled. "Now if only we could make money with a circus act," she said. She bent down, gave him a quick hug, then pulled his leash from her back pocket to hook it on.

"You don't normally put him on the leash, do you?" Penny asked.

"No," she said. "Not since I moved here, but he is leash trained. I just figure, every once in a while, I should do it to keep him in the habit."

At that, they stepped out on the creek pathway, and a streak of orange bolted toward them. Nan's huge Maine coon cat had come with Nan's house. He was part of Doreen's family now. "Goliath, want to go for a walk?" As usual, the cat largely ignored her.

From the veranda at the back of her house, Doreen could hear Thaddeus calling out, "Wait for me. Wait for me."

Doreen chuckled. "I guess Thaddeus wants to come too." The large beautiful blue-gray parrot with long red tail feathers had also been part of Doreen's early inheritance along with Nan's house. *What would I do without them and Nan to keep me company?*

Penny seemed fascinated as Doreen squatted down, waiting for the bird to waddle to them. She stretched out her arm, and Thaddeus hopped onto the back of her hand and sidestepped all the way up to her shoulder. Once there, he brushed his beak against her cheek. She gently stroked his back. "I wouldn't go without you, big guy."

As if he understood, he nudged her a couple more times and then settled in. Just as she was about to take a step, he said, "Giddyup, giddyup."

She turned to look at him and said, "No way am I following *your* commands."

He twisted his head, looked at her, batted those huge eyes of his, and said, "Thaddeus go."

"Yes," she said in exasperation. "You can tell you'll be going somewhere," she said. "You're already on my shoulder, and we're already out of the house."

And then he seemed to settle without more arguments. As she glanced at Penny, her new friend tried to hold back her chuckles. Doreen rolled her eyes. "It's pretty bad when the bird treats me like some sort of old gray mare," she snapped. "Oh, wait." She returned to her house, reset the alarms on the front and back doors, and then rejoined her animals and Penny. "Now let's go for a walk."

"I heard the beeps." Penny glanced back at the house. "Do you always set an alarm when you go for a walk? You don't look like the nervous type to me."

"Normally I wouldn't. But I have an antiques dealer coming tomorrow to look at a few pieces," she said, carefully fudging the truth. "I would hate for anybody to go inside and help themselves."

Penny nodded. "Oh my, no. When I think of all the hours George and Nan spent arguing about her antiques ..."

"Why arguing?" Doreen asked.

"Because George thought she should sell them, and Nan said she had another plan in mind."

Doreen's heart warmed when she thought about Nan's *other* plan. "Yes, Nan was holding on to them for me," Doreen said with a wistful smile. "My grandmother is pretty special."

"Oh, she's special all right," Penny said, chuckling. "George used to come home from one of his visits, and, although he'd be brighter and full of laughter, he'd say Nan was especially crazy."

"A lot of people have told me that she fell somewhere in that realm," Doreen said. "I am afraid she's losing some of her memory now though."

"She's probably not taking all those supplements George told her about. They worked like a charm for her."

"What kind of supplements?"

Penny shrugged. "I'll take a look. I have the notes at home somewhere. George always had a fascination with natural remedies. Nan was having trouble even back then."

"And they helped her?"

Penny nodded emphatically. "Oh, yes. George used to comment on it all the time."

"If you could get me that list, that would be awesome," Doreen said. "I have absolutely no idea about supplements. And I really don't like doctors."

"No, once you deal with something like George's heart condition," Penny said, "you consider how much the medical profession actually knows. Obviously they're helpful a lot of the time, but, on some occasions, it makes you wonder if they aren't just pushing drugs."

"Exactly," Doreen said. "But if you had supplements that worked instead, that would be huge."

"I think it's the same list he gave me, so I can certainly find out when I get a moment," Penny said. "Do you think Nan would take them again?"

Doreen nodded. "Particularly if I say it was the same stuff George used to give her."

"That might work," Penny said. "Those two really did get along like a house on fire. Nan was pretty distraught at George's funeral."

"I'm sure she was," Doreen said. "One of the hardest things about getting old must be watching all your friends die before you."

"Very true," Penny said. As they walked up to Penny's house a good half hour later, Penny motioned and said, "If you want to come in for a few minutes, I can look for that list."

Doreen brightened. She'd been looking for an excuse as it was, since she had never been invited inside anyone's house in town other than Nan's retirement home and then Doreen's murderous neighbor Della's house. Doreen nodded and said, "Sure. Thank you very much." Together, the five of them trooped into Penny's home.

Chapter 2

Sunday Afternoon ...

INSIDE PENNY'S HOUSE, Doreen looked around. It was stuffed with pretty floral-patterned couches, large floral paintings and, yes, ... floral rugs. It was also pristine. "You haven't started packing, have you?"

"It's not like I've sold my house yet," Penny said in a dry tone.

As Doreen looked at Penny's big living room, it wasn't really cluttered, but it was overstuffed with mementos. "If you got a staging crew or a Realtor in here," she said, "I'm pretty sure they'll insist on all the pictures coming off the walls, all the stuff being moved off the countertops, hauling out the big hutches you've got. Realtors can be quite brutal."

Penny's jaw dropped. "You know what? I was thinking about bringing in a stager to see what they'd charge me. But it sounds like you know a lot about it."

"Not necessarily," Doreen said, "but I've watched lots of those shows on TV. And my husband did a lot of buying and selling."

"Right," Penny said.

Doreen could almost see that, in Penny's mind, those

disqualifiers just raised Doreen's status several notches. Doreen didn't understand how that worked because, of course, people should be doing their own investigation and research on this type of thing before deciding. Besides, in Doreen's mind, she should be demoted, not promoted, for her husband's activities. "Have you picked out a Realtor?"

"Absolutely. I'm going with Simi Jeron," Penny said. "I've known that family for thirty years or more."

"Oh, good," she said, "that should make it easier. Ask her about staging and decluttering when she's here."

"She's already been here once, but we haven't signed any paperwork yet."

"That's when the boom will get lowered," Doreen said, chuckling.

"I hope not," Penny said, walking into her kitchen, approaching a large cupboard and opening it up. She took out a small notebook sitting on top of the box of vitamin bottles, brought it to the kitchen table, and sat down, flipping through the pages. "Ah, here it is," she said, "a page just for Nan." She held it up and then read from it. "Vitamin D, ginkgo, B12, and I'm not sure what this other one says."

"Do you mind if I take a look?" Doreen asked, holding out her hand. Penny handed over the notebook. As Doreen looked at it, she said, "I'm not sure what that is either. May I get a copy of this?"

"We'll photocopy both sides."

While Penny made copies, the animals, although curious about the inside of a new place, didn't appear bothered. Mugs wandered; Goliath dug on the rug, his tail twitching; and Thaddeus sat quietly on her shoulder, and that worried her the most. He seemed to be huddling awfully close. She reached up and murmured to him. He leaned into her touch.

"Thanks," Doreen said as she accepted the sheets from Penny. Doreen gave the list a casual glance, wondering if Nan would even listen to her. Maybe if Doreen found the right time to speak with her grandmother. Still, she pocketed the list and followed Penny back to the kitchen, where Penny tucked the book back into the vitamins corner.

"Must've been nice that George was so interested in health," Doreen said.

"A lot of good it did him," Penny said bitterly, and she winced. "I'm sorry. I shouldn't have said that."

"I guess you're angry he died, huh?"

"Isn't that the stupidest thing?" Penny said. "Even after a year, I still look around our house, and I get mad at him. We had all these plans for retirement, all these things we would do now that he wasn't working anymore, and here he up and dies on me."

"Can't you do those things on your own?"

"I could," Penny said, "but I don't really want to. They were things we would do *together*. They were *our* plans."

"Versus *your* plans?"

Penny froze for a moment and slowly nodded. "Very insightful." She glanced at her watch and said, "Oh, my goodness. I have to run to meet someone."

"Oh, of course. Sorry," Doreen said. "We'll get out of your hair and let you get on then." Goliath had taken up a seat in the middle of George's big recliner. Doreen scooped him into her arms, and, with Thaddeus still on her shoulder, Mugs trotted behind them. "It was a nice visit," she said, "and I'm glad I had good news for you in the end. Now your life can get back to normal."

As Doreen stepped down the front steps, Penny said, "Once again, thank you. I will definitely sleep better now."

With a half wave, Doreen watched as Penny, her purse in hand, got into her vehicle, reversed out of her driveway, and headed down the street. Though Doreen knew she should leave too, she stopped on Penny's driveway. She *really* shouldn't do what she was thinking of doing. But it was pretty damn hard to talk herself out of it. With a shrug, she decided it would worry away at her, so she might as well put her mind to rest.

She put Goliath down and headed into Penny's backyard, where Johnny had had his favorite place to sit. Doreen didn't know why Penny's echinacea bed was bugging her, but she thought she'd read somewhere how echinacea was used in all kinds of medicine. It certainly wasn't—as far as she knew—a killer, but anything could be a killer if you took too much of it.

Doreen made a quick trip through Penny's backyard, mentally jotting down what was here—marigolds, lilies, calla lilies, black-eyed Susans. None were flowering yet. Daisies were with buds ... This would be a lively garden when summer hit. She really appreciated the wide variety, even a few straggling tulips. She stopped and stared at them and shook her head. "Why are you guys drooping over like that?"

She stopped to study the short stalks of an echinacea clump reaching for the sky. They wouldn't bloom for another month or two, and this bed was far too crowded for them to do well. Then belladonna and foxglove had mingled in the patch too. *Drat.* She was hoping some of these plants wouldn't be found here. So was their presence that bad? She couldn't tell. But, since the same poisonous plants lived in Nan's garden, ... possibly Nan and George had shared a love of poisonous plants as well as antiques?

Glancing around, Doreen noted how little shade the

echinacea plants would probably get during the daylight hours backed up against the fence as they were, which wouldn't help their growth. As she dropped down in front of the massive green patch—at least three feet across with dozens of plants in here—she frowned, realizing their roots would be completely twisted together. Echinacea plants loved company, particularly its own family, but, at some point, they would fight and hate each other—just like every other family unit could do.

Too-close confines caused too-much strife.

She checked the ground around the roots, unable to help herself, and realized they were also very dry. The ground was poor here, with many rocks noticeable in the soil. Even garbage. She pulled out a small piece of plastic from the edge and tossed it aside. Echinacea *could* survive in crappy soil. A lot of plants *could* survive. But the intention of a garden was not to have them survive—it was to have the flowers thrive. And again, as she glanced around the backyard, she thought what had once been Penny's pride and joy was probably just a constant source of work and bad memories now. As Doreen walked past the echinacea, she thought she saw something else burrowed in the center of one of the plants. But, from the park side of the fence, just then, a man asked, "Hey, what are you doing back there?"

She popped out of Penny's backyard gate guiltily, leaving the gate open for her animals, and plastered a bright smile on her face. "I walked home with Penny," she said, "but she had to take off. I just wanted to get a quick look at her garden. She has done so well here," she said, injecting a bright warmth to her voice.

The man looked at her suspiciously.

She looked him over, from the top of his six-foot frame

to his dirty sneakers, and held out her hand. "I'm Doreen Montgomery, and who are you?"

Reluctantly he shook her hand. "I'm Steve."

"Steve?"

His frown deepened. "Just Steve."

She nodded and said, "Well, if you see Penny, and you want to tell her that I was in her backyard, that's fine," she said. "She knows I'm a crazy gardener too. I was checking out her echinacea."

"Echinacea?" he asked doubtfully, looking at the green splotch against the fence.

"Echinacea," she said firmly. "We were talking about mine at my house earlier."

At that, his face seemed to settle, and his shoulders sagged as if with relief.

"Not to worry," she said. "I'm not a thief. I'm the one who helped solved Johnny's disappearance."

At that, awareness came into Steve's eyes. Of course Mugs's slow approach, his head lowered and moving from side to side like a pissed-off bull, drew more attention to Doreen. So did the orange streak that raced between Steve's legs, and he grinned. "Now I know who you are."

Thaddeus, not to be outdone, squawked, "No you don't. No you don't."

"Yeah, sorry about them," Doreen said. She gave Steve a quick finger wave. "And now I'll head home before my critters decide they like Penny's garden better than mine."

Steve watched as she and her animals ambled toward the creek. "Why are you walking along the creek?" he asked, calling behind her.

"Because I love it," she said. "It's my favorite place to walk."

He shrugged and said, "Nothing but dirty water down there. It's full of ducks and all kinds of waterfowl."

"Hopefully I'll see some today."

"You won't catch me walking through the water that's their toilet." And, with that, he headed off.

She walked a few more steps and turned to look back. He strode away, not having explained his presence at Penny's property. Doreen frowned and thought about that, then sent Penny a text. **Stopped to take a quick look at your echinacea plants. A stranger named Steve came up and didn't seem terribly friendly. Wasn't sure what he was doing in the park behind your place. Just a heads-up.** And she left it at that.

"Come on, Goliath, Mugs ..." Thaddeus squawked as he waddled toward her, but then Mugs came racing forward with Goliath on his heels, and, in a surprisingly quick move, Thaddeus jumped on Mugs, screaming at the top of his lungs, "Giddyup, Mugs. Giddyup, Mugs."

Doreen just shook her head with a loving smirk on her face. *My family.*

By the time Doreen had reached her little bridge that would lead to her backyard, Thaddeus had long given up riding Mugs, subsequently walking. But now he was tucked into the crook of her neck, swaying with her every step. She crossed the bridge as her phone beeped with a return text. **He's a lovely neighbor, but he doesn't like strangers. That echinacea is doing terribly. As are some of my more specialized plants. Suggestions?**

Doreen grinned. Perfect entrance to find out more. **Absolutely. Maybe we'll have tea another day and check it out.**

Anytime.

Chapter 3

Sunday Late Afternoon …

B ACK AT HER place, Mack drove up as she stood on the
front step. Corporal Mack Moreau, the most interesting man in town and the most infuriating. He followed the
legal line, even when she wanted him to bend it just an itsy-
bitsy bit. Still, she had to admire him for that stance.

He did know right from wrong, and that was more than
her devious ex had understood. As Mack walked toward her
house, he lifted the small bag he carried.

"Did you bring everything we need? Because I'm starving."

"You're always starving," he said, striding forward to the
kitchen. "I'll get started. You can make coffee."

Obligingly, she was happy to do that as she finally had
confidence in her ability to make a good cup of coffee. As she
watched Mack, he first washed his hands, and then he took
the cold pasta from the fridge. "What's in the bag?"

"Artichokes," he said with a smirk. "As ordered."

She gasped in delight and watched as he popped the top
off the jar and pulled out four of the oddest-looking things
she'd ever seen. Her smile fell away. "I don't know what

those are."

He stopped, looked at her in surprise. "Artichokes?"

She shook her head. "I'm not sure if we're talking about the same thing here," she said delicately. "Because the artichokes I know look like a pine cone."

He chuckled. "Absolutely, whole artichokes do look like that. These are artichoke hearts." He said, "Surely they didn't put the artichoke leaves into your pasta."

She frowned and said, "I don't know. What do the leaves look like?"

"Pine cone petals," he said bluntly. "Could you eat them? Or did you scrape them through your teeth?"

She shook her head. "No, I ate them as part of the dish."

"Then what they gave you were the artichoke hearts."

"Oh," she said, and, then in a small voice, she asked, "Why do pine cones have hearts?"

He looked at her, and she watched his mouth work as he tried to hold back his mirth. She glared at him, her hands on her hips, and warned, "Don't you dare."

But it was too much. He sagged into the nearby chair, his arms wrapped on his chest, and then, like a balloon that had been blown up too tight, he howled with laughter. She stomped toward him and swung her arm back, but he leveled a look at her and said, "Don't you even think about it."

She snorted and stepped back and said, "How did you know?"

When he saw the glass of water in her hand, he just stared at it. "You wouldn't really have dumped that on me, would you?"

She just watched him with the same level look, and he chuckled again. "I don't know if pine cones have hearts or not. Artichokes do," he said. "Next time, if I think about it, I will bring a whole artichoke, and we will dissect it."

"Okay," she said, happy with that. "You'd have made a good teacher, you know that?"

"It was my second career choice," he said, "so thank you."

"The public school system lost out when you went into the legal side of things."

"Let's hope I've caused more damage to the criminal world," he said, "than I would have caused to those young vulnerable minds."

She thought she knew what he meant but wouldn't worry about it. Because, all of a sudden, she saw a piece of artichoke that looked almost like what she was used to. She picked it up and delicately put it between her lips, tasting it. And then she beamed. "Oh, my goodness, this is it." And she ate the whole thing. He cut several more and moved them off to the side. She picked up one that had more leaves than the soft-heart part. She asked, "Can you eat all of this?"

He nodded. But she could see which part was the soft heart and which was the start of the inside leaves. She ate that one too, and, after it was all gone, she said happily, "That's divine."

"Can't say I've had much of them myself to know," he said, popping one into his mouth, but he nodded. "So let's start with the pasta." He pointed at the leftover spaghetti noodles. "Now we can leave them whole."

"I don't think so," she said. "They're stiff and cold and will be impossible to eat like this." She shook her head. "That's not the way the chefs made their pasta salad."

Mack grabbed a bowl, poured some olive oil in, and rubbed the noodles and the oil together with his hands. Almost instantly they separated into nice wobbly noodles.

"Now," he said, "you can chop them, or you can use scissors."

"Ah," she cried out, "I have the perfect tool." And she reached into one of the kitchen drawers and pulled out a large pair of shears. He looked at her in surprise, and she said, "Hold up the noodles."

So he held up one clump of pasta lengthwise, his fists holding opposite ends, and she snipped the pasta in between his hands so that the noodles were now in thirds. He nodded and said, "That works perfectly." With the cut noodles in another bowl, he added Italian dressing. She watched in amazement as he then added a splotch of mustard. When he had it all mixed up together, she delicately dabbed the end of her baby finger into the salad and tasted it. She beamed. "How can you just do that?"

He chuckled. "Lots of trial and error."

"Maybe lots of trial," she said, "but I highly doubt there was much error."

"You'd be surprised," he said.

With enough noodles cut for the two of them for dinner, he tossed the artichokes in on top, brought out three Roma tomatoes, cut them into bite-size pieces, and added them. He opened a can of black olives, drained it, then added half the can while Doreen watched in fascination as a meal so similar to what she used to love was created in front of her. When he brought out the feta, and she saw a solid block, she cried out in surprise.

He looked over at her. "And how does your feta normally come?"

"In perfect little squares," she said, frowning. "But that one is huge."

He nodded. "Do you have a flipper?"

She brought him a metal spatula. He looked at it and said, "Perfect." He cut a slice off the block, then cut that piece into small cubes. She smiled with delight. "You know what? If I had any idea that this is all the chefs at my husband's place used to do," she said, "then we were paying them way too much."

Mack gave a shout of laughter at that. "I don't know about that," he said, "because they were obviously very good at what they did, or your husband wouldn't have kept them around."

"True enough, but he went through one every six months or so," she said. "He really was fussy."

"I'm not surprised," he said, but he kept it to that.

Then she already knew his opinion of her ex. She wondered about bringing up Mack's brother, who'd offered to look into the mismanagement of her divorce case by her own divorce lawyer—then decided against it. She didn't want to ruin a lovely dinner.

He tossed the ingredients lightly and said, "Anything else you want in here?"

"Pine nuts," she said.

He looked over at her and said, "I didn't buy any. You didn't mention those before."

"Oh," she said and then shrugged. "Looks good to me."

"Let me check the fridge," he said. He headed there, opened the door, and spied the green onions. "Perfect." He brought one out, diced it into very small rings and tossed it on top. "Now, how about some plates?"

"I found these in the back of a drawer last week," she said, coming out with two brightly colored, almost garishly colored bowls in orange and red. "I wasn't sure what they were supposed to be, but I thought maybe they would be easier for something like this."

He chuckled. "Those are pasta bowls."

She looked at him in amazement and said, "But why ... why are they ..."

"It was a phase," he said. "Everybody had them. We would toss the pasta in a larger bowl and serve it in these."

She nodded with understanding. "Yes, that makes sense. We used silver chafing dishes at every dinner."

That raised an eyebrow, but he didn't say anything else after that. He served up their pasta salad and handed her one of the two bowls. "Where would you like to sit?"

She glanced at the kitchen table and back to him.

He motioned outside on the deck. "It's a beautiful day. Why don't we sit out there?"

Chapter 4

Sunday Late Afternoon ...

DOREEN BEAMED AND stepped outside. She set her bowl on the veranda table and walked back inside to get cutlery and water. When she returned, she found Goliath had claimed her seat. Thaddeus was on the back of her chair eyeing her bowl, and Mugs had already taken up residence underneath the table, in case something dropped.

Mack said, "We still have red wine from last night. We never did have a glass with the meal." He poured two glasses, and they sat on the deck with their pasta salad and red wine.

Doreen munched on the pasta salad and moaned in delight. "This is delicious. And so different from last night," she said. "And it was so easy. To think you cooked the noodles for two meals at the same time."

"That's just being smart with your time," he said.

She nodded and reached for the glass of wine. She lifted it up and said, "Cheers."

"Cheers," he said, "and congratulations on solving yet another case."

At that, she beamed at him, took a sip of wine, and sputtered.

He took his sip, rolled it around in his mouth, and swallowed. He placed his glass down, looked at her, and asked, "Are you okay?"

She gasped for air, nodded, and said, "But maybe you'd like my glass too."

He dumped her wine into his glass. "Absolutely."

She sighed. "I was really looking forward to that too."

"Did you not like it?"

She opened her mouth, then closed it.

He winked at her. "It's obviously not the brand of wine you're used to. I did warn you it was a cheap wine and perfect for cooking," he said. "Still, I never learned to differentiate between wines. I'm more of a beer guy."

"In that case I'd rather have a beer too," she said.

He stared at her. "You drink beer?"

She frowned. "I think so."

"You think so?"

She nodded. "At least some of the drinks I had were mixed with beer, I think," she said slowly. "And the wine is okay. I did tell you," she said in a rush, "that I didn't like *red* wines."

"Yes, you did," he said. "Maybe we'll try a white next."

Relieved, she sat back. "Yes, that would be great. I didn't mean to insult you," she said, chewing on her bottom lip.

He just smiled. "How could it insult me to know I get to have both glasses myself?" He lifted his glass.

"You can have the rest of the bottle too."

He looked at her and said, "This is the rest of the bottle."

She sighed. "I don't remember you cooking with the wine."

"I put it in the sauce, when I added the noodles to the

salted water last night, somewhere around the time Hornby was being difficult."

She curled her lip up at that. "Please tell me that he'll never get out of jail again."

"No, he won't. Not with three murders under his belt."

"What about Susan?" she asked. "Do you think we need to check on her death?"

"No," he said. "I already spoke to her doctor. Her fatal breast cancer wasn't her first bout. It had been a recurring problem for her over a good ten years. She finally lost the battle."

Doreen winced at that. "Cancer is the devil," she said softly. "I'm so sorry for her."

"The doctor said she also had a long history of drug abuse after the accident."

"As if maybe she felt guilty?" Doreen said with a nod. "As if maybe, in her subconscious, she understood what had happened?"

"I wondered that myself," Mack said. "But no way we'll ever know for sure—not now."

She nodded. "It's still sad."

"It is, indeed," he said. "So what did you find out at Penny's?" he asked out of the blue.

She almost choked. When she cleared her throat, she looked at him and asked, "What are you talking about?"

He narrowed his gaze at her. She worked hard to put that look of innocence on her face, but it wasn't working when he just narrowed his gaze a little more. Then he tapped his bowl with his fork and said, "Doreen ..."

She sighed. "You're mean," she announced.

"I'm mean?" he asked in astonishment. "This is two nights in a row I've cooked you meals."

She winced. "Okay, so now that's really mean."

He shook his head and said, "I wonder if I'll ever understand you."

"Of course you will," she said. "What's not to understand?"

"So, I'm mean for cooking you two meals," he said, "and then I'm really mean because why?"

"Because you brought it up," she explained patiently. "That was just an added little twist to the mean stake you plunged into my heart."

His lips twitched, and he chuckled. She glared at him. He held up his hands in peace. "You have an interesting turn of thought," he said.

She frowned at that. "That sounds like something Old English."

"I was trying to be nice," he said in exasperation. "Never mind. I'll eat my dinner."

"Oh, good," she said and proceeded to eat too. When she lifted her head again, he was watching her.

"You did that on purpose, didn't you?"

She stared at him and said, "I don't know what you're talking about."

Just then his phone rang. He groaned, put down his fork, pulled out his phone, and said, "What's up?"

"You need to go down to Rosemoor," said the person on the other end.

Doreen could hear the voice from where she was sitting.

The dispatcher said, "A ruckus with a couple of the pensioners."

Doreen gasped.

"Don't tell me," Mack said. "Let me guess. Nan is involved, isn't she?"

The dispatcher on the other end laughed. "Absolutely. Something to do with winning another bet, but Richie seems to think he should get half of the earnings."

"Oh, good Lord," Doreen muttered and stood. She walked into the kitchen, grabbed her purse, and said, "Hate to eat and run, but I'm gone." As she raced out the front door, Mugs barked like crazy at her sudden movements. She could hear Mack shouting behind her, "Doreen, you get back here."

Like that would happen.

Chapter 5

Sunday Evening...

DOREEN PARKED AT Rosemoor and headed toward Nan's little corner suite, taking the stepping stones as fast as she could. She landed on the back patio and tried the glass door, but it was locked. "Drat," she said. She rapped hard, but no answer came from within. She quickly made her way around the flagstones to the main front door of the retirement home just in time to see Mack pulling up.

He glared at her.

She raised both hands, palms up. "What?" she asked. "I have to protect Nan. You're not allowed to upset her." The look of astonishment on his face had her groaning. "Not that you would knowingly try to upset her ..."

He just shook his head and said, "Come on. Let's see what's going on."

"I already know what's going on," she said glumly. "Nan probably put bets on Alan Hornby."

"I did not." Nan's strident voice carried across the foyer, where at least a half dozen other residents of the home had gathered.

Richie said to Nan, "She should resolve this. She's your

granddaughter."

"Somebody called the police," Nan said, rolling her eyes. "Like we need their help."

The other residents muttered their assent.

Mack just sighed. "Somebody called the police because there was a ruckus," he said. "You can't blame me for showing up and doing my job."

Nan looked mollified. "At least you brought Doreen with you."

"No," Doreen cried out, rushing toward Nan. "I came ahead of him."

Nan looked from her to Mack. "What do you mean, ahead of him?"

"We were having dinner," Doreen said, "when dispatch called in. As soon as I heard what was going on, I raced out in front of him."

Nan's expression turned crafty. She faced Richie. "See? I told you."

Richie surprised Doreen as he clapped his hands in joy. "We'll make double the money on this one, Nan," he cried out in almost a hooting manner.

Doreen looked at Nan and then at Richie and again to Mack. "Did I miss something?"

"I doubt it. Come on, Nan. Let's have a little talk." Just then another vehicle pulled up. Mack said, "Looks like Darren is here too."

"Oh, no," Richie said. "Time for me to leave then." And he turned and tried to hustle away, but Mack grabbed him by the trailing end of his bathrobe and said, "Nope, that won't happen, Richie. If you call the police in, you'll deal with the consequences."

"We didn't call the police," Nan said. "Why would you

even think that?"

"I'm sure you didn't," Mack said, obviously striving for patience. "But, if you caused such a ruckus that the police are called, then you have to deal with the consequences."

"Why didn't you say that in the first place?" Nan asked. She looked over at Richie and grinned. "Maybe they'll cuff us and take us to a jail cell." She held out her wrists. "I've never been arrested before."

Doreen stepped forward and said, "Yes, you have, Nan."

Nan turned to her granddaughter and said, "*Shh*, you didn't have to tell him that. It was such fun last time. I just wanted to repeat it."

Richie looked at Mack and put his hands out to be handcuffed too. "If she gets to be arrested, I do too. No way I'll die without having experienced what jail is like."

Darren walked through the door, a cop Doreen recognized but didn't actually know. He took one look at Richie and said, "Granddad, what are you up to?"

Doreen snickered.

The new arrival looked at her and groaned. "Of course you'd be at the bottom of this one."

Outraged, she said, "I came to protect my poor Nan."

He snorted at that too. "The last thing *your poor Nan* needs is protection," he snapped. "She's led *my poor granddad* down a criminal path."

Doreen's jaw dropped as she watched Nan cuddle up with Richie. "Oh, good Lord," she said, "I really don't want to know what those two are up too."

"Oh, yes, you do," Mack said. He grabbed her by the shoulder and gently nudged her forward. "Remember? You wanted to get here to protect your Nan."

She glared up at him. "I might just go home and finish

my dinner," she said. "And, since you didn't finish yours, I'll eat yours too."

Nan laughed. "You two sound like an old married couple already," she said, pure delight on her face.

Richie nodded. "They do, indeed," he said. "They do, indeed."

Even Darren chuckled. "Now you're done for, because once these two get to matchmaking, you know what happens."

"They can just stop whatever matchmaking they've got in their minds," Doreen said, raising herself up to her full height. She glared down at her Nan. "Nan, you will not go there. Do you hear me?"

Nan tried to look appropriately subdued and then lost it and cracked up. She patted Mack on the hand and said, "Dear, you go home and finish your dinner. We'll be just fine here."

"I can't do that," Mack said with a heavy sigh. "As much as I wish I could. Who called the police?"

Doreen heard a faint voice. She turned to see Maisie, standing off to the side with a little finger wave.

"I did."

"And why did you do that?" Mack asked Maisie.

Maisie took a step back.

Doreen stepped in between the two of them. "Lower your voice," she ordered Mack. "Maisie is shy and easily scared."

He looked at Maisie in surprise but gentled his voice. "So, Maisie, what were these two doing that bothered you?"

She sniffled and patted her cheeks, as if not sure what to say now that all attention was on her.

"Of course it would be her," Nan muttered from behind

Doreen. Doreen spun and glared at her. Nan stuck out her tongue in response. It was all Doreen could do to not laugh. She turned again and said, "Maisie, do you want me to walk you back to your room? I'm sure all of this is pretty upsetting."

Maisie looked pathetically grateful.

"Where's your room?" Doreen asked.

"I'm down at the far end," she said.

"Good. Let me walk you there," Doreen said. "What's upsetting you?" She knew all the rest of the people gathered in the lobby watched their progress.

Maisie leaned closer and whispered, "Your Nan is not very nice."

Doreen bit her tongue on that one. "She has her moments," she said gently, "but her heart is as good as gold."

"Maybe," she said, "but I'm not so sure about that. Joe and I broke up. He wants to get back together with Nan."

Doreen looked at Maisie and saw tears in her eyes. Doreen remembered how Nan had felt when Maisie had come traipsing into her room, talking about how Joe needed his sleep *afterward*. Doreen sighed and said, "Love triangles are difficult, aren't they?"

Maisie's eyes welled up. "Yes, they are," she whispered.

They arrived at Maisie's door. She opened it up and stepped inside. Even from the doorway, Doreen had a hard time with the smells coming from the room. "You do like incense, don't you?"

"Oh, no, that's air fresheners," she said. "I absolutely love the smell of patchouli."

"Oh, how nice." The inside of Doreen's stomach twisted. If there was one fragrance she couldn't stand, patchouli was it. "Anyway, I'm sure Mack needs to talk to you because you called the police. Just tell him what you know, and it'll be fine."

"Thank you," Maisie said. "I really do appreciate your kindness."

"It's easy to be kind," Doreen said. "But please don't lie. You have a reason for saying what you need to say, and you have every right to feel safe here." As she stepped back, she saw Mack striding toward her. She motioned at the room and said, "Maisie's waiting for you."

He went to say something, but Doreen shook her head, again pointed at the open doorway. He nodded and stepped in. "So, Maisie, can you tell me what's going on here?"

Doreen smiled at his nice, strong, official voice because, even though it sounded businesslike, it was very gentle. She chuckled at that. Even Mack could be trained apparently. With that thought uppermost in her mind, she headed back to the open area where people still milled about. In fact, the numbers had doubled. She glanced around, looking for Nan, but saw no sign of her. See approached Richie, talking to Darren. "Richie, where did Nan go?"

"Probably gone to lie down, I expect," he said. "With all this ruckus going on, we all need our sleep, you know?" he said, scowling at his grandson.

Darren just pushed his hat back, pinched the bridge of his nose, and said, "And I'd be happy to go home and finish my own dinner, but every time *you* get into a ruckus here, they call *me*."

"Well, they shouldn't, should they?" Richie snapped. "They should be calling whoever is on duty."

"We're a small precinct, Granddad. When it comes to family issues, we try to leave it for a family member to handle."

"Huh. So how come Mack always comes for Nan?"

Darren grinned. "You know the answer to that."

Doreen heard Richie's comment and Darren's answer. She wanted to pipe up and ask for clarification herself when somebody else said, "I don't understand."

Richie turned and in a smug tone said, "Because Mack is always looking out for Doreen."

"Ah," commented the other resident, who Doreen didn't know. "Well, that makes sense. Those two are really an item, aren't they?"

Doreen shook her head, stepped forward, and said, "If you don't mind, I'll go see my Nan then." And she turned her back on the gossip and headed off. She really did hate gossip.

"No problem," said Darren. "Pretty sure Mack will be along in a few minutes."

Her back stiffened. She looked over her shoulder to glare at him, saw his big grin, and promptly turned and walked down the hallway to Nan. Doreen needed to do something to stop this gossip and to stop it fast. Now if only she had an idea of how to do that.

Chapter 6

Sunday Evening...

DOREEN WALKED INTO Nan's suite and sat down across from her on the small couch. "Nan, stop causing a disturbance at this place," she announced. Then added carefully, "And I want you to stop the gossip about Mack and me."

Nan poured them each a cup of tea, then looked at her granddaughter, her eyes twinkling, and said, "Do you now? And why is that?"

"Nobody likes to be gossiped about, Nan," Doreen scolded lightly. "You know that."

"I never bother about gossip," she said with an airy wave of her hand. "But you have to learn to live a little, my dear. You should care about what it is you're doing in the moment, rather than worrying about how other people will see it. Besides, people always talk. It's human nature."

Doreen's shoulders sagged. She figured this would be one of those life-lesson talks. She firmed up her tone and said, "It's nobody else's business what I do."

"As long as you keep finding bodies and solving all these cases," Nan said with a shake of her finger, "people's tongues will wag. Of course it makes sense that they'll automatically include Mack in that discussion."

Nan had a point. Doreen just didn't want to think about it. "What did you do to cause the ruckus?"

"It had absolutely nothing to do with Richie's and my discussion," she said complacently. "But smart of you to figure out Maisie made the call because she was upset with me."

"That's a waste of official city resources," Doreen said quietly. "What if somebody needed the police across town?"

"There're other cops," Nan said. "Besides, I wouldn't waste police man-hours like that. You'll have to talk with Maisie about it."

"I would," Doreen said on a groan, "but I doubt she'll listen to me any more than you are."

At that, Nan tilted her head to the side, considered the problem, and then nodded. "You're right there. Maisie does like drama."

"That was a lot of drama in the reception area," Doreen said, "between you and Richie for sure."

"Oh, dear, that's just fun. When you get to be our age, there aren't a lot of other things we're allowed to do."

"Fun?" Doreen asked. She shook her head. "I admit that fun has a different meaning for different people ..."

"Of course it does," Nan said supportively. She patted Doreen on the hand and smiled at her. "For you, solving cases is fun. But so many people wouldn't want anything to do with that. They wouldn't want to get into trouble, get into danger, cross the law, find bodies, or any of that stuff," she said. "Where you, my dear, appear to be perfectly suited for it."

Doreen winced at that. "I admit it is interesting work."

"Admit it. You think it's great fun."

"Does that mean something's wrong with me?" she asked, suddenly worried.

Astonished, her grandmother shook her head. "Absolutely not. You're blessed, honestly."

"Blessed?" Doreen wondered if Nan was going off on one of her tangents when she continued.

"Yes, you found something that's fun, that is exciting, that gets you out of bed with a bounce every day. You've always loved gardening, and so the gardening has led you to another even more exciting hobby."

"Sure, but it's hardly a hobby."

"What would you call it?" Nan challenged. "People are coming to you now."

"Just this once," Doreen protested. "Let's not take that too far."

"Sure. Sure, sure," she said, chuckling. "This week one person, maybe another one next week. Who knows? In six months, you could be getting dozens of people contacting you."

"Well, they can't do that if they don't know where I am," Doreen said. "The only reason Penny did is because she heard about me after I found Paul and because of the fact he went missing twenty-nine years ago, which is the same amount of time her brother-in-law had been missing."

"Of course, and she was a local, so she knew about Paul's case," Nan said, nodding. "You know what you should do?"

Doreen picked up the cup of tea Nan had placed in front of her.

"You should set up a website."

Doreen almost sprayed the tea from her mouth. "A website?"

"Absolutely. Call it something like ... *Finders Keepers.*"

That just ... was so ... *wrong* that Doreen couldn't even begin to formulate an answer.

"Maybe not that name exactly," Nan said, tapping her chin thoughtfully. "Give me a little bit of time. I'll come up with something catchy for it."

"I'm not trying to drum up business for this hobby," Doreen said. "That would be terrible."

"Why would that be terrible?" Nan looked at her in surprise. "Seriously, you could make some good money doing this."

"I'm not a licensed PI. It's only fun because I get interested in the case, and I dig until I can get to the bottom of it," she admitted, probably for the first time to herself as well. "But it won't be the same if people want me to do all kinds of stuff that doesn't appeal."

"Oh, that's a very good point," Nan said. "We'll need to add some explanation that you only take on cases that appeal. Then everybody'll try to make their situation as interesting as possible, so you look into their case."

Doreen didn't think she wanted this to go any further. "How about we just shelve that idea for a while? It's been a crazy-enough day as it is. I'm really, really tired. I didn't plan on coming down here now. For heaven's sakes, I only solved this Alan Hornby problem this morning. I haven't even had a chance to think straight today."

"That's good," Nan said, her voice firm. "Full days are good days. And, once you get to my age, and you realize how empty some days are, you will be pining for those days again."

"Oh, dear, that's probably quite true." She was sorry if Nan was bored much of the time.

"Besides, this way," Nan added, "you forgot all about the antiques leaving tomorrow."

At that, Doreen brightened. "Right. I'd forget, and then it would hit me every once in a while throughout the day, and I realize it's tomorrow."

"So now you go home. Just rest, don't worry about the website, don't worry about finding another case, nothing at all," she said. "If I hear of anything interesting, I'll let you know. In the meantime, you focus on getting those antiques out of your house, okay?"

"Sounds good to me," Doreen said. Plus she didn't want to think about Penny and the crazy thoughts Doreen had been having about the death of Penny's husband. Doreen placed her empty teacup on the table, gave her Nan a gentle hug, kissed her cheek, and said, "And you stay out of trouble for once, please?"

Nan's twinkling eyes said she had heard but had no intention of listening. As Doreen got to the door, Nan called out, "What about the animals? Why didn't you bring them?"

"I raced out of the house so fast that there wasn't time."

"I miss them," Nan said. "Bring them next time, please."

"I will," Doreen said, and she stepped out into the hallway, thankful the reception area was empty now. Once outside, she noted how late it was. She took several deep breaths, looked up at the moon and the sky, and shook her head.

"That went well," Mack said from beside her.

Startled, she turned to look at him. He sat on one of the big brick planters at the front of the building, his arms across his chest. "Are you done here?"

"I am. I've been waiting for you." He inclined his head. "Are *you* done here?" he asked.

She nodded and sighed. "I do love her, but …"

"We all love her," he said firmly. "Don't worry about the *but*s. They happen with all of us."

"Do they though?" she asked.

He chuckled and said, "Come on. Let's get you home again."

"It's so late," she said with a yawn. "I'm glad we got dinner in first. … At least *some* dinner."

"Me too. And it was good. I really enjoyed that dish. It was new for me."

"I still have to clean up the kitchen." She groaned. As she got to her car, she turned to look at him. "Are you heading back to the office?"

He shook his head. "If you want, I'll come and help you clean up the kitchen. Otherwise, I'm heading home to bed."

She waved him toward his vehicle. "Go," she said. "I'll just put the food in the fridge and leave the dishes until morning."

He nodded, and they parted ways.

Chapter 7

Monday Morning...

WHEN DOREEN WOKE up the next morning, her head felt heavy, her body achy. She wasn't sure what she'd done to deserve this, but it probably had to do with sleeping on her mattress on the floor. As she lay here, she remembered what today was. She bolted upright, bounced out of bed, and raced into the shower. Today, Scott, the antiques guy from Christie's, was coming with a crew to pack up her furniture.

Out of the shower, wrapped in a towel, she remembered how she hadn't cleaned up the kitchen fully last night. As she glanced around her bedroom, she hadn't taken the time to clean up the mess in here either. She needed to do more before the movers could come in and pack up everything. Why the devil had yesterday been so busy? But, of course, it had been crazy between Alan's visit and then Penny's visit and last night's impromptu visit with Nan. Doreen hadn't had much time to herself all day. And Mack had come for dinner and had made an absolutely wonderful meal for them. She wondered if she could sneak in some leftovers for breakfast because she sure didn't have much time otherwise.

She glanced at her watch and winced. It was already nine a.m. She was seriously late.

She quickly dressed, her hair brushed back in a ponytail with short tendrils flying loose around her head. She collected her dirty laundry, ran downstairs, and put on a load of wash so at least it was out of the way, and returned to her bedroom to straighten up as much as she could. She had so many of Nan's clothes yet to go through, and her bedroom was still filled with so much clutter. She made the bed—her pallet on the floor—as best she could and then went downstairs again.

As she got to the bottom, she found Thaddeus sitting on his roost in the living room, staring at her wide-eyed. She walked over, reached out a hand, and he hopped onto it. She cuddled him up close, brushed the feathers on his chest and neck, and said, "Good morning, Thaddeus."

"Good morning, Doreen," he cheered.

She gasped. "When did you learn my name?"

"Doreen, Doreen."

She giggled, feeling inordinately pleased. "Well, finally," she said, "and I like you too." She dropped a kiss on the top of his head and walked into the kitchen. She put on coffee first and foremost, as Thaddeus worked his way up onto her shoulder, so he could sit on his preferred perch and watch as she worked. With the coffee on, she turned off the alarms on the security and walked into the living room, wondering how much she had to clean up before the moving men got here. Everything was so chaotic in the house presently, and Christie's would be taking out such big pieces that she knew the moving men would have to create a wide path, leaving behind a mess by the time they were done.

With the minutes racing by, she filled the kitchen sink

with hot soapy water and cleaned up the dishes from the previous night. She had told Mack it wasn't a big deal, but, now that she'd overslept, she felt pressed for time. She knew it wouldn't matter to the appraiser if her dishes were done, but somehow it mattered to her.

With that done and realizing she was doing this backward, she checked in the fridge for some food. Just a little bit of that pasta salad was left. She brought it out, looked at it, wondered if she should eat it straight from the fridge or at room temperature. She decided to heat it up a tad and tossed it into the microwave for a couple minutes to take the chill off. Smiling, she then sat down with a cup of coffee and ate the dinner leftovers from the night before. She worried Mack would be upset with her. Although she was pretty sure he wouldn't be, she wondered why she felt so distressed about the idea. Finally she couldn't help herself. She took a picture, sent it to him, and texted him. **Leftovers for breakfast. Hope it's okay.**

Instead of texting her back, he phoned her. "Why wouldn't it be okay?"

"You paid for it, and you made it, and you barely got one meal's worth of it yourself," she explained.

He sighed heavily. "We still have a long way to go with you, don't we?"

She frowned at the phone. "I don't know what you're talking about."

"I'll explain later," he said. "When is your appraiser coming?"

"I don't know," she said, "and I slept late, so I felt like I had to get some food down, then look at what else I need to do. I admit to feeling fairly stressed."

"Don't panic. They're likely to be there for hours," he

said. "Didn't they say they could be there a couple days?"

"It's possible," she said. "It depends how much trouble they have. I'm sure the smaller pieces won't be an issue, but the bed and the couch ... Well, I don't know."

"Aren't you supposed to look for the provenance stuff?"

She gasped. "I forgot all about it. I gotta go." She hung up and ate as fast as she could, which was a damn shame because the food was so good. Finally she slowed herself down and said, with Thaddeus staring at the tomato on her plate, "I don't need to race through everything."

"Doreen, Doreen."

She looked at Thaddeus. "What would you like, Thaddeus?" But he'd already snatched a piece of green onion off the top of her plate and had run to the other side of the table with it. She smiled. "Not sure you'll like that," she said. "It does have a bit of a bite."

Slowing herself a little more, she finished her plate at a more reasonable rate. Then she got up, tossed her plate and fork into the hot soapy water, and turned around to take care of feeding her three animals before cleaning the rest of the kitchen. Finally she filled her coffee cup and took a deep breath. "At least that should be clean enough." She checked her phone to realize the battery was almost dead. She'd forgotten to plug it in last night. "Damn."

She went upstairs and put it on its charger. In ten minutes she could get a decent amount of charge. What she didn't want was to have Scott Rosten call her and not receive his call. While she was here in her bedroom again, she took the opportunity to pick up more boxes for Goodwill and brought them down to the front stairs. She hadn't been able to take it all in her last trip there. She wasn't sure she'd gotten all of the items together for Wendy either. Doreen headed upstairs once more.

"Wendy." She frowned and glanced at her phone on the charger. "You never called me back after I dropped off that last load on Friday."

She wondered if she should give Wendy a call. Doreen understood she'd gotten there early at opening time, but Wendy was supposed to get back to her after going through the latest boxes of Nan's things. If Wendy couldn't sell some items, she would call Doreen to pick them up. And now, of course, it was early on a Monday, so not the best time to call Wendy either. Doreen frowned at that. "Maybe your life is as crazy as mine is," she said. "I don't know how people do it all. They have work. They have children, and yet, still sometimes all this craziness piles in on top." She shook her head. "I just have me to look after."

At that, Mugs barked.

She looked at him and grinned. "And you," she said. He was on his back, lying on her mattress on the floor, all four feet in the air, content. She reached down and scrubbed his belly, and he just sighed with happiness. She chuckled. "We should be doing more cleaning up in here. The moving men can't even maneuver around all this stuff." She figured she could clean out more clothes from the drawers and dressers. She still had boxes she hadn't had a chance to sort through yet.

Frowning, she decided to move those boxes into the spare room, at least the stuff that had come out of the dressers and the vanity. She didn't want to rush the job of going through Nan's clothing as there was money to be found. Who could forget Nan's habit of leaving money in her clothing? Still, Doreen needed to clear out some of the clutter in here.

With that done, she heard vehicles outside. She looked out the front window, and, sure enough, Scott was here. She ran down the stairs and opened the front door. She beamed up at him. "Hey, I wasn't sure how early you would come."

"I tried to call earlier, but the phone was busy," he explained, "so I just came straight over. I hope that's okay?"

Her head bobbed a yes. "Sure is. Come on in, please. I'm so terrified of things going wrong that I couldn't wait for you to come. It's been a very stressful weekend," she said.

Scott chuckled. "Well, we're here now," he said.

She looked behind Scott to see the men with him. "Oh, good, you brought four men with you," she exclaimed.

"Yes, I figured it was probably easier to bring more men and see if we could get it all done today than stay in town and have just two of them."

"I'm amazed it would take that long actually," she said, "because a moving truck and a couple guys could have it all out of here in an hour."

The foreman just looked at her.

She winced. "I guess you have to take better care of these things than that?"

Scott nodded. "Absolutely we do," he said. "I'd get shot if we were to do a half-assed job. Besides, with a set like this, you know it's very special."

"I hear you," she said. "I'm still looking for the paperwork though. I am hoping, maybe once you get the biggest pieces out, I will have a little more room to keep searching."

"We will get to work on that," he said. "So you go off and do whatever you need to, and we apologize ahead of time if we'll be in your way."

"It's fine," she said, smiling. "Let me rephrase that—I'm just happy you're here, so let me know if you need anything." And she turned and left them to the living room.

Only she couldn't. She kept looking into the living room to see them gently removing drawers, packing up drawers, wrapping up legs of the coffee table, but not until after they'd taken a great deal of photographs of every angle and every side of the designated pieces. They worked in pairs of two—one photographed and then they wrapped, taped, and had the first pieces moved to the truck outside. Finally Scott walked over to her. "Are you curious or worried?"

"Both," she said, chuckling. "Curious because I didn't understand how much you would baby the furniture. But, when you wrapped up this furniture, then covered it in Bubble Wrap before placing it in padded blankets, ... I'm amazed," she said.

"While it was in your possession," he said, "it's gently worn. But, once it comes into our possession," he said, "we don't want any more damage to occur. We'll get our restoration people to take a look at the pieces at the auction house too."

"Restoration?"

"Some of the scratches can be easily fixed," he said. "Some of the pieces might need oiling. Others might need a little bit of refinishing. You can try to sell them all as they are, or we can get them fixed up and then sell them after that. I can give you quotes on both."

She nodded, her mind in turmoil. "You know I'll go with the one that doesn't require money up front, don't you?" She wrapped her arms around her chest, seeing her dreams of a big payday going out the window. But it figured—nothing came free.

"Neither come with cash up front," Scott said with a shake of his head. "We wouldn't do anything unnecessarily anyway. But you want to get top dollar for these pieces. And, in this case, we'd give you a quote for the work, get the work done, and then sell the pieces. So the money required to pay for the work done would come out of the profit."

"Oh," she said. "Well then, I'll wait and see the quotes."

"Good enough," he said. "You'll get a decent amount for these pieces," he said, "but, if they're in better condition, and if they look new and shiny, you'll get more. It's amazing how the public responds to the bright shiny look."

"I understand," she said slowly. "Just like anybody else, I'm more susceptible to something that looks shiny and new than something that looks old and beaten."

"Old and beaten is fine, and, if it can be made shiny and at least look well maintained, that's a huge difference," he said. "It can't ever be made *new* again. That's not what we're selling either. We're selling antiques, things that have lived and survived for a long time with wonderful care. Filling in a few scratches and giving it a coat of oil or buffing out some bigger scratches and putting on a stain that matches is not the same thing. But, because of the age of the antiques, everything has to be matched, so that could be expensive. We wouldn't do that unless it was something you specifically wanted done."

She shook her head. "I wouldn't want anything that would decrease the value of the antiques, and it sounds like some of those would."

"Some methods used would, yes," he said. "I would definitely not go in that direction myself."

One of the men called him. He walked over, and they huddled over a chair, looking at some marks on it. She chewed on her bottom lip, watching them, worrying about it. When they stepped back and continued taking photographs, she wondered if she could ask what was wrong and then realized she would just slow the process. With this many men, they could get everything out of here today, and she needed that. She wanted these pieces to be in their hands, where they were responsible for keeping them safe. And, for that to happen, she needed to back off and to let them do their thing. She walked into the kitchen, poured herself a cup of coffee, and said to the animals, "Let's go outside, guys. We're in the way."

Mugs hadn't settled down at all. He'd been wandering around the living room. He'd recognized Scott but wasn't so sure about the other men. One of the men didn't like dogs, and that had added its own difficulty. Some of her husband's cohorts hadn't liked pets, and she'd been required to keep Mugs away from her husband's office. Now she pulled out a leash because Mugs kept going back into the living room. She gave the leash a rattle, and he came running. She hooked him up and called for Goliath, who just stared at her from the bottom step of the stairs, his tail twitching as if to say, *Yes, I'm here, and?*

Chapter 8

Monday Midmorning...

DOREEN SIGHED. "COME on, Goliath. Let's go outside. We're in the way." She propped open the door and headed down the steps, hoping that Goliath would *choose* to follow. It was pretty hard to order that cat to do anything. So far, Goliath did what he wanted. When it lined up with Doreen's wants, they were both happy, but that didn't mean that he would choose to be agreeable today.

As she walked down the path toward the creek, Mugs at her side, Thaddeus on her shoulder, Goliath streaked out past her.

She chuckled. "See? I told you it was a good idea."

He just shot her a look that said, *Whatever.*

At the creek she stopped and wondered what she was supposed to do now. She was restless. The moving men were doing what they needed to do. And she wanted that to happen, but, at the same time, they would be hours. She couldn't just sit and relax. She didn't really feel like gardening, although she should be doing that. Instead she found her feet, almost as if by rote now, heading toward Penny's house. Doreen groaned as she arrived at the spot where she'd normally cross the creek. "We don't always have to go in this direction. You know that, right, guys?"

Mugs was already trying to cross, but the leash wasn't giving him much leeway. She sighed and said, "Come on. Let's keep walking beside the creek." And she walked past the crossing spot. Once Mugs realized they were changing direction, he raced eagerly. She just smiled. It was always nice to have company, and these trips were fun for the animals too.

She was trying to avoid Penny and that persistent nudge in the back of Doreen's mind that maybe something wasn't quite right there. But Doreen had no basis for that, and the last thing she wanted to do was look too closely at somebody who could be a friend. Doreen didn't have any friends, and it was a novel idea to find somebody at this time of her life. Her other "friends" had been deemed appropriate for her lifestyle back then. Her husband had vetted them all, and they were usually trophy wives of businessmen he worked with. She'd thought that was what friendships were. But, as soon as she'd gotten involved in that messy divorce, everybody had distanced themselves from her, helping her realize there was really no such thing as *friends* with that group.

Now, even though Penny was that much older, it was still nice to know Doreen had somebody she could maybe go have a cup of tea with outside of her own grandmother, and, to be honest, Doreen hadn't had the time or the interest in getting out and socializing with anybody else. She'd been so busy working on these cold cases that she hadn't put any effort into fitting in here. Penny had definitely helped in that regard. In fact, that made Doreen feel very good.

Then, of course, her mind zipped to Steve. At least Penny didn't seem to be too perturbed that Doreen had been in

Penny's backyard. Which was good, but Doreen felt like she'd pushed the limit there, and now she needed to back away. She walked along the creek, her thoughts scattered as she tried to avoid thinking about what was going on at her house. She needed that furniture gone and for Scott to give her the names of other antiques specialists to contact about the little stuff Doreen wanted to get rid of as well.

Speaking of the little stuff, she still had to figure out exactly what that thief, Darth, had taken from her house that wasn't found in the back of his truck. Plus, he had to be working with someone. Doreen would like to know who that was. She wanted to attend Darth's trial too. She trusted Mack to return the items they knew had been taken, but there could be so much more missing than she knew. So she sent Mack a text. **Re Darth, what else did he steal from me? Who's he working with? When's his trial?** Doreen had pocketed her phone to hear a beep almost instantly, pulling out her phone once more, surprised to get a response so fast from Mack.

I'll let you know what I can let you know as we figure it out.

Typical Mack. Finally having worn herself down with all those thoughts, she stopped at a particularly shallow spot in the creek, where she kicked off her sandals and walked into the water. It was a beautiful sunny day, and, if nothing else, it was lovely to be by the water and just listen to the delightful soothing sounds for a few moments. She found a particularly large flat rock and sat down, kicking the water, deliberately splashing Mugs, who danced around barking at her. Goliath sat on a high flat rock beside her. Thaddeus entertained himself and her by hopping from rock to rock. "You guys are allowed to play," she said, "but you're not allowed to find anything."

"Why shouldn't they?" a man said from behind her.

She turned to see Steve and frowned at him. "I'm surprised to see you here."

His eyebrows rose. "Wow, and here everyone says you are friendly. I gather we got off on the wrong foot?"

She shrugged. "You weren't terribly friendly yourself the last time I met you."

"I'm sorry for that," he said, "but you were skulking around Penny's house. I do like to keep an eye out for her. She's a dear friend."

Wondering if she had, indeed, behaved suspiciously at the time, Doreen admitted, "That makes sense, but you scared me."

"Oh, my goodness," he said, walking a few feet south of her and sitting down on a nearby rock "I didn't mean to." Then he frowned, adding, "Well, maybe I did. I did think you were perhaps up to no good."

His tone was light, and his mannerisms were so different than last time that she almost believed him. She had no reason not to believe him. She nodded and said, "Well, in that case, hi."

He chuckled as he watched Thaddeus peck away at a piece of driftwood. "I don't think I've ever met anybody who went for walks with three pets like yours."

"They like to go with me everywhere," she said warmly. "They certainly make my life interesting and fun."

"I'm sure," he said in amazement. "And the cat?"

"Goliath *chooses* to come with me," she explained. "He's a character, and he loves to watch the creek."

"You can get him in the water?" he asked in surprise.

"Oh, gosh, no, but he does love to sit here and enjoy the

view with me, whereas Mugs here," she said, motioning toward her basset hound, "I don't think he's happy unless he *is* wet." And just then Mugs jumped farther into the creek, his ears floating on the surface as he barked, happily swimming.

"You don't worry about him floating away?"

She shook her head. "He's a good swimmer. And we've spent lots of days playing in the creek."

"I haven't seen you around here before," he said.

"I'm from farther down the creek," she said. "We don't normally walk up this far. But this morning I just wanted to get out of the house."

"The walls crowding in on you?"

"You could say that," she said with a wry smile. "Sometimes you just need a change."

"You are Doreen, right?"

She nodded. "Yes, I'm sure I told you that before."

He just smiled. "You're wary now. Why?"

"Because I don't want to find out you're a reporter or something," she said. She looked at him, suddenly suspicious. "What do you do for a living?"

He gave a bark of a laugh at that. "I'm a lawyer," he said.

Instantly she could feel herself withdrawing. "Oh."

"And a wealth of emotion is in that exclamation," he said gently. "I suppose you don't like lawyers either?"

She wrinkled her face. "I'm sure some are okay." She hopped to her feet, gave him a bright smile, and said, "I really do need to head back though. It was nice meeting you again." She tried to make it sound like she wasn't running away, but, when he laughed, she realized she'd failed. "I don't mean to be rude."

"But you just can't help running away. I admit that I

don't usually get that kind of a response when I tell people I'm a lawyer."

"I'm going through a nasty divorce," she said. "My lawyer shafted me."

He grinned amiably. "I'm a corporate lawyer," he said. "I don't handle divorces."

"Understood," she said. "Besides, not all lawyers are the same, I'm sure."

He chuckled and stood. "Anytime you want to go out and have coffee," he said, "I promise I'll prove to you that I'm not the same as every other lawyer."

She smiled and said, "Maybe, some time. Thanks for the invite."

And she turned and walked down the pathway. She deliberately didn't turn around, but she could feel his eyes boring into her back. She should have gotten his last name. "Just Steve" wouldn't cut it. And already she wondered if she could contact Mack about him. See if this guy was on the up-and-up or if he was a shyster, like her ex-lawyer was. But then why would Mack do that? It wasn't like he had the right to investigate people without cause, right? But, if she had Steve's last name, she could do a lot herself.

As she walked past Penny's, she wondered about asking Penny about Steve, then thought that was stupid. Still, Doreen pulled out her phone and sent Penny a text. **Hey, I just ran into your friend Steve on the creek. Interesting guy.**

Her response came back pretty quickly. **And he's single and wealthy**, Penny texted. **You could do worse.**

At that response, Doreen replied, **I can't remember his last name. I know he's a lawyer, but I can't place him …**

Albright, Penny texted. **He's a high-profile lawyer,**

does corporate stuff, she wrote. **He's a really nice guy.**

Interesting, Doreen answered. **Thanks for the name. Now at least it'll stop bugging me.**

No problem, Penny said. **Maybe you want to come over, and we can discuss my garden sometime.**

Sure, she said. **I'm on the creek right now.**

Come over then. I'll put on the teakettle.

With that firmly shifting her direction, Doreen back-tracked on the easier rocks to get across the creek and headed toward Penny's house. She didn't know where Steve was now, and she dared not look. As she made it to the other side, she saw Steve heading toward Penny's too.

He stopped, looked at her, and raised an eyebrow.

Doreen shrugged. "I was talking to Penny. She invited me for tea."

"Right," he said. "That's where I was going too." And he fell into step beside her.

Although she felt a little awkward because she wanted to ask questions about him, there wasn't much she could do about it. As they approached Penny's house, Penny opened her front door and laughed. "And look at that? The two of you. Together. Come on in."

But Steve just shook his head and said, "No, I've got to head into town. I was just walking her to your place. We'll talk later, Penny," and he gave a wave and took off.

Doreen watched him leave, and, as she turned back around, Penny's face twisted with bright curiosity. "Well, you're definitely interested," she said in delight. "He's a good man."

"Maybe," Doreen said with a smile. "But the fact that he's a lawyer isn't in his favor."

At that, Penny laughed. "Maybe," she said, "but he

doesn't do the kind of work that most of us would think."

"Maybe," Doreen said, "but still. So what's this about your garden? Have you made some decisions about what you want to do?"

"Your idea for a memorial is lovely," she said warmly. "And I have signed the contract with the Realtor to sell the house."

"Oh, interesting," Doreen said in surprise. "That was fast."

"Yes, I'll probably head back East, closer to my daughters, find a condo near them," she said, "but I'll see."

"When's the sign going out?" Doreen asked, turning to look around.

"I think in two days. They need a contractor to install the sign. And we've got a photo session coming up."

"Did you ask about having the house staged?"

"She only said, if I wanted to, I could."

"What about the clutter?"

Penny shook her head. "She didn't seem to think that was a problem."

Inside, Doreen frowned. "Interesting," she said cautiously. "From everything I've read and heard, a house sells better when it's sparsely furnished, so it shows lots of space and lots of room for the new buyers' own possessions."

"Maybe," Penny said, "but, at the moment, I'm good with this. Hopefully somebody will offer close to full price, and I'll get to leave real fast."

Thinking her friend was probably dreaming on all accounts but not knowing for sure, Doreen just smiled. They took their tea outside to the back garden and continued their discussion of all kinds of options, from buying new plants to just rearranging some. "And you're okay to have the memorial here, even though you're selling, correct?"

"I'm leaving this stage of my life behind, and I'm leaving them both behind so ..." She shrugged. "That seems like a fair thing to do."

"Do you want to plant a small bush or more flowers? What are you thinking of?"

Penny pointed out the edging around the echinacea. "Those are stamped bricks. You can't really see it from here because the plants are so overgrown, but I thought maybe I'd do something in this really rough spot here and maybe put a small tree—a weeping or red maple or something," she said. Then she gave a half laugh. "The weeping part is probably apropos."

"Absolutely," Doreen said. She walked over to the echinacea, happy to have a chance to take a good look with Penny here, and bent down to pull out one of those stamped bricks Penny had mentioned. "These are quite pretty. If you hose them off and took a steel scrub brush to them, they'd clean up nicely."

"Maybe," Penny said, "but that sounds like an awful lot of work. I won't have much time because we'll have the Realtor's showings coming up fast."

"That's true," Doreen said. "And remember. Regardless of what you do, the new buyer could rip it all out."

Penny nodded. "But I'm doing this for me," she said firmly.

"Good enough," Doreen said. She stood and stepped back. "You should have fun with this project."

"Actually ..." Penny hesitated. "I was wondering if I could hire you to do it."

Doreen looked at her in surprise and delight. "Pay me to do what exactly?"

"I don't have a lot of money," Penny said, "but I was thinking, for a couple hundred dollars, you might be able to do something nice."

Doreen schooled her expression to not show the joy she felt screaming inside her. "When would you want it done?" she asked cautiously.

"The sooner, the better. I was thinking the backyard, if that's where you think it should be, although there is that unfinished bed in the front."

"Let's walk out there and take a look." Doreen walked past the echinacea and said, "Do you just want a tree, or do you want to move some of these plants out there too?"

"I'm not sure. I'm at a loss now. I thought I knew what I was talking about when you first came out, but now it seems I have more options than I first considered."

"No problem," Doreen said. "I can definitely help you come up with something nice. But, if we make it too complicated, it will take more time."

"No," she said. "I definitely don't want to make it complicated then."

In the front yard was a round garden with a very sad-looking bunch of flowers. "Why don't you take that little weeping maple in the back in the center and move it up here?" Doreen said. "Although I don't know, are you planning to put something like a little rock or stone or bury something to show it as a memorial?"

Penny shook her head. "No, this is literally just for me, but this bed is looking pretty sad, and, for curb appeal, I suppose it would be the best place for this to happen."

Doreen thought about it and said, "It's pretty crowded where the maple currently is. It would make a better statement here. If you want, I can make sure the soil here is decent first before we transplant that tree. Then I could move the stamped bricks from the backyard to create an edging look."

"I thought George put some around this front bed. They must be covered up."

"That's one less thing to move then," Doreen said, smiling.

Penny look thrilled. "And you can do it soon?"

"I can't start today," Doreen said. "The moving men are in my house, packing up the antiques. That's one of the reasons I came out for a walk. To get away from all the chaos."

Penny nodded. "They can be quite disruptive, can't they?"

"Absolutely. I could probably stop by tomorrow and get started. Do you have shovels I can dig with?"

Penny nodded. "You know what – I do. There are lots of gardening tools around."

"If you have anything like that which you want me to put in," Doreen said, "why don't you bring it out when I start digging, and I can figure out what should go where and maybe create something George would have liked."

"This is sounding better and better," Penny said, clapping her hands. "George always thought this whole bed should be redone, but I never really knew what to do with it because nothing seemed to grow well."

"I can handle that," Doreen said confidently. "Collect all the stuff you think George wanted to plant here, and it'll just be George's bed."

"Thank you," Penny said. "I guess I'd like to make it George's and Johnny's bed."

"If you have a rock you want to paint something on,

then do so," she said. "Maybe take a couple flat rocks and, with a permanent marker, write their names or their initials—something to memorialize them. Put down all three of your names because you're leaving. Once you sell the house, you'll be part of the memorial," she suggested.

Penny looked intrigued with the idea. "That's not a bad idea either. Okay, I'll see you tomorrow morning then," she said as her phone rang. "I have to go inside and take this."

Nodding, Doreen handed Penny the teacup, called the animals to her, and waited until Penny had dashed inside the house. Doreen stood here for a few long moments, studying the bed. It had dead grass in the front, which meant it wasn't getting water on a steady basis. She should have asked Penny if any underground irrigation was here because that would make a big difference too. She moved a couple of the rough rocks sitting on top. This would be hard work. Something she hadn't really understood before she had said she'd do this job. Although it would be a lot of work, it was also a lot of money for her.

Not only that, it was her second gardening job. Feeling lighter and happier, she called the animals back out to the creek, and they headed home.

Chapter 9

Monday Noon …

AS SOON AS Doreen walked into the kitchen, she noticed the almost deafening silence. She raced to the living room, but it was empty. She dashed out the front door to see the men packing some of the living room furniture into the truck.

Scott saw her and said, "There you are. We've got everything but the couch packed up, and then we'll work upstairs in the bedroom. But we wanted to get these smaller pieces in first."

She looked at the big panel truck and nodded. "When I came in the kitchen door, I couldn't figure out where you guys were."

"Not to worry," he said. "We're still here. It will definitely be an all-day event. Still, we have hope we can get out on time."

"Perfect," Doreen said, leading the way back into the house. With the coffee table and the two pot chairs now gone, there was more space. "Also, I was hoping you could give me some names of other antiques' experts to ask about some of this little stuff." She pointed to the knickknacks. "I already had a thief come in and steal several pieces, and they're now being held by the police as part of the investigation."

Scott's face showed worry. "Oh my," he said, "that's terrible."

"I know," she said. "We caught him in the act, so that's the good part, but he had a list already that he was collecting, and that was not so good. He also knew about the bigger pieces of furniture, so I'm really glad you came today to get this stuff. It's been a tough weekend waiting."

"I am too then," Scott said, "and I'll definitely email you a couple names. I said I'd do that before, didn't I? I'm so sorry, my dear. I must have forgotten."

"It's not a problem," she said. "At least the other items are small, so they should be easier to ship out."

"Unless they need to be shipped somewhere farther away."

"True," she said. "But I don't want to worry about that until I know more."

"I'll think about it. Let me keep working. This big couch will take a fair bit of time. I know the four men will handle it themselves, but I do want to oversee the process," he said, sounding worried and looking back toward the living room window.

"Sure. You do that," she said. "I'll put on a fresh pot for you."

"If you wouldn't mind," Scott said. "I know the men would definitely like a cup. We'll also take a break after the couch and get some lunch."

She nodded, and he walked back outside. She put on a fresh pot of coffee, but she poured the old coffee into her cup and microwaved it. It was still so hard for her to waste food.

She knew it was stupid because she was about to put another pot on but no reason why she couldn't have some of the old and these guys have the fresh coffee. They were the ones working hard. She certainly wasn't.

When the coffee was done, she peered into the living room. The men were busy wrapping and packing and taping. She watched in fascination as the entire couch was bundled up securely. The sense of loss in her heart surprised her. She really would miss that piece. Not because it was comfortable to sit on because it wasn't. Not because it was her style because again it wasn't. Not because it was a piece she had loved to look at because yet again it certainly wasn't. But it was a piece of her heritage, a piece of her ancestry, and that gave her an unexpected sense of loss. When the men tried to pick it up and carry it out, she winced. "Will it fit through the door?"

Scott came to her side. "Let's hope so," he said, watching the men as they tried to angle the couch to test the fit through the front door. Scott asked, "Do those living room windows open?"

She nodded. "They certainly do."

With the men still trying to fit through the couch through the front door, she opened up one of the big windows. Scott halted the men and pointed. The men all nodded, backed up, and proceeded to maneuver the couch through the open window with two men inside and two men out. Doreen had such a sense of relief when the couch was finally loaded into the truck that she stood with her hand over her mouth in disbelief.

She closed the window, and Scott said, "You might want to leave it that way. I'm not sure how to get the bed out yet."

"Oh my. I forgot all about that," she said. "I hate to admit it, but I was afraid that would be an issue from the start."

He nodded and motioned at the living room. "This room looks incredibly empty now."

She danced around in a circle, her arms wide. "This looks much better." Several pieces of paper were on the floor that had fallen when they'd dislodged the couch. Doreen bent and scooped them up. One said *Penny Jordan* on it. She laughed and held it up, "I just had tea with Penny Jordan."

Scott looked at it and smiled.

She pocketed the first piece and took a look at the second one. "Interesting," she said. "Plants are listed here."

"I don't know anything about plants," Scott said.

"I do," Doreen said, "but I definitely don't use these for what they're meant for." He looked at her in confusion, and she then pulled out the piece of paper with Penny's name on it. She frowned, turned it to read the chicken scratch notes on the other side.

"What do you mean?" Scott asked.

"Foxglove, digitalis, belladonna," she read. "All plants used for medicine."

"Nothing wrong with that, is there? All of our traditional medicine came from herbs and plants at one point. At least until the pharmaceuticals could create designer versions of them."

She nodded, folded the pieces of paper, and put them away. What she hadn't told him was they were in Nan's writing, and that meant Doreen needed to ask Nan what the hell this was all about. And how long ago had these plans been discussed.

Scott said, "If you've got that coffee ready,"—pointing to the men—"they're ready to take a break."

As she watched, the four men hopped from the truck,

and, instead of coming toward the house, they pulled out sandwiches from a bag.

She called out, "If you want a coffee to go with that ..."

The men all nodded. She walked back into the kitchen, poured four cups, and she and Scott took them out to the men. Outside they all sat and talked as the men ate big sandwiches. "Did you get those locally?"

"Yes," Scott said. "At the deli just down off of KLO Road."

"I know a little mall is in there," she said. "I haven't had time to do very much exploring."

"You should check out the deli," one of the men said. "These are really good."

She nodded, and her phone rang. Seeing it was Nan, she said to Scott, "I'll be right back." She headed inside as she answered her call. "Nan, I was just about to call you."

"Good," Nan said. "Did the antiques guys show up?"

"Yep, the living room has been packed up. And just as they took out the couch, I found some papers on the floor in your handwriting."

Nan laughed. "Of course you did. You could find all kinds of stuff now. What did these papers say?"

"Penny Jordan and a bunch of plant names," she said slowly. And she named them off again.

"Oh, yes," she said. "I remember that. Penny and I were talking about plants that were harmful to have in the garden."

"But these aren't always harmful, Nan," she said. "And so many people who have them in their garden are none the wiser."

"No, but I think Penny was asking for another reason." Blissfully unaware of Doreen's sudden gasp of surprise, Nan added, "Besides, I told her these could kill someone."

"Interesting," Doreen said as she pulled out the pieces of paper and looked at them closer. "Did she have a reason for asking?"

"Of course she did," Nan said. "I always figured she killed George. I was just waiting for you to prove it."

Chapter 10

Monday Afternoon ...

THAT AFTERNOON WAS even more nerve-racking than the morning. The men from Christie's hadn't taken a break until late, and Doreen was pretty antsy by the time they finally got back to work. With the living room cleaned out, she was smiling a sigh of relief, but she knew the upstairs would take equally as long. The bed was a huge problem. She led the way, and the men started working on the vanity. When she heard muttered curses, she decided she needed to be anywhere but here. She crept downstairs and stood with her hands on her hips, taking stock of the living room. "Mugs, what do you think we should do from here?"

Mugs just woofed at her side, but he kept going back upstairs to where the men were. She'd been forced to clip a leash on him and keep him with her all the time. He wanted to "help" everyone. With no major living room furniture to sit on now, she put a couple odd chairs she presumed had zero value into the middle of the room and brought out the vacuum to give the rug a thorough cleaning.

The rug was another piece she thought was supposed to go too. It was supposed to be extremely expensive, but that didn't mean Christie's was interested in it. She gave it as good a cleaning as she possibly could and then worked all around the rest of the living room. The remaining two upright chairs—looked modern.

She found it odd that Nan had even bought them. But maybe it was at a different stage of her life, and she was looking for something more contemporary. Three lamps remained, one that was pretty rickety, and Doreen wasn't sure it had any value, and the other two weren't bad, if she could find something to set them on. And, of course, that was another problem. She had two pot chairs, but was that all she wanted in here? Using the vacuum brush, she cleaned behind the door, around the base of the stairs, and down the hallway, making sure she got as much of the living room itself back to prime sparkling condition. With the chairs set off the rug, she waited until Scott came down to ask him about the pieces. She was gratified when he appeared, talking to one of the guys, only to have his gaze catch on the rug, and a slow smile dawned.

Her fist gripped the vacuum handle as she waited for him to bounce down the last few steps. Hesitantly she said, "I know it's not part of the set, but I don't know if it was you or Fen who said the rug was valuable."

Scott wasn't talking now. He had a magnifying glass in his hand as he studied the weaves and the hooks—was that the right word for the loops of rug as it pulled through? He had the corner flipped over so he could see the backing on it. One of the other men bent down, and together they muttered. Finally Scott straightened and said, "Are you attached to this?"

She gave him a droll smile. "No," she said. "Is there a good reason to not be attached to it?"

"About fifteen grand worth," he said. "Maybe more, I can't really tell yet. It needs a good cleaning, but I don't want you to do it," he rushed in.

She frowned at him. "Meaning, I might ruin it?"

"I can't say," he said, "but we have to determine what these fibers are and then give it the proper cleaning for that material."

Considering she probably would have just taken a vacuum mop—one of those cheap rentals from the grocery store—and scrubbed it over, she was glad he'd said that.

"If you can get fifteen thousand for it," she said slowly, "then you should try."

"Don't forget we have a commission on that too."

She mentally backtracked the fortune coming down to a nice little windfall. She said, "It's pretty nice."

"It is," he said, appraising it closely. "There is a chance," he said, "that it could be worth more, but I have to clean up some of these corners in order to see."

She bent down to the corner he was talking about. "It looks like a signature is there. Why would that be?"

"Artisans used to put their signatures in as a series of special stitches when they finished a piece, signifying it was their work," he explained. "But somewhere along the line this has been rebacked or a new backing put on it."

"Or it was put on at the same time?" she suggested.

"That's possible too," he said. "Which would put it around the late eighteenth century."

She looked at him, her eyes round. "And yet, it's only worth fifteen thousand?"

"No, no," he said. "I didn't say that. It could be worth three times that. I don't know. It depends on what the signature says, which is why I don't want you to clean it. Any solvent you use could potentially damage not only the fibers but wipe away this signature. I can take it with me, and we can try."

She nodded. "I know Fen said it was valuable, but I don't remember if he gave me any figure. I'll check my notes."

"Not to worry," he said. "Once we get all the pieces back to Christie's, I can get it assessed by another specialist and give you a full accounting."

She nodded. "That would be lovely if you could," she said with a beaming smile.

He turned to the two men with him on the main floor and said, "Because this is here and ready, I suggest we pack it and load up before we start in on the other pieces up in the bedroom."

They nodded, then headed to the truck, pulled out more packing blankets, and she thought some tissue paper or something. She watched in amazement as the entire surface of the rug was covered with the tissue, and then it was slowly rolled lengthwise, the long side forward, until the entire rug was packed up into a tight bundle. Then they took the packing blanket and wrapped all around the outside. Finally it was tied together and the ends closed off. And before she knew it, even though it had taken at least an hour, if not two, it was tossed onto the men's shoulders and carefully carried outside to the truck.

Some sort of old rug had been left behind, had been underneath the nicer rug. She pointed at it and said, "Why would that be down here?"

Scott looked at it, made a funny face, and said, "People do weird things. Maybe it was to protect the good rug from the flooring."

She wasn't sure why any rug should be protected from the wood flooring that she now saw definitely needed refinishing. She grabbed the vacuum again as Scott headed back upstairs, and the two moving men came back from the truck and joined him. She vacuumed all around the old ugly piece of rug, wondering if she should just toss it. Mugs, hating the vacuum hose, finally came over and sniffed as soon as she shut it off. She looked at him and said, "It smells weird, doesn't it?" He sniffed to the point he was actually lifting a corner of it. "Hey, hey, hey," she said, pulling him back gently. "That's pretty strong snogs you got there, buddy."

But he strained at the leash and refused to be budged.

Sighing, she pulled the vacuum handle back, laid it gently down on the hardwood floor. Now she was worried that this old rug had value too, and she crouched beside Mugs at that corner he was sniffing at and lifted it up. As she flipped it back, she stared in amazement. There appeared to be an inset handle flush within the wooden floor, all stained with the same finish. She sure wouldn't have seen it without moving out all this furniture and the rug under the rug. But for Mugs's barking, she wouldn't have noticed, it was so well done.

She slowly rolled back the piece of junky rug, realizing Scott was quite correct; it was just a piece of old tattered something or other that didn't even have a finished edge. Somebody had just cut it and put it down and then placed a good one on top of it. It was also very thin. She rolled it up carefully, and, since it wasn't too big or too heavy, she dragged it outside on the porch and laid it over the front railing. Then she came back with the vacuum and cleaned up all the dirt and dust underneath it. How was it even possible there was so much? Mugs alternated between straining at the leash away from the vacuum and toward the secret space. The only reason she'd had any idea the handle existed was because of him.

She also didn't want the men upstairs to know about it. Not until she inspected it further. She walked back over to the spot, her fingers gently going over the piece of wood that appeared to lift and, checking around to make sure nobody was watching her, she tried to pull up the handle. But it wouldn't budge. She frowned, looked at it again, and gently tapped the wood all around it. She heard a hollow echo. Excited, she walked into the kitchen and came back with a butter knife. She wasn't sure this was the best thing to do, but, considering the condition of the floors, she thought it worth a try. She gently scraped along the edges of what she thought was a handle. But, even after that effort, again when she pulled, nothing shifted. She frowned and said, "Well, Mugs, we're wrong sometimes. It looks like it's this time."

He just shot her a look as if to say, *No. I'm not wrong. You're wrong.*

Just then she heard footsteps again. She bolted to her feet, picked up the butter knife, and casually walked back into the kitchen, placing the knife in the sink. As she returned to the living room, the men were gently carrying the vanity mirror outside, followed by each of the drawers wrapped up in what appeared to be more Bubble Wrap. As they came back in again, they brought rolls of more Bubble Wrap. She watched in amazement. She wanted to go upstairs and see what they were doing but knew her bedroom would be chaos with so many people in it.

Just then Scott came back down. He whistled at the living room and said, "I can't believe how big this room is now." She watched his gaze dart around. He glanced over the hardwood floor straight to the pot chairs, grimaced before focusing on her. But he didn't appear in any way to notice the flooring. He motioned at the chairs. "I guess that'll give you something to sit on until you figure out what else you want in here."

She smiled at him. "And I gather from your response to seeing them, they have zero value."

"I'm sure they have value to someone," he assured her. "But not in the antiques world. Those are cheap knockoffs from anywhere in the last ten years. Hardly any historical value." He looked around. "You've done incredibly well, particularly adding the rug to this collection of yours going to Christie's." He stood in the middle of the living room and said, "Of course the floor is pretty damaged."

"That's not what I expected," she said. "I figured the rug would have protected it."

"That just goes to show you the floor had a lot of use before the rug was laid," he said, "and maybe that's why your Nan bought it. Not only for its antique value but because her living room floor needed to be redone." He pointed at the scratches and the dullness to it. "But it is true hardwood," he said, "so you could get it refinished, and it would look splendid." He smiled as he looked around. "Right, and I never did give you those names of somebody to look at the small stuff, did I?" He walked over to a vase that had blue-and-white markings. "I don't think this can be a Ming vase," he said, "but it's sure a nice copy."

At the term *Ming*, her ears perked up. "If it was real, huge money would be involved, right?"

He chuckled. "Thousands again. May I?" he asked as he reached up a hand.

She nodded.

As he lifted it, there were sounds of rattling on the inside. She shrugged and said, "I've never even looked inside."

Holding it gently, he slowly reached his hand in and came out with several huge marbles. He chuckled. "Remnants of the children who lived in the house," he suggested. "And this is why I love antiques. Because some people have such irreverence for them that they become common household items that everyone, including children, can enjoy."

He handed her the marbles to hold, and she stared at them. They were bigger than she remembered from her childhood. She wasn't even sure these could be classified as marbles because something appeared to be inside them, maybe like a bug or whatnot. She shrugged and stuck them in her pocket.

She waited with bated breath while Scott studied the vase. He looked inside at the base and then at a mark on the bottom. "Well," he said, letting out his breath slowly. "I'm not the expert on this, but this might be the real thing." His tone was so dazed, as if this was the last thing he expected.

She stepped forward and said, "Really?"

He nodded. "I need a place to lay it down, so I can take some pictures, and I'll contact a colleague of mine."

At that, she wanted to jump around and scream. Instead, she picked up her phone and called Nan. "Hey, Nan?"

"Oh, I do love having you close," Nan cried out cheerfully. "What can I help you with now?" she asked. "Did you get any closer to finding out if Penny was a murderer?"

"No, no, no," she said. "That's not what I'm calling about. Remember that big blue-and-white vase on your mantel?"

"Oh, that Ming vase?" she asked in a loud voice.

Scott's head turned and looked at Doreen's phone, and then he glanced up at her. "Ask her if she has a receipt," he said.

"I heard that," her grandmother said. "Not sure about a receipt. I had it appraised for insurance once though," she said thoughtfully. "I'm not exactly sure where that is either now."

Doreen just closed her eyes and pinched the bridge of her nose. "I'm still trying to find any paperwork," she said, turning to look around the living room. "Now that the living room furniture is out in the truck, I felt sure they would be here somewhere."

And her gaze went to the floorboards she had tried to lift. "Do you know anything about this vase, Nan?"

"Sure, I picked it up at a garage sale years ago," she said. "I thought it was lovely, and then one of those antique road shows came through town, and I asked one of the experts. He tried to buy it from me back then," she said. "For quite a bit of money, as I recall."

"Do you remember how much money?" Doreen asked.

"Oh my, this was quite a few years ago now, and I think he offered me seven or eight thousand dollars."

Doreen's gaze locked on Scott's, and his eyebrows shot up. He nodded slowly. She smiled. "Do you have any problem with me selling it?"

"Of course not, my dear. I told you. All those antiques in there are your inheritance. And you need to probably sell them all sooner rather than later. You need the money now, not when I die," she said. "Besides, things in that house probably need to be fixed."

"You can certainly see the wear and tear on the living

room floor now that the rug is gone too."

"Oh, right," Nan cried out. "I forgot about the rug. I paid a pretty penny for that quite a few years ago."

"Yeah, we could use receipts for that too."

"They're all together. Whenever you find them, you'll find them all," Nan said cheerfully.

"Any idea where she got it?" Scott asked from her side.

"Nan, do you remember where you got the rug?"

"Somebody who was selling off his antiques, dear. He tried to tell me it was worth a lot of money. I figured it was just him telling me that he needed more than I was offering. You know what negotiating is like."

"But did he have any proof?"

"Nope, I don't think so. That's why I wasn't too interested in paying a higher price," she said. "Of course he tried to tell me there was some sort of mark on the underside. But all I found was some washed-out names. Really wasn't a whole lot there to prove what he was saying. But he was also dying and trying to clean out his property before his family came in and sold it all for pennies."

"That makes sense," Doreen said. She looked to Scott and lifted her shoulders as if to say, *What else can I ask?*

Scott nodded and said, "You need to find those receipts."

"Oh, is that the appraiser there?" Nan asked through the phone. "Hi, I'm Doreen's grandmother." And didn't her voice turn flirty? Doreen just rolled her eyes.

"Yes, this is Scott Rosten here," Doreen said. "He's the man from Christie's."

"You might as well have him take the vase and get it properly appraised," she said. "I'm sure somebody at Christie's will know the value of it. You know what? You can be a specialist in a certain area of antiques, but it's pretty hard to be a specialist in all of them, and that's why I didn't know anything about the rug. It's the only rug I've ever bought, but I loved it." She said, "Did you recognize the hummingbirds all through it?"

Doreen winced. "I don't think I did," she said. "Over the years it got rather dirty."

Nan said thoughtfully, "Speaking of which, I don't think I ever cleaned that rug. I wonder if that devalued it."

Scott piped up. "You probably retained the value because you didn't," he said. "Now we can treat it properly and get it cleaned up without damaging it."

"Oh, good," Nan said. "I always did hate housecleaning."

Chapter 11

Monday Midafternoon ...

DOREEN HUNG UP from her conversation with Nan, watching as Scott carefully photographed everything he could on the vase. She couldn't believe what a gold mine this house had become. And all of it had been Nan looking out for Doreen. She could feel tears pricking the back of her eyes.

"What was this about whether Penny is a murderer?" Scott asked.

Doreen tried to brush it away but knew that curiosity was best killed right at the moment. "Somebody just mentioned that a neighbor's husband had a heart attack, but his symptoms didn't look like a heart attack."

"A lot of things can cause a heart attack," he said, "and murder is usually for the most basic of reasons."

"Money, greed, and passion," she supplied.

"And power," he said, tilting his head at the house. "He who controls is often the one murdered."

She hadn't thought about it that way. As she traipsed outside, watching the beautiful vase be packed up in the back of the big truck, she couldn't understand how mentally she'd shifted to thinking the vase was beautiful, when before, on the mantel, it had been just a vase. Back inside she watched Scott studying everything else on her mantel. "Let me know if anything else is of interest," she said in a dry tone. "I'm sure a year's worth of dust covers everything."

"That's often how antiques are treated," he said. "At least the ones nobody knows have value." He picked up a couple small vases and replaced them and then turned back to her. "All I can say is, at the moment, I'm not seeing anything else."

"I presume the lamps are no good or not worth anything?"

He looked at them and shook his head. "No, much too modern for anything I'm interested in. The pot chairs, the lamps ... are all yours."

"What about the dining room?" she asked. "It's full too. Do you want to take a look?"

He looked at her with interest. "I don't think we ever discussed the dining room."

Nan's house was laid out in lots of small rooms. Not Doreen's preferred style. Doreen led the way through the living room to the parlor on the other side. Scott stepped in, and she could hear him suck back his breath. She turned to look at him as he stared at the dining room table. "So I guess I'm eating in the kitchen forever now?"

He ran his fingers through his hair. "I must have been so dazed by the living room furniture," he admitted, "that it never occurred to me to venture into an adjoining room." He turned and looked back at the door and said, "It was shut, wasn't it?"

She nodded. "Yes. I was wondering about taking off the door and widening the opening so we could have a more open concept."

"As long as you're not trying to keep the natural heritage of the house, I would," he said. "I know this was a charming house in its day, but all the closed-off rooms make it darker and smaller looking, doesn't it?"

"Absolutely," she said. She watched as he walked around the dining room. His gaze was on a huge candle thing in the center atop a long runner across the table, and then his hands gently stroked the table itself. She watched as his focus jumped from one chair to the next, as if counting. And then he took the chair closest to him, crouched beside it, and tilted it slowly onto the floor so he could look underneath. She pulled out her phone and texted Nan. **Is the dining room set worth anything?**

Nan sent back a bolded caps text with lots of exclamation marks.

YES!!!!!!

Doreen sagged onto the closest chair. "You know I haven't even had a meal at this table yet?"

"Good. It's a completely different maker," he said, "and not as valuable as your living room set, but it's certainly a very nice piece, and the fact that you have all eight chairs ..." He shook his head, almost as if at a loss for words. "We won't be finished today, my dear," he said, straightening up. "I'll do a little bit of research on this set, and we're still finishing your bedroom." He glanced at his watch. "It's already three o'clock."

"So tomorrow too then?" She wasn't trying to be pushy, but she was desperate to know if this table was worth money and if he would take it. She hated the avarice rising up within. She looked at the table, deciding if she liked it or did she just not care? It was very dark, and that she didn't like.

She much preferred light wood, like the light pine cupboard, which Scott hated. Even oak would be better. "Is this mahogany?"

He sat back and nodded. "It is, indeed. And very much the color of its era." He checked the upholstery on the chairs and said, "I'm not sure this is the original upholstery though. I'll do some research on that."

She nodded, realizing that would, of course, devalue the set. But maybe not a lot.

Scott sighed and said, "How is it I didn't know about this room before?"

"Because we were so busy," she said, "talking about that big set from the living room and the rest of it in the master bedroom."

He nodded. "I'm not even sure we can get all this done tomorrow, but we will do our best. All of it has to go back to the warehouse and be crated. And then it'll be airlifted."

She raised her eyebrows at that. "Sounds expensive."

He nodded. "It is, indeed. But it's also mandatory."

She had no clue either way and wasn't about to argue with him. She checked the upholstery on each chair. "Well, all the chairs have the same upholstery."

He looked at the table and said, "Another leaf goes with this. Any idea where it might be?"

She looked around the room. "Two hutches are here, but I don't see any table leaf stuck behind them. I'll text Nan again."

He followed her, his hands going over to the hutch. "This is a matching set to the dining room," he cried out happily. He just stood and stared for such a long moment that she realized this really was a surprising discovery for him.

She turned to the nearby piece of furniture and asked, "And that sideboard, is it also?"

He looked at it and frowned. "It's close, but it's not a match."

She could hardly be disappointed when apparently the dining room table and eight chairs and the hutch were all a matching set. "So maybe the sideboard got lost somewhere along the line," she said, "and this was an easy replacement? It looks the same to me, but I guess to your trained eye it's not."

He shook his head. "No," he said, "and it appears all of these drawers are also full. Let me take photos. We'll leave here soon for the day," he said. "They're preparing the lowboy dresser up there and the vanity," he said. "I'm not even sure we'll get the bed apart today. We don't have the right tools. A couple newer screws were put in which we don't have the right heads for, and we definitely want to make sure we use the right tools for every piece."

She nodded. "As long as you get the rest out, then that's something."

He said, "So I've only got about an hour more here, and I promise we'll be back tomorrow morning." He stared at the dining room set in fascination, then looked at her. "You do want to sell it, right?"

Her head bobbed. "While you're gone," she said, "I'll pack up everything in the drawers, if I get time. I really don't know what to do with all the china though." As she thought of that, she thought about china handed down through the ages. "I'll ask Nan if these are sets from my great-great-grandmother." She hadn't heard back from her latest text to Nan about the table leaf, but Doreen sent her grandmother another.

At that, his eyes lit up. He walked over to the hutch, opened up the glass doors, and pulled out a piece of china, a small cup with a saucer. He flipped it over and let out a low whistle. "It's Royal Copenhagen's Flora Danica," he said. "And that is also a lovely find. Each of these pieces would have been hand-painted." He turned back to her and said, "Your Nan has done a very special thing by making sure everything in this house has value. And she's done right by giving it to you now. It's much better than waiting until somebody dies. If she wasn't around, you might not be doing this. You could have just brought in a junkman and tossed it all."

She hated to admit it, but that was a possibility.

He deliberately backed up and said, "If you don't mind, I'll take a bunch of photos. Back at the hotel I'll have some discussions with colleagues. I'll take some photos of those pieces on the mantel too. A couple items there I just don't know about."

She nodded. "Nan had eclectic taste. She not only liked some antiques but she really liked some modern pieces."

"That makes her not a collector but somebody who enjoyed life," Scott said warmly. As he stepped back, her phone rang.

"I have to take this, if you don't mind," she said. "It's Penny."

"The murderer?" he asked with interest.

She winced. "I hope she's not."

He chuckled. "My dear, how could you possibly know?"

She didn't say anything but headed to the kitchen. "Hi, Penny. How are you?"

"I just realized how chaotic your day likely is," Penny said. "I shouldn't have called. You must have the appraiser there."

"It is chaotic. But the men are almost done. What can I do for you?"

"The Realtor said, if we're doing any yardwork, we should do it fast, like that front garden bed. She agreed we should do something with it. Curb appeal opportunity is huge, and, once the photos are taken and people come to view it, it has to be in essentially the same condition."

"So, you want me to come today?" Doreen asked, wincing as she glanced at her wrist and the time. "I suppose I could get an hour in this afternoon. Scott is leaving soon, and I seem to have a bundle of energy I'm trying to wear off just from the excitement of the day."

"Isn't it lovely to find out you're getting money?" Penny said enviously. "And, if you could come by, that'd be awesome. At least then, once you start, you'd know what to do to get the rest done tomorrow and the next day."

"When is the photographer coming to take photos of the house?"

"Wednesday," Penny said.

Wednesday. "Ouch," Doreen said. "That's a lot of work to be done tomorrow."

"I believe he's coming early afternoon. Maybe even at noon."

Doreen groaned. "That's a ton of work. Okay, I'll come this afternoon as soon as Scott leaves."

She hung up and turned to see her vanity making its way down. At least, she presumed it was from the size. She couldn't see anything of it because it was completely wrapped up in packing blankets. Scott was muttering to himself in the dining room, and she didn't dare mention the basement or the garage. But she was pretty darn sure the garage was full of garbage. Still, how could she possibly know if she didn't check it out or have Scott look at it? With all the antiques still in the house, she needed to be wary of intruders too. She'd hoped it would all leave today, but now that they had found more, apparently not. Just then her phone rang. It was Mack.

"Are they gone?" he asked.

She stepped out on the veranda and said, "No, and they can't do the bed today."

"Oh," he said, "well, that's too bad."

"Something about missing certain tools, how some of the bolts have been replaced over the years, and one they don't have the right tool for."

"Makes sense," he said. "And, of course, they don't exactly travel with a ton of tools."

"Right," she said. Cautiously she added, "He also thinks the dining room set could be valuable."

Mack was silent for a moment, and then he chuckled. "You know what? I'm not sure I ever saw your dining room set. You keep the door to the dining room closed. Only if you go around through the kitchen do you see it. And it's always been one of those stately rooms nobody ever uses."

"Exactly," she said. "So he wants to do some research tonight. He's taking photos of everything right now, and then they'll come back in the morning to work on the bed and potentially the dining room set."

"Well, you must be thrilled."

"Thrilled and still terrified," she said, "because that means I have to keep the place safe and the pieces in good condition until he comes back tomorrow."

"Right. That's why I called. To make sure things were going to plan."

She stared out at the garden and said, "I have a favor to ask."

"What's that?" he asked, his tone almost like he had returned to work and was only paying partial attention.

"Can you take a look at the autopsy report on George?" She said it in such a rush she wasn't sure he understood.

Silence was on the other end. "George Jordan?" he asked cautiously.

"Yes," she said, "and I know … I know this sounds stupid. It's just something I found in my living room and something I saw in Penny's garden. I'm about to head up there as soon as Scott leaves and do some work in her front bed because she's just listed her house, and they want to come and take pictures on Wednesday."

"Hold on," he said. "You're not making any sense. Why are you working on her garden if you're now asking me about the autopsy report on her husband?" he asked, his tone sharp. "Do you suspect she might have murdered him?"

"I'm not sure," she said, "but the thought won't leave me alone."

He groaned. "You can't go looking for trouble everywhere. And how on earth would you possibly sign up to do gardening work for her if you think she killed her husband?"

"Well, I figured it was, one, for the money," she said drily. "Remember that thing I need on a regular basis?"

He snorted at that.

"And, two," she said, "it might be a way to find out more." At that he exploded. She winced. "Obviously I'm not going to do anything dangerous."

"You don't know the meaning of the word dangerous," he said in an ominous voice. "I will look. But," he said, "you're not in any way, shape, or form to bring it up or to mention it or to do anything that'll cause Penny to think that's what you believe of her."

"Of course not," she said with feigned innocence. "That would just be mean."

He snorted at that. "Also something you don't understand. You're the nicest damn person I've ever met." And, with that, he slammed down the phone.

She heard the heavy *clunk* and winced. "Well, nice job again, Mugs," she said, feeling a body up against her leg. Only she looked down to find Goliath winding through her legs.

She pocketed her phone and picked up the cat in her arms. "I'm sorry, baby. You don't like all these strangers in the house, do you?"

She buried her face in his neck while giving him a good scratch along his face and his ears. His heavy guttural purr kicked in, and he rubbed hard against her neck and head. She leaned against the railing, and, sure enough, Thaddeus, who had been quietly sleeping upstairs until the men had gone into the bedroom, had flown out the back door and was even now walking back and forth on the railing. "I promise, guys, things will calm down soon."

She just didn't know how soon. Thaddeus hopped up onto her shoulder and cuddled in close. Now she had Goliath in her arms, who reached out a paw, as if to swat Thaddeus off her shoulder. "No jealousy, you two," she ordered. "I'm tired. It's been a very long day, and apparently I have a lot of heavy physical work to do now too." She groaned at the thought, but, at the same time, it might help her understand something more about George's death. Although she had no clue how or why, and she had absolutely no motive for Penny to kill George, Doreen couldn't let go of the idea …

Chapter 12

Monday Late Afternoon …

EXHAUSTED, BUT KNOWING she had to get started anyway, Doreen grabbed a bottle of water and put it in a small pack. She had pocketed her phone and Mugs's leash. He came running at the jingle, and so did Goliath. She looked down at Goliath and grinned. "I really should get you a harness."

He just shot her a look and reached up, stretching along the kitchen door. "Yes, we're going out," she said. Right now the house was silent. The Christie's guys had finally left, but they would return tomorrow morning. She went through the motions of packing chunks of cheese and an apple, then filled her water bottle. She locked the front door and set the alarms, slipping out the back door just in time. With Thaddeus on her shoulder, she followed the creek toward Penny's house.

When she arrived, Penny was out front, looking at the bed in question. When she saw Doreen, she cried out, "Oh, good, I was so afraid you wouldn't be able to come."

"I'm here," Doreen said. "Unfortunately it's been a very long, tiring day."

"Right, and, because of the photographer," she said, "we don't have much time." She had a couple shovels, and apparently she would work at Doreen's side. Doreen couldn't be upset at that. She needed the help to get this done so fast. With the animals milling around the center of the yard, Doreen and Penny dug out the plants currently in the bed. "So, are we moving that Japanese weeping maple?" Doreen asked.

"Maybe," Penny said, "although I was wondering if we should just do flowering shrubs."

"The maple is a statement piece," Doreen said. "But we are taking a chance transplanting it. It's not that they're difficult, but they can be touchy. The other concern I have is that you don't appear to have any water here, no underground irrigation. Is that correct?"

Penny nodded. "It does get hit by the sprinkler though."

Doreen assessed where the water lines were. "So, sprinkler or spray?"

"There is a pop-up sprinkler head on that side," Penny said. "It hits this area."

"Well, that's something. If you were looking to put flowering shrubs in here, they should be ones ready to flower in order to have color this year, but the transplanting could also set them back many months."

Penny's face fell. "I was hoping to put in echinacea."

"We can put some of it in. They are past green at this point so a good choice," Doreen said, "but we should take a fair bit of dirt with those plants to make the transition easier."

They walked to the backyard and looked at some of the perennial bushes. "That isn't a bad idea though," Doreen said. "What you really want is something that'll flower over the next few months while the house is being shown, correct?"

"Right," Penny said, "and that front bed's not very big, yet ... I don't know what to put there."

"How about we do a mix of black-eyed Susans, echinacea, daisies? You have painted daisies here, and their bright pink would offset the lovely purply-pink of the echinacea and the white of the daisies. And, of course, black-eyed Susans are yellow, and they look ready to bloom, but they will come a little later. I can't guarantee they'll all come out at the same time but instead will produce interesting color all summer."

"It would be better if we had some come in stages, right?"

"Exactly." Doreen walked back to the bed in the front yard, studied the size, and guessed it was about six feet by six feet. "This isn't very big," she said. "We'll dig down quite a bit more and need to get some peat moss and topsoil. This is really rocky soil here. The flowers or the maple won't take well to this transplant if we don't boost the soil condition. Do you have a tarp?"

Penny looked at her in surprise. "Sure, but why?"

"Because we have to dig out all this rocky ground," she said, "and you've got a nice driveway here that I don't want to ruin with lots of dirt. If you have a tarp, we can shovel it onto that and then drag it someplace to get rid of it."

Understanding, Penny disappeared into the garage, and then she opened a double garage door so she could walk out that way. It was the first time Doreen had seen the inside of Penny's garage. Doreen didn't want to be resentful, but the fact that it was empty and held a vehicle made her very envious. "I wish my garage looked like that," she murmured.

Mugs woofed at her side; Goliath had stretched out on Penny's porch steps in the sun, and Thaddeus snoozed on the railing beside him.

"This was George's domain," Penny said. "Any time we wanted to do carpentry work or renos or repairs, we'd move the vehicles out, and then he'd have this as his shop."

"Looks lovely. It's also incredibly neat and clean."

"Well, that was George," Penny said, laughing. "He always had to be busy. I think it had to do with stopping his mind from wandering in the direction of what happened to his brother."

"Understandable," Doreen said. She anchored the digging fork into the ground and went to help Penny tug out a big tarp. "It doesn't have to be a big tarp," she said cautiously.

"It's the only one I've got," Penny said. Finally they spread it out beside the garden bed. Mugs was now lying in the shade, ignoring them. Indeed, the tarp was at least ten foot by ten foot, but Penny shrugged and said, "Like you said, we can't get everything all dirty with this little project."

They started digging, removing the rocks, but it was hard work. Penny took the digging fork and loosened up a bit of the bed and then took the shovel and carefully lifted the rocky soil and tossed it onto the tarp. The deeper she went, the more dirt and even more rocks there were. She groaned and said, "Maybe that's why nothing is growing here."

"I think so," Doreen said. By the time they had the entire garden bed down a good foot, they found even more rocks. But she turned and said, "Any chance you have a pickax?"

"Are you strong enough to use one?" Penny asked in

surprise. "I do have one. George used it, but I can't remember what for." She walked back into the garage and came out dragging a large pickax.

Doreen sighed. "Well, here goes nothing." She took it in a firm grip, hefted it over her head, and forcefully pounded it down. If she let it just drop, the bounce would ripple up her arms and destroy her shoulders. But this way she took the blow all the way down, and she could feel it in her back too. But it did seem to make a dent. She did ten more of those strikes and then sat back, saying, "That's hard work."

By the time the rocks were mostly dealt with, the sun had gone behind some clouds. Doreen said, "Well, we didn't get very far, but honestly this is more than I expected to get done. And it's not quite dusk yet."

Penny, sweat dripping down her face, had been sitting off to the side for the last bit, catching her breath. "Do you think it's deep enough? It just seems to be filled with more rocks."

"I gather a lot of Kelowna is built on rocky ground," Doreen said. With the digging shovel she cleaned out the last of the loose rocks. "You know what? We're probably fine here. There is ground underneath, and it looks like we're hitting a bed of clay. We'll use the pickax to just loosen that up, and then we'll drop some good soil in on top to help it replenish that ground." She looked at it and frowned. "You need to get some really nutritious soil in here."

"What do you mean, I need to?" Penny said. "Can't you pick up a bag?"

Doreen chuckled. "How much do you think one bag will fill?

Penny groaned. "Can we take any from the back garden? I don't really have any money to bring in something. The delivery fee will be incredible."

"Probably about fifty bucks," Doreen said absentmindedly. She looked at the back garden. "I could steal some. Let's go take another look." She grabbed her shovel and headed into the backyard. That woke up the animals, and they all raced to her side.

The entire backyard had a perimeter garden, and it was about four feet away from the fence that completely closed it in. Doreen walked along to a couple spots, found a place where nothing was growing, and asked, "Do you remember what was in here?"

"I think the dahlia bulbs didn't do well here."

Doreen stabbed her shovel into the ground and smiled. "Well, it is soft," she said. "I could certainly move a bunch of this over and maybe buy six or seven bags for the top."

"If you could do that, that would be much better."

"I can only do it," she said, "if you have a wheelbarrow."

Penny disappeared into the garage and came back with a wheelbarrow.

Doreen smiled. "Okay, tomorrow I'll move some dirt from here to that front bed. I'll be here first thing in the morning, or as soon as I can. I know my packers are coming back in the morning." She frowned. "Maybe I'll leave them to their own devices while I do this." But she hated to do that.

"I'll head inside now. I'm exhausted," Penny said, wiping her face. "I'll see you in the morning then." And she walked away, leaving Doreen standing in the back garden with her shovel still in the dirt.

Chapter 13

Monday Evening ...

EVEN THOUGH TIRED, with the animals flaked out all around her, Doreen hadn't left Penny's backyard yet. Her animals had done as much running around and dancing, then snoozing, as they could, so they would be more than ready to head home whenever Doreen was ready. She currently inspected the bed of echinacea in the backyard, where Doreen saw a leaf that didn't belong.

She bent down with her cell phone out and took a picture of it. She wasn't sure what it was. Regardless, she could take some echinacea from here and put a little in the front bed. She needed more than one plant in order to make a color splash, but, if she left each transplant fairly small, they would all grow and multiply quickly, and the bed would be full in no time. But still, often new owners came in and ripped out whatever landscaping was here, so it didn't make sense to put too much time or effort or money into this one curb-appeal project, especially with the short time limit involved.

Plus she'd just accepted the price offered, but she hadn't expected all the rocks in the soil, nor having to haul the dirt from the backyard garden to the front bed. Still, it was her fault for not defining exactly what she would do for the money.

She'd done enough today. Slowly she walked back out to the front garden, stopped to survey the work she'd done, taking a couple photographs, although the lighting was wrong. What did she expect with dusk approaching?

And then, with the animals in tow, she strolled back to the creek. As soon as she got there, she stepped into the deeper water, bent down, washed her hands, and then washed her face. The creek water wasn't necessarily clean, but it was cool, refreshing, and helped with the sweaty feeling. When she was done, she stepped back out to see Goliath sitting on a large rock and Mugs sitting in the middle of the creek, just looking at her.

"Come on, Mugs."

Thaddeus, who walked along with them, had hopped from rock to rock to rock. Even now he sat beside Goliath, waiting for her. She and Mugs, both bedraggled and wet, resumed walking. "Let's go home."

By the time she got home, she felt an overwhelming fatigue and relief. "I didn't bring anywhere near enough food," she muttered to the animals as she headed up to the house. She stepped inside and turned off the alarm, took a look at the time, decided it was too late for coffee, and put on the teakettle. "If I still have any energy by the time I come out of the shower," she said, "I might have a cup of tea." She probably needed food; otherwise she likely wouldn't sleep through the night. But first she needed that shower.

She headed to her stairs but stopped at the living room, shaking her head, knowing her bedroom would be way worse. When she got up there, because the massive bed frame was still there, it didn't look all that much different. The vanity and the dresser were gone, leaving large empty places where they'd stood, but she knew everything else had been rearranged to get to those pieces. She walked into the bathroom, stripped down, and stepped under the hot water. It took three shampoos to get her hair clean, and she hadn't done anything about cleaning and drying Mugs.

This was when she wished she had the servants around. If she'd come home tired and the dog wet, two servants would take care of the dog, so he didn't track water and mud across the house. And, of course, her job had been to step into a shower and to make herself perfect looking for whatever was going on that evening. As she stepped out of her en suite bath, a towel wrapped around her, she leaned against the door for a long moment, just resting. "Those were the old days," she muttered. "The good news is, you don't have to be perfect tonight because nobody is here but us."

She put on her pajamas and walked back downstairs. Although technically spring, it had been a hot summerlike day, and she could almost feel the humidity from the shower cloaking her skin by the time she made it to the kitchen, but she was too damn tired to care. She made herself a couple pieces of toast—well, really one piece for her and one piece for Mugs—topped each with peanut butter. Then, along with her tea, took it all with her and sat outside on the deck, enjoying the cooler evening air. Even if she had had the food to make more for dinner, she didn't have the energy to prepare it or to eat it. Mugs matched her almost bite for bite on her hot toast. How was it that he loved peanut butter as much as she did? She quickly consumed her food and then went inside to get a piece of cheese and an apple. By the time she was done with that, she was too tired to keep her eyes open.

She pulled out her phone, checking for messages, and saw Mack had called her. She listened to the message and frowned. She was too tired to deal with him. She flicked through the images she'd taken, looking for the one of the strange leaf among Penny's echinacea. But her phone wasn't the best way to study these. Doreen took her tea back into the kitchen, transferred the images to her email, and opened them up on her laptop.

As she went through them, she stopped at the image of the backyard garden. Something was shining in the corner, near the echinacea. That made no sense because she'd been there and hadn't seen anything. But it had also been at that weird dusk hour, so it might have been hard to see. So why had her cell phone photo picked it up? Maybe because of the flash. She'd also taken several photos of Penny's garage to remind herself that a garage could look like that. Doreen had so much work ahead of her in Nan's garage that it was exhausting even to think about it.

Then she looked at the close-up picture of the echinacea bed with the odd leaf, and she blew it up even larger so she could take a look at the leaves on the inside. She could bring a piece home and check it out a little closer when she started digging in that bed, but it almost looked like foxglove. It was often mistaken for a weed—before it flowered, that is. Honestly hydrangeas, a common flowering shrub, could be some of the most dangerous plants, and Penny had several of those. But then so did Nan.

As Doreen took a look out the window at her back garden, even in the moonlight, she saw dozens of plants in her own backyard which were likely dangerous. But she never once considered Nan was a murderer. So why was Doreen so suspicious of Penny? Doreen opened her browser, brought up Penny Jordan's address, and then went back several years on the city satellite map images to see what Penny's yard had looked like before. Doreen found very few changes had been made in the last ten years.

About fifteen years ago or so ago, that front garden bed had been created per a Google Earth picture date stamped from back then, revealing a big gaping hole in the ground. She frowned as she saw it was much deeper than the hole they made earlier today. Why was that so deep back then? There was no need to go very deep, but obviously the rocks were still there, which meant that, for some reason, George had put all those rocks back in the hole again.

She hadn't done any research on George, outside of how that info pertained to Johnny or Penny. Doreen should look up birth records and marriage licenses.

Just then her phone rang. It was Mack, and she smiled. It would be nice to hear his voice. "Hey, Mack," she said, but there was no way to hide the exhaustion in her tone.

"Sounds like you did too much today," he said. "Did you go to Penny's?"

"I sure did." She explained the problems they came across.

"You were using a pickax?" he asked in astonishment. "You have any idea how sore you'll be tomorrow?"

"You mean, on Wednesday," she said, "because tomorrow I have to go back and do more. Wednesday the photographer's coming."

"I understand Penny needs to get top dollar for her place, but she could have hired somebody else."

"And yet, you know I need the money, so …"

"I sure hope you get a decent price for those antiques, so you don't have to do jobs like this again."

"You and me both," she said, "but you know what? For a while I'll probably keep accepting them because, in my head, I feel like I need them."

"So the packers are coming back in the morning?"

"Yes, but I don't know that they'll get to the dining room," she said. "But they'll be coming and packing up the bed."

"It's pretty exciting for you, on many fronts. Just make sure you're not looking to continue the excitement of the cold cases by dreaming up something that doesn't exist."

She winced. Was she doing that? "I won't."

With that call done, she flipped through the pages of the search she'd started. She always found that supposedly the most relevant stuff on a search came on the first screen load, but some interesting things could be found when you went deeper through the search-related links. Somewhere in the back she found a notice that Penny and George had gotten married. She smiled, and then she saw Penny's last name: Foster. "Penny Foster," she said. "Interesting."

She did a search for Penny Foster and came up with multiple sites, one of them involving a dead brother and his father. She hoped that wasn't the same Penny, but it would explain why the big teddy bear everybody had called George had appealed to her. Doreen found mentions that the father, Randy Foster, had abused the son, Anthony Foster, and he'd eventually died from his injuries. Doreen found that pretty horrible too, and now she couldn't possibly bring it up with Penny. But it did make her much less suspicious in Doreen's mind. With that last thought, she headed up to bed and crashed.

Chapter 14

Tuesday Morning ...

DOREEN WOKE UP feeling like crap but went down-stairs, making herself a cheese omelet, just like Mack had taught her. She needed enough protein to work on Penny's project. While she sat here in the kitchen eating, the doorbell rang. She checked her watch to find it was nine a.m. already. Holding her coffee cup, calling out over Mugs's din of barking, she walked to the front door to find Scott.

He beamed at her. "So do you want to sell the dining room table too?"

She eyed him over the brim of her coffee cup and then nodded. "Yes, I do."

He nodded happily, rubbing his hands together. "Good," he said. "I couldn't get any research on the fabric covering the chairs, so I'll take some better photographs, and I'd much rather do that back at the office, where I have access to more information. But, even with the possibility of it being reupholstered, it's still a really nice piece."

"Take it then," she said, "but that means you probably won't get it all done today, will you?"

"We'll try," he said. "I have two other men with me today."

She looked up at six men behind Scott. She motioned them all in and said, "Go for it," and then remembered she was supposed to empty the hutch. She groaned and said, "If I give you boxes, will you empty everything for me?"

"If you want to sell the hutch, yes," he said. "I'm not sure about the second piece."

"That sideboard did have empty drawers," she said, "so maybe we can transfer everything from the hutch over to it. If not, I'll give you a few boxes. Unfortunately I have to be at a friend's house."

Scott nodded. "Not to worry," he said. "We'll be fine. We'll get the table and the chairs all out of the dining room first, and that will give us space to empty out the hutch." And, with that, he started barking orders, and the moving men dispersed through her place.

Mugs, more confused than ever, sat at her feet and whimpered. She crouched down and said, "It's okay. This is the last day of craziness."

"Unless you find more pieces," Scott said cheerfully.

"I better ask Nan about that."

He poked his head around the corner and looked at her in astonishment. "You haven't yet?"

She shook her head. "No, but I need to. She'd know which pieces are the most valuable."

"I would think so," he said. "Call her while I'm here. Who knows what you might find out?"

Trouble was, Doreen was out of time. She looked at her menagerie, and she couldn't leave them with the moving men in the house, which meant she'd take them to the garden center with her. But that would eat into her time. Better that she head out now and get the gardening work done first. Avoiding it wouldn't help. "I'll call her while I'm walking up to my friend's house," she said.

"We'll be here when you get back."

She stopped and asked, "No chance of hidden drawers in this thing, right?"

He shook his head. "Not likely. I was just looking at it. I won't see any hidden letters like last time or any more treats."

"If you take it apart and find something …"

"Absolutely we'll save it for you. Don't you worry. We know this is part of your heritage."

Even him saying that made her feel guilty all over again. She grabbed several apples and figured she'd buy some food while she was out getting the potting soil. She also grabbed a bottle of water and filled her travel mug with coffee. And then calling the animals, she headed out the back door and walked toward Penny's house. As she did, she called her grandmother. "Nan, did you know that dining room table is valuable?"

"Of course it is," Nan said brightly.

"What else should I tell the appraiser about?"

"All of it, silly."

Doreen shook her head, about to object to Nan's lack of specificity, when Nan spoke again.

"How are you? You sound terrible."

Doreen rolled her eyes at that. "Thanks, Nan. That makes me feel so much better."

"Didn't you sleep last night?"

"I slept like a log," Doreen said, rotating her stiff shoulders as she walked. "The trouble was, I'd done a lot of heavy physical work at Penny's first. Found a ton of rocks in that bed. I'm on my way up there now. She's paying me to put together a nice front garden bed for the Realtor's photos tomorrow."

"And what are you doing for her?"

Doreen explained, and Nan said, "So it'll just be a green bed for the photos then?"

"Yes," she said, "because nothing is in bloom, unless I can get her to buy a couple annuals."

"You can also put some dianthus or something around the bottom just to show a spot of color."

"The problem is, Penny doesn't want to spend any more money than she has to," Doreen explained. "And I certainly understand that. She's looking for a small memorial to improve that bed, which was an eyesore."

"Right. That eyesore has been there for a long time though."

"Yes, I looked on Google Earth, and, about fifteen years ago, it was a great big hole originally. Maybe from sewer work. I don't know for sure."

"So somebody turned it into a rock garden? That's a better answer."

"I could certainly put in sedums and some hens and chicks," Doreen said thoughtfully. "But I don't think Penny has any of those in her garden in the backyard. She didn't want to buy any either. And that front bed is a big-enough space that she'd spend a fair bit of money to fill it."

"Like you said, she's selling the house. So just snag what you can from the back garden—without making it look like you stole from it—and do what you can," Nan said cheerfully.

"Did you know Penny before?" Doreen asked.

"What do you mean by before?"

"Before she married George."

"Yes and no," Nan said.

"Meaning?" She and her animals were already at the place in the creek where they crossed. Thaddeus sat on her shoulder, so Doreen picked up Goliath under the belly, listening to him howl as she carefully stepped across the rocks. Mugs had no intention of staying dry and dove into the middle of the creek, working his way over. When he popped out on the other side, she joined him.

"Just that she was a young woman, originally from the lower mainland, and, of course, she had some family problems we knew about but didn't really know the extent of," Nan said.

"Apparently her father was abusive."

"Yes, I believe he killed her younger brother. We always said that was why George was perfect for her. George was a very gentle soul."

"Right," Doreen said. "What happened to her father?"

"No idea. I think he went to jail for a bit, and then he just disappeared. Maybe he's dead."

"Well, that's probably a relief for Penny at least. Particularly if she was afraid of him. Afraid he'd come back into her life."

"She was afraid of him," Nan said. "But that was a long time ago."

"True, but some things stay with you."

"I think that's why she was close to Johnny, because she had lost her own brother so young."

"How old was he, do you know?"

"It was one of those sad cases where he'd been abused a lot, so he was small for his age, but I don't really know all the details, dear. You could ask Penny though."

"Yeah, well, I won't do that," Doreen said. "I can hardly

walk up and say, 'Hey, Penny, I'm investigating your family. You want to give me all the gory details?'"

"Why not?" Nan said testily. "You know how much easier it would be if people were honest?"

"I can't argue with that," Doreen said. "Don't suppose there would be anybody in the old folks' home who would know, would there?"

Nan chuckled. "I feel like I'm a really good source of information for you."

"I was just thinking about Richie's age and how much he might know about Penny and maybe Penny's family."

"Not just Richie but possibly Maisie," Nan said thoughtfully. "But that would mean being nice to her."

"Nan, it's not hard to be nice," Doreen chided. "Remember that you're not supposed to get into any more trouble."

"Which means I need to avoid Maisie," Nan said. "Something about that woman just sets me off."

"Okay," Doreen said hurriedly. "Don't talk to Maisie then. Maybe ask Richie."

"I can do that," she said, and she hung up just as Doreen approached Penny's place.

Chapter 15

Tuesday Morning ...

A T PENNY'S HOUSE Doreen headed straight for the backyard garden where she'd taken the pictures last night, looking for whatever had been shining in the photograph, but she saw no sign of anything. With a shovel she stabbed the area where she thought she had seen it and found a small piece of laminate. Like from an ID card. Since it was a corner with no markings on it, she tossed it aside. *I'm wasting time.* She glanced around, looking for Penny, but saw no sign of her.

Penny didn't have to stay here and watch or work alongside Doreen; it was just a matter of whether Penny wanted to get the work done in time or not. Realizing there was no help for it, Doreen opened the garage door, pulled out the wheelbarrow again, and saw Penny's car was gone. When empty, the garage appeared huge. It looked so much like a man's domain that she could understand how this was George's space.

She put on the gardening gloves still on the workbench, and one of them caught on a drawer. The drawer popped open. She went to close it but saw a small leather-bound journal facing her. Glancing around, and knowing she had absolutely no business opening it, she picked it up and flipped through it. It looked to be in a man's handwriting. She'd seen Penny's handwriting on the letter she'd sent her, and this wasn't it.

And then she saw something about Penny in here. Realizing she shouldn't read it, Doreen put it on top of the bench and closed the drawer, then grabbed the wheelbarrow and headed to the backyard. As she dug away, gathering soil from the backyard to transport to the front yard, she couldn't stop thinking about that journal. She filled the wheelbarrow with as much dirt as she could handle, turned around, and walked it slowly back out to the front yard, where she dumped it in the garden bed. She did this four more times; then she grabbed her water, wiping the sweat off her forehead, and returned to where she'd left the journal.

She took off her gloves, flipped though the book again. No name was on it, but it appeared to be ramblings all within the last year of George's life. There were sporadic dates as well as lots of entries with no dates. Toward the end was a single line: *I have no choice.* Hearing a vehicle, Doreen dropped the journal back into the drawer, pulled up her water bottle, and stepped out as Penny drove into the driveway.

She waved and honked and pulled up beside the garden bed. She hopped out and said, "I knew we were short on time, so I picked up the extra soil, so you didn't have to."

"Good," Doreen said, delighted at Penny's thoughtfulness, making her own actions feel that much worse. "I wasn't sure how I would manage it all. I've moved five wheelbarrows full of soil from the backyard garden. Take a look and see if you're okay with how I've been taking out the dirt."

Penny nodded and said, "If you want to bring the wheelbarrow here, we can unload this."

Doreen nodded and brought over the wheelbarrow, wondering how she'd become a heavy laborer. She had less muscle than so many people. She lifted and moved the potting soil bags to the wheelbarrow and then dropped them off beside the new garden bed. She took the shovel and smoothed around the dirt. She looked to Penny and said, "Do you have a hose?"

"Of course." Penny went into the garage again, brought out a hose, hooked it up to a water tap just outside the large garage door, and handed the other end to her.

Doreen soaked down the dirt she'd brought here, wondering how she could open up a discussion on Penny's family. "I'll get a couple more wheelbarrows full." She shut off the water, grabbed her shovel and wheelbarrow, and headed to the back. Penny came with her.

Doreen said, "I noticed how much space is in your garage. It's amazing that you don't have all the junk like I have in mine."

"They're probably about the same size garages too," Penny said, looking over her shoulder at her garage, still open. "I don't even notice it. I never go in except to park and to go through to the house. Now that I'm selling though, I imagine I'll have fun trying to clean out George's stuff."

"Have you still got all his stuff in the house too?"

Penny shook her head. "No, I cleared out all his clothing and most of his personal belongings. I gave it all to Goodwill. But something about the garage is a bit daunting."

"I might be able to help you," Doreen said. "But I admit, for the moment, I'm pretty busy."

"Well, if you have time," Penny said in delight, "it

would be lovely to get a spare hand or two. I figured I would just open up the back of the car and fill it and take it all down to Goodwill. If you want anything here, you're welcome to have it."

"Maybe I'll take a look a little later," Doreen said. "I'd love to recreate that same setup at my garage."

"Absolutely nothing in there I want," Penny said, "so help yourself. Take it all if you want. Including the benches as far as I'm concerned. I'll run out and grab some groceries. I meant to do that before, but I figured you would be here working and needed the potting soil first." On that note she drove away again.

Doreen immediately stopped what she was doing, picked up the journal, and stuffed it in her little bag. That was one thing she definitely wanted. She returned to her work, and, by the time Penny came back, all the dirt from the backyard had been moved over, all the potting soil bags had been emptied and mixed in—but for two bags still left on the side to heap around the transplanted plants.

She next moved to the black-eyed Susans, finding two lovely little clumps to transplant. She brought them out to the front yard carefully in the wheelbarrow and planted them across from each other. She was thinking of a sundial type of a system. With both planted, she again went to the backyard, hunting out more options. She found two smaller clumps of daisies, just starting to bud. They were kind of late for her, but the clumps were really compacted, which would explain it. She hoped they would survive the transplant. Even if they didn't bloom right now, they certainly would pick up and do well next year. Daisies were like that—they were hardy.

The animals made every trip with her until they slowly dropped to the side and just watched her.

Doreen straightened, rubbed her shoulders, and pulled an apple from her bag. She munched away as she wandered through the garage. While Penny wasn't here, Doreen went through all the drawers, looking for anything else of interest. But there didn't appear to be much. She found lots of sandpaper and metal files and stuff. She was fascinated by the tools and really would love to have a bunch of them because she had so many renos to do. She wasn't all that handy herself, or at least didn't know if she was or not, but she couldn't even begin to determine that if she didn't have tools. She'd find a way to empty her damn garage so she could get it set up like this.

On the walls were boards with holes in them, full of hooks and tools hung in neat and tidy rows across the wall. There were hammers and chisels and so much more—everything one could possibly want. If Penny wanted to get rid of it, well, dare she hope Doreen could have it all? Just then Penny's vehicle pulled back in again. She turned and waved as Penny pulled up into the garage. Penny hopped out and said, "See what I mean? There's just so much of it."

Mugs came over to greet Penny.

Doreen nodded. "I have so much work to do on my house, and I really could use what's here."

"Take it all then," Penny said. "I've already asked my daughters, and they don't want anything, not to mention the fact they're back East, so it'll be much harder for them to get stuff."

Doreen pointed Penny to the new bed as they both walked to the garden and said, "This is what I've done so far. What do you think?" She explained which plants were which and what else she planned to do.

Penny nodded enthusiastically. "We should have done

this a long time ago," she said. "When you consider how overgrown those plants are in the backyard, they probably should have been divided a long time ago."

She walked back to the car, unloaded the groceries, and said, "I've picked up some doughnuts. I'll come out with a cup of coffee for you and a doughnut in a few minutes."

At that, Doreen laughed and said, "Thanks, I could use the sugar." And she returned to the back garden. She studied the painted daisies, but they weren't in great shape, and they would be much smaller. With that thought in mind, she found two small ones and put them together at the front of the new bed.

And then she wanted the echinacea, and these plants would be smaller at the beginning but would grow higher, so she wanted them at the back of the new bed on both sides. So she went to the big pile of echinacea at the rear gate in the backyard. It wasn't that it was in any better shape, but it happened to be the clump she was interested in. She gently loosened the roots and divided off several good-size plants. She wouldn't mind having three for along the back of the front bed because, when it came to blooms, they were really stunning. She didn't know the height of the daisies that she'd put in. She was used to daisies that grew a good three feet high. There might be some adjustments down the road, depending on what the garden looked like when the roots fully took. Moving carefully, she brought the echinacea clumps to the front.

Just then Penny popped out of the front door with a cup of coffee. She looked at the echinacea and said, "Oh, I thought you would take it from the good bed."

"That's one of the reasons why I took it from the one at the fence back there," Doreen said. "They didn't look to be doing too well there."

"I thought we were trying to make this prettier though," Penny said, worrying at the bed. "Oh, you found the painted daisies. Those are pretty there."

"Yes," Doreen said. "Do you have a birdbath or a centerpiece of some kind? We discussed the weeping maple, but I don't think that's a good idea now."

"I have a tall lamp. It's solar. I took it out from the backyard because it was in danger of being completely overgrown. Let me see if I can find it." She placed a cup of coffee down on the ground where Doreen could reach it and disappeared.

Doreen took a big slug of water followed by a sip of coffee. Goliath snoozed on the porch steps; Mugs was at her feet, content. Thaddeus had taken up residence at the railing again. She reassessed her day's work. Time was speeding by, and she still had to fix the holes in the back gardens where she'd taken all these plants. She personally thought a nice centerpiece and some white rock around the base would really set off this new bed, but she'd also promised to give this bed some sort of a finished edge.

Once she was done with the transplanting, she could dump the rest of the potting soil in and around and pack the plants in tight. She wiped her forehead and decided she should check her phone. She'd turned it off while she was working, and, sure enough, there was a call from Nan. Glancing around, she called her grandmother back. "Hey, Nan. What's up?"

"Are you working at Penny's?"

"Yes," she said, taking a couple deep breaths. "And it's hard work. But I'm hoping to be done today."

"I thought you didn't have to be done until tomorrow."

"I forgot about the brick edging to finish off the new bed," she said with her shoulders sagging. "It'll be tomorrow before I'm done for sure."

"Anyway I did hear some news I thought you'd like to know," Nan said. "Well, you know Penny was from the lower mainland. That's where he died."

"Who died?" Doreen asked, trying to follow the conversation.

"Penny's brother, and I guess eventually her father, although I don't know of what."

"Thanks for this. I can call you back when I get home tonight, particularly if you have any more information for me."

Nan lowered her voice. "Can't talk now, can you, huh?" she asked in a loud raspy whisper.

Doreen groaned. "Not really."

"Okay, fine," Nan said, "interesting," and, with that, she hung up.

Doreen wanted to scream. *Interesting* was a heck of a hook to end that conversation on, but leave it to Nan to add a bit of drama to the moment. Doreen wondered what betting pool Nan was setting up on this one. But her deadline loomed, and she really wanted to be done with this job. Before it did her in. She also had to get home to the guys working on the antiques. So it was a good thing she had tomorrow morning still.

Just then Penny came back with a very tall solar garden lamp. She said, "This used to have a big cement block that it gets screwed into, but I don't know where the block went."

Doreen looked at it and said, "This is lovely and would look wonderful in the center." She placed it in the middle of the bed for a look.

"That's really nice," Penny said again with a big smile. "I don't know why I didn't do this before."

"We do need something for a base to support it. What about the cement thing around back at the corner of the house?"

Penny looked at her in surprise and darted out of sight. She came back a little later, rolling a great big round cylinder. "I don't know how you managed to see this," she said, stopping near the bed, out of breath, "but it's exactly what I was talking about. The holes are a bit dirty though. I don't know if we can clean them out."

While Penny rested for a moment, Doreen had her hold the lamp. Then Doreen got the hose and cleaned the holes in cement base. "Do you have any bolts?"

"Somewhere," she said doubtfully, "but I don't know where."

"Do you mind if I look in the garage?" Doreen asked.

Penny nodded. "Like I said, you can have anything you want in there."

"Then I want it all," Doreen said, laughing. She opened drawers until she found a couple bolts, looked at them, and nodded. She came out with nuts, bolts, and washers. She tried them for size and said, "Look at that? They fit."

Together the two women put the bolts through the lamp base and into the big cement block, and then, with a washer and a nut on the other side, Doreen manually tightened each down. She had to go back to the garage and get a wrench in order to tighten them all securely.

"You're really handy, aren't you?"

Doreen chuckled. "Don't tell my ex that," she said. "He thought I was useless."

It took the two of them to lift the block and lamp into

place in the newly redesigned bed.

Doreen realigned it and said, "Penny, walk over to the end of the driveway and see which way it looks best."

With Penny at the driveway telling Doreen to turn it slightly left and then a little more until finally she was satisfied, Doreen pushed down the block as deep into the bed as she could get it and then packed the displaced dirt up and around it. Afterward she sat back and looked at it. "You know something? That looks really nice."

"Just imagine when it's full of flowers," Penny said, smiling. "Now we just need a border." She looked at what was there and said, "I know something's already there, but it's half buried in the dirt and looks pretty rough."

"Well, maybe we can just hose it all off." Doreen grabbed the hose and washed the bricks on the outside edge of the bed. It would be easier on her if she didn't have to create a new border and could instead just clear off the old one. She turned to Penny and said, "Do you have a nozzle where I can get a harder spray out of this?"

At that, Penny looked doubtful. "I can take a look on the backyard hose," she said, "but I don't think so." She went around to the back, while Doreen used her thumb to make a more forceful spray. Soon she found the ring of bricks, almost completely buried under the dirt. But she worked harder at uncovering them because this would save her a ton of time. As it was, she would go home now. She could finish this up in the morning.

Penny came back and said, "No, I don't think so."

Doreen nodded. "This brick edging will take a couple hours to clean up, and I have to go home now, but we've done a ton today. How about I come back early tomorrow morning? I can have this looking pretty decent before the photographer gets here."

Penny smiled. "It's after six o'clock. Do you think your movers are gone?"

Doreen looked at her in shock. "Is it after six? Good Lord, I'm seriously late. I will see you in the morning." And, with that, she scooped up the leash hooked on Mugs and called Goliath, who was lying in the far corner of the garden, as far away from the hose's water spray as he could get. She tucked up Thaddeus onto her shoulder, and she raced home. By the time she got there, she was out of breath, and Mugs, who had run all the way with her, panted heavily. She groaned when she saw the house was dark and closed. But, of course, the movers wouldn't have known to set the security alarm. Sighing, she opened the back door and stepped in.

Chapter 16

Tuesday Early Evening ...

DOREEN TOOK OFF her dirty shoes, left them on the deck, and called out, "Scott, you here?" Of course there was just silence. She pulled out her phone and dialed him. "Hey, I'm sorry I missed you."

"Not to worry," he said. "We've left you boxes and boxes of stuff to go through, and I've taken pictures of the china. I'm not sure if it's worth selling or not, but I do have somebody I can ask. It was a very long day. We got your bed, the dining room set, and the hutch. I'm pretty sure you'll probably find more, and, if you do, please let me know. I did take a quick glance around. I didn't snoop, and I didn't see anything at first glance, not like when I saw the dining room table," he said warmly. "But I know you said there's a basement and a garage too."

"Yes," she said, walking through to the dining room. "I'm in the dining room right now, and I can't believe how big it is without that table here."

"Having a hutch on either side and the table really took up a lot of space," he said. "You'll see we left the sideboard and lots and lots of boxes for you."

Indeed, at least eight boxes were on the floor. "Thank you," she said. "I should decide if I want to keep the china or let it go too. If keeping it, I need a place for it." In her mind, she added, *hence the hutches.* He had left her one, but she wasn't sure if it was big enough to hold all this.

"Like I said, it might be valuable. Well, I know it is valuable," he corrected himself. "But I don't know if it's valuable enough that you want to part with it."

"What value are you thinking?" she asked.

"Probably three to four thousand. Potentially more but I can't be certain yet."

She looked down at the dishes and said, "Absolutely I want to sell them."

"Okay," he said. "When you have a moment, put all of the set off to one side and let me know exactly what you have for inventory, and I'll confirm with my specialist. I saw a bunch of extra serving dishes and platters, and that all helps with the value too. And, like I said, if you have any other questions or if you find any other pieces, let me know. It's been lovely dealing with you, Doreen."

She smiled and said, "Don't forget. You owe me a ton of paperwork too."

He chuckled. "Check your email. There are receipts for everything we've picked up yesterday and today, and I left paper copies of everything for you as well. And, if you get a chance, it's really important before the auction that we find any provenance dealing with these pieces."

She groaned. "I know. I just haven't had a chance."

"Or space apparently, but I feel like I almost emptied your house. I was feeling pretty bad when we took out the dining room table because, with the empty master bedroom, the empty living room, and now the empty dining room, you look like you have no furniture at all."

"That's just fine," she said firmly. "I still have an old kitchen table and chairs, and I have a couple chairs in the living room that will do until I figure out what I'm up to. Besides, I needed to clear everything out in order to fix the living room floor." Suddenly remembering what that was all about, she walked back over to the living room and stared down at the wood. "I'll call you as soon as I know anything more."

She thanked him and hung up. She stood here, rubbing her face, wondering how her calm, boring life had become so cluttered. She really hadn't needed Penny's added job, but she knew her friend needed help, and Doreen really did need the money. Plus she potentially got a garage full of tools to boot. But now she was exhausted. She walked back to the kitchen, put on the coffeepot, and sagged in a chair. Immediately the animals came toward her, hollering, and she realized they were hungry too.

As she finished feeding the last one, she heard a vehicle on the driveway. She walked out to the front to see Mack. She opened the door and smiled at him. When he hopped out with a large pizza box in his hand, she cried out in joy. "I sure hope you plan on sharing that," she said.

He grinned at her. "Hey, you probably have enough food in there that I could make another big pasta dish, and chances are you haven't touched all that pasta sauce either, have you?"

She nodded. "I didn't know what to do with it," she said. "I ate the leftover spaghetti salad, but the rest of the food is still here."

"We'll cook tomorrow," he said. "But tonight I'm too damn tired, and you look terrible."

"Thanks," she said bluntly. "I just came back from working on Penny's garden. I haven't even had a chance for a shower. I completely missed Scott leaving."

That's when Mack stepped into the living room. "Wow, does this room ever look different."

"Yeah, what about this one?" she asked, and she led him through the door into the dining room.

Mack whistled. "This is a huge room."

"I know," she said, "but all the dishes are on the floor, and now Scott tells me those are valuable too."

Mack chuckled. "You sound so despondent, and yet, this house has been such a gold mine."

"I know," she said, "and now I worry that somebody'll come and steal the china."

He nodded solemnly. "Go get a quick shower, and I'll set up the pizza on the kitchen table."

She shook her head. "I don't think I can. I need food. I'll just wash up in the sink, and then we'll eat."

And that's what she did. So, even though her hair was dusty and dirty, and her bones were so sore and her muscles so fatigued, like warm melted butter, she sat down at the kitchen table and reached for the biggest slice. The funny thing was, he let her.

As soon as she had her piece, he picked up the second biggest. She ate slowly, savoring it with her eyes closed.

"You realize it's almost seven, right?"

She nodded. "Penny had promised me coffee and a doughnut this afternoon, and I got the coffee but no doughnut, and I had only taken a couple apples with me. I had planned to pick up soil and my lunch at the same time, but Penny surprised me by making the soil run. I did make an omelet before I left, but I was late leaving this morning.

Scott was here with extra men to take the dining room stuff. It was just chaos. And then I got to Penny's place and had so much work to do there before the deadline," she said, her voice gaining a little strength as she explained.

Mack asked exactly what she was doing for Penny, so Doreen told him. And then she said, "She also said I could have anything I wanted out of the garage because, if she sells the house and she's moving back East, she'd just get rid of it at Goodwill."

"Is there anything you want?"

"You know," she said, tilting her head and looking at him thoughtfully, "I think I do. She has a lot of tools there. I used a bunch to get her a garden lamp set up in a block of cement. Obviously it already had predrilled holes, but she had a good drill and several circular saws, even hand saws, and I don't have any of that."

He looked at her and asked, "Do you know what to do with them?"

"No, not really, but I found bolts and got them on using a wrench," she stated firmly. "And what I don't know I can learn."

"Exactly," he said. "I'm quite happy about this."

The thing was, he hesitated. She looked over at him curiously as she took another bite of dripping hot melted cheese and closed her eyes again in joy. When he didn't speak, her eyes flew open, and she said, "What?"

He frowned, but a glint of humor was in his gaze as he said, "Where will you put it all?"

She snorted. "I did think about that, and, of course, the answer is, *in my garage*. Except that my garage is full."

"Maybe this weekend we'll tackle it," he said. "Can you still find time to work on my mother's garden?"

She barely held back the groan because that was the last thing she wanted to do, but it was her weekly job, so it was what she did. She nodded. "I have to finish Penny's tomorrow by noon. The photographer is coming early afternoon, so I'm just cleaning up the brick, cleaning up the yard, making sure it all looks pretty, and then I'll fix up the backyard from where I pulled the flowers and the extra dirt. But I should be done by twelve. I'll take Thursday off and will go over to your mom's Friday before noon as usual."

"So maybe Saturday we should take a look in your garage."

"That would be very nice. I'd love to get that door open and to figure out if the contents are garbage or valuable."

"From what I saw, it was garbage," he said bluntly.

"I know. That's what I saw too. But I was hoping maybe something of a useful nature was in there."

"Once you figure out how much other stuff here is valuable, maybe hold a garage sale for what's left."

"That's a great idea. I'm just not sure how to do one. I haven't been to one myself."

He slowly lowered the piece of pizza in his hand and said, "What?"

"That was far too beneath my husband's stature," she said, mimicking her ex. "And I haven't had a chance to do anything here," she complained good-naturedly. "Apparently something and some people have been keeping me busy."

At that, he chuckled. "Okay, definitely Saturday," he said. "I'll pick you up, and we will go garage sale shopping. There are always lots of garage sales in town during the spring and summer."

"Maybe we should do that, then come back and take a look at the garage," she said thoughtfully. "And can the sauce hold until then? If tomorrow doesn't work out?"

"If we freeze it, it could," he said. "I'll warm it up again, but you don't want to let food sit for more than five days in the fridge."

She nodded. "Five days, got it." But she wondered if she actually did. It seemed like the days were running past her so fast that she didn't have a clue if she was coming or going.

Chapter 17

Wednesday Morning ...

WEDNESDAY MORNING, DOREEN woke up, her body protesting as she forced herself out of bed and into a hot shower. Today she had to be finished for Penny's sake, and then she wanted to come home and just settle into her own space. It felt odd right now, as if all the men had left some sort of foreign energy behind. Not that the place was full of testosterone or anything, but it just felt like it wasn't her own. Of course the fact that so much of the furniture had been stripped out also made it feel unusual.

When she was finally dressed, she couldn't find any more energy to dance down the stairs. Instead, she dragged her sorry butt all the way down, one step at a time. She was saddened to see Mugs looked exhausted too. "Hey, Mugs, we'll only be there for a few hours today." Goliath was lying at the bottom step and refused to move.

Using the banister, she hopped over him, wincing as she landed on her feet, the motion jarring up her legs and back. That wheelbarrow and she had not gotten along very well yesterday. This was the most physical work she could remember ever doing in her life. And she needed food, as in a decent amount of food. But she also felt very short on time.

She slapped together a large sandwich and sat down with that and a fresh cup of coffee. She'd fed the animals, so they would be good for the trip too. She kept her phone on Silent, not wanting to be disturbed with anything else that she had to get done. She needed to focus on Penny's place, and then she wanted to do nothing more than come home and collapse. She'd have said collapse on the couch, but she no longer owned one. She gave herself a head shake and said, "Hey, this is huge for you, so let's just get this job done and move on."

She made herself another sandwich to bring with her because yesterday she hadn't had anywhere near enough food. And then, with her coffee in her travel mug, she opened the door, and amazingly all the animals perked up.

"Come on, guys."

Thaddeus, however, was looking for a ride. He walked up her arm to her shoulder and tucked in close. She chuckled, and then she thought about whether she needed to reset the alarm and decided that being tired was no excuse. Still a lot of china and other items were inside that she had no idea how valuable they were. She also needed to ask Nan if more valuable stuff was around and get a real answer this time. Particularly among the mess in the garage.

She reset the alarms and then led everybody out the kitchen door. The trip was slow, even though she was trying to push it to get there, but she found it hard to force her legs to move with any kind of enthusiasm.

Once there, she put her sandwich and coffee mug down and started in on the bricks. She needed a steel brush, the hose, and a rake, and it took two hours to get all the bricks cleaned up and nicely set. She was happy to see the tall lamp in the middle, standing straight and true. The good-size cement block gave the lamp a secure base.

Finally she was done. She stepped back, wiping her face. She was now covered in mud from the water used to clean up the bricks. She shut off the water and reached for her coffee cup and then took several steps back to look. So far, she had seen absolutely no sign of Penny.

Or of the animals. They'd all hidden in the shade at the side of the house. It seemed like they wanted her to finish this job too. It was nowhere near as much fun as solving cold cases.

As she stood here, wondering if the bed was good enough, Penny drove up behind her.

She hopped out and said, "Wow, that looks lovely. I noticed this morning just how much that lamp sets it all off." She pointed at the bricks. "I don't know how you got them so nice and shiny. I had no idea they could look like that."

"They'll darken once they're dry," Doreen said, "but they're looking pretty good. I'll tidy up the backyard for pictures."

On that note, she picked up half her sandwich, munched through it for energy, and, when she was done, with Penny having long since disappeared into the house, Doreen grabbed the rake and carefully covered her tracks. In the backyard, she started at the first clump she had removed and carefully moved dirt and some of the rocks around to hide that she'd just stolen parts and pieces. Then she took the rake and carefully gave the space between some of the larger open areas a bit of a rake to make it look better. When she was done, she could feel her shoulders sagging again. She walked the wheelbarrow back to the garage, putting it where it belonged, and hung up the rake. Then she took pictures of the garage and everything that was in it.

Penny came out just then, holding two one-hundred-dollar bills in her hand. "As much as I can't afford it, you did such a phenomenal job that I'm delighted. Here."

Doreen thanked her and pocketed the money. She knew all about offering and not affording. She pointed to the garage and said, "Are you serious about letting me have this stuff?"

"Absolutely," Penny said. "And probably the sooner, the better. It's fine for showings, but I'm sure the Realtor would say it would be better if the garage were empty too."

"Right," Doreen said. "The question is whether the workbenches are attached or not." She lifted the edge of the first one and nodded. "So these can leave too."

"It would make a lot more space in here for whoever buys the house," Penny exclaimed. "So the sooner ..." And she cocked an eyebrow at Doreen.

Doreen chuckled. "Yep. I have to go home and try to sort out my house, and then I'll get into my garage. I presume you're okay if I have a week or two to get George's stuff cleaned out?"

"Sooner would be better. If you need some tools, like right away, feel free to come back. I don't lock the garage, so anytime you want, come on in. Open up that big door and start moving stuff."

Doreen smiled in delight. "Thank you," she said sincerely. "That's a huge help."

The two women waved at each other as Penny said, "I've got to go," and headed to her car again. "Apparently there's more paperwork for the Realtor to sign."

"There's always paperwork for that stuff, but you're good to go for the pictures now." Doreen picked up Mugs's leash, hooked him on, grabbed her travel mug, and said, "I've got to head home myself."

"And I've got to be back for the photographer in an hour."

The two women separated with Doreen heading toward the creek, the animals finally moving with some energy as they realized she was done and they were heading home. She was fascinated that she had been gifted an entire tool shop. She could already hear her husband's disparaging remarks as to why she'd want it since she didn't know how to use anything. But maybe it would help a lot if she could have the tools for somebody else to use while working on her house.

And she hated to say it, but a part of her thought maybe she could sell some of it and get more money. It made her sound greedy, and that wasn't how she wanted to be viewed. She wondered how to move the entire workshop to her place, including the workbenches and all those boards with the hooks. She should talk to Mack about that. At least she'd taken a ton of photos, so she could put it up in her garage the same way.

When she finally got back home again, she propped open the kitchen door for some fresh air and put on more coffee. She washed up, made herself another sandwich, and then slowly walked through her living room and dining room. It really would be nice if she could take out the wall between the two rooms. It depended on how they'd built it though. She didn't know if a retaining beam was up there, if that wall was structural, and she wasn't even sure how to find out. She opened the door to the dining room and walked through. She still had all the dishes to deal with and the sideboard Scott hadn't taken. Yet some of the clutter was gone.

She opened the door and walked through to the kitchen. She had a complete circle layout with the laundry room right beside the kitchen. She walked in and opened up the door to the garage. She flicked on the light switch and just stared, groaning. "It would be easier to look at this," she said out loud, "if we could open the big doors." But she would wait for Mack for that.

Speaking of which, she heard a vehicle coming up the driveway. She walked out to the front to see Mack parking in her driveway. He hopped out, and he held two items that she could identify through the clear Bubble Wrap, the snow globe and the vase that Darth had stolen from her place. She smiled. "You guys don't need them anymore?"

"All the photos have been taken for evidence, and they've released these back to you."

She held open the door while he carried them in, and they unwrapped both pieces and placed them back on the mantel. "You need somebody who can give you a hand with the little stuff, don't you?"

She nodded. "Scott was supposed to send me some names, but I don't think he has yet." She yawned unexpectedly, then apologized. "I finished Penny's garden this morning, so I admit that I just want to sit and veg for the rest of the afternoon."

"Considering your dining room looks like it does, … maybe fix that up first …"

"It was in the back of my mind to sort more of that too," she said. "Or sorting my bedroom. The more I get cleared out, the more I realize there is more to clear out."

"You'll get through it," he said in a commiserating tone. "I got off early today. Have you eaten?"

"I had another sandwich," she said, "but, if you're offering food, I'm happy to eat again."

He chuckled at that and said, "I thought we could take some of that spaghetti sauce, if you haven't frozen it all yet, and turn it into something for dinner. I have a green salad and a sauce dish in mind."

"Absolutely. Are you staying here until dinner then?"

"No, I can get it started, leave it to simmer, and then come back in a few hours. I'm taking my mom to her doctors."

"Is she all right?"

Mack nodded. "Just checkups, prescription refills, that sort of thing."

And that was what he did. She watched in fascination as he brought out this big, thick, rich meat sauce he'd made before, turned up the temperature ever-so-slightly until it warmed up, and then he added some more spices and more tomatoes.

"Is there enough for more spaghetti?" she asked hopefully.

He shot her a look. "I can pick up some pasta, if that's what you'd like. But maybe we'll have that on Friday."

"I'd love that," she said. "And, while you're there, can you get me several packages, please? I'll pay you."

He just waved his hand at her offer of money.

She pulled out the two one-hundred-dollar bills and said, "I'm not sure what I'm supposed to do to break these. I guess I go to the bank."

He looked at them in surprise, and she explained, "This is how Penny paid me."

"Well, good for you," he said. "But, yeah, the bank. Otherwise one of the big grocery stores will accept them. A lot of the little stores won't take anything that big in case they're counterfeit."

She looked at the money with suspicion.

He just chuckled. "Hey, that's not your problem," he said. "I highly doubt Penny had that money sitting around. She probably just got it from the bank and brought it to you."

"Maybe," she said, "but I would have preferred smaller bills."

"Money is money," he said cheerfully.

"True enough," she said and pushed the money back in her pocket. "Maybe I can get a few more loads to Wendy too. I need to see her anyway. She was supposed to call me about my last load—if she didn't accept some of it—and she never did, and I didn't have time to follow up."

"So just leave this sauce to simmer for a couple hours," Mack said. "I'll do a little more grocery shopping." He opened the fridge, took a good look, and said, "We still have a fair bit here. We just need more pasta." She nodded, and he said, "I'll see what I can find." He waved a hand, and, just like that, he was gone.

Since she had eaten something, and this was too hot to snack on—which she shouldn't do anyway, but it was so hard because it was like a thick, rich, meaty soup—she grabbed a cup of tea and headed upstairs. The mattress looked so damn inviting. The trouble was the rest of her room looked like a nightmare. With the dresser and the vanity and the bed frame and night tables all gone, every-thing was on the floor. She didn't have a place to put a lamp. She literally had nothing left.

In the spare bedroom she had two night tables, so she moved one to her master bedroom, shifted the mattress on the floor so it would at least look like it belonged with the nightstand, and, with one of the lamps from the spare bedroom, she could have some light. She stood in the center and looked around. "Do I work on the clothes in the closet, or do I work on the stuff in boxes in the spare bedroom?" she muttered. She'd moved a bunch of that stuff off the floor in her bedroom into boxes and then off to the spare bedroom to make some room for the movers. She was just spreading around the mess instead of handling it. But, with the dresser out from the back of the closet, she literally had nothing to put small items of clothing into now. "That probably wasn't the best idea, was it?"

But, in her heart of hearts, she knew there was no way she wouldn't sell those pieces of a very large and expensive set. "Speaking of which, a piece is still missing," she muttered to herself. "He said it was the tallboy. Or a highboy. I think either name can be used. I need to keep an eye out for that."

She dove into the boxes in her spare bedroom, sorting what she could, pulling out everything she had absolutely no wish to keep, and anything that was clothing went back into the box to take to Wendy's. Doreen laughed and chortled as she collected a further $183.46. Then she packed up four boxes of clothing and set them off to the side for Wendy. She had another two boxes of stuff that she hadn't decided if she was keeping. At least she more or less had the floor cleaned up in her spare bedroom.

Then she went to her closet. With another double handful of hangers pulled from there, she sorted through them on the bed in the spare bedroom, becoming a bit more of a pro at this process. She went through more pockets, found lots more small change and small bills, chuckling in delight and thinking about how much fun this was, comparing it to her grandmother finding the chocolates in her own grandmother's furniture. Same idea and probably worth about the same amount to each child at the time.

Keeping two items, she put fifteen more into a pile for Wendy and did it again and then did it again. By the time she'd finished the front rack, it was time to stop. She'd been so busy sorting that she'd not bothered to count the money, and her bowl was looking mighty abundant. Such a wonderful gift. She checked her watch and thought, *I could run to Wendy's right now.*

Picking up two piles of clothes to sell on hangers, she carried them down and laid them over the back of the pot chairs in the living room, went to the car, opened up all the doors, and carefully moved the boxes inside and then rearranged all of the hanging clothing on top. By the time she was done, she could feel her energy sagging yet again. But she could smell the spaghetti sauce too. She walked back in, stirred it, and shut it off. If nobody would be here, no way would she leave that fire devil to burn on its own. She feared she'd have no house to come back to.

With Mugs in tow, she locked up the other two animals and headed to Wendy's.

"There you are," Wendy said as Doreen walked in. "I was expecting to hear from you before now."

"I've been a little busy," Doreen admitted.

Chapter 18

Wednesday Late Afternoon ...

"SORRY, I'VE BEEN *very* busy," Doreen corrected. "I did bring more boxes and more clothing, if you want them."

Wendy nodded. "Yes, but I don't have any time to sort right now. It's been crazy busy at the store. Maybe that's a good thing?"

"For you, it certainly is," Doreen said.

"I've had multiple pieces sell since we brought in your last load. This time, I'll give you a big closet rod on wheels," Wendy said. "If you can shuttle that out the back door, just hang up your items and bring them in that way."

So, they put it at the back door, and Doreen unloaded what she had on hangers; then she brought in the boxes. "I honestly don't know what to do with this stuff. I hope you like it." She opened the first box and pulled out silk stockings. Wendy's face lit with delight. Then Doreen pulled out the lingerie and skimpy nightgowns and some items she didn't even understand. She held one of them up, and Wendy chuckled.

"Those are old garter systems," she said. "They're making a comeback too. I'll be able to sell this stuff easily. It's less of a size issue. It's more of a taste thing."

"I imagine it is," Doreen said. "I can't imagine it's terribly comfortable."

"Ah, but for special events ..." Wendy said with a cheeky grin. "Leave the boxes. I'll sort through them, and, well, I'll let you know as we go."

"I thought you would call me on Saturday," Doreen said.

"I'd planned to." Wendy nodded. "I'm sorry. I just got so busy. I don't know what's going on, but business has been very, very good."

"Any idea if much of my stuff is selling?"

"Let me take a look at the books." She pulled out her big ledger account and brought up Doreen's page. "Actually," she said, "I owe you over four hundred dollars so far, payable at the next quarter."

Doreen was stunned. "Seriously?"

"Absolutely," Wendy said. "You've given me hundreds of pieces so far. I wouldn't be surprised if you don't get two or three times that before we're done."

"Sounds lovely to me," Doreen said in absolute delight. With a wave of her hand, she went back out to her car. There she talked to Mugs. "Isn't that fantastic?"

Wendy knocked on the window. Doreen rolled it down and said, "Sorry, did I forget something?"

"No," she said, "not at all. I just wanted to remind you that it'll still be a few months before you get your money."

Doreen smiled and said, "I know. That's why I'm doing gardening jobs in the meantime. I was working for Penny Jordan for the last two days, getting her house ready for photos so she can sell it."

Wendy stared at Doreen. "She's selling her house?"

Doreen nodded. "I think it's just too much after George's death."

"She's had a lot of death in her life," Wendy said slowly. "I'm glad George was good to her because she had a pretty rough upbringing from what I hear."

"I heard something about that. Apparently it was an abusive household, and then a younger brother died at her father's hands or something."

"Penny and I went to school together."

Doreen felt her stomach twist with excitement. "Seriously? I often wondered," she said, "what Penny was like when she was younger. It must have been pretty rough losing her brother."

"She alternated between anger, sadness, more anger, and more sadness," Wendy said with a decisive nod. "It was rough on everybody. And then when Johnny went missing, well ..."

"I'm sure that was hard," Doreen said quietly. "And, of course, since then she has lost George."

"Absolutely, and there was some talk about that too," Wendy said, her gaze going directly to Doreen's. "But you haven't heard anything about that, have you?"

"Heard what?" Doreen asked, hedging.

"Just some talk that maybe she helped George on his way."

"Like a mercy killing?" Doreen asked.

"Maybe, yet nobody really talked about it much. Just that Penny and George had had some pretty vicious fights throughout the years."

"Sure, but like everybody seems to say, George was good to her and for her."

"Yes," Wendy said. "But Penny has a *very* good male friend … But that makes me sound like I'm being hard on her, and that's not how I meant it. I'm sure the police would have known if anything untoward came up about George's death."

Doreen nodded. "I'm sure they would," she said. "Besides, what possible reason would she have to hurt George?"

"Losing Johnny was always a big elephant in their marriage, not knowing what happened there," Wendy said. "Imagine having something like that sitting there, eating away at you while you wondered what happened, the same unanswered questions always a part of your marriage. That would not have been easy."

"No," Doreen said. "I don't imagine it would have been."

On that note, Wendy said, "I've got to get back into the store. Talk to you later." And she turned and went inside.

Chapter 19

Wednesday Late Afternoon …

BACK HOME AGAIN, Doreen let Mugs inside the house. As she stood here, she looked around and said, "I know we cleared out a ton, and this floor is basically empty, but honestly it's still too full for my liking." And then her gaze landed on the inset handle in the floor.

She walked into the kitchen, pulled out a butter knife, and came back, trying again to scrape the handle free. What she didn't want to do was damage the floor, and she didn't want to end up breaking the handle either. If it was a handle. She was on her hands and knees, intent on gently loosening up the floorboard when Mack asked, "What are you doing?"

Startled, she looked up to see Mack standing in the doorway, frowning at her. He had a bag of groceries in his hand. She motioned at the floor and said, "Doesn't that look like a handle to you?"

He looked down at the floor and said, "Hang on." He put his groceries on the kitchen table and walked back over again. He bent down and said, "Did you dig this in?"

She shook her head. "No. I've been trying to clean all the dirt out. But you can see the outline here," and she traced what looked like a handle that should lift up.

He nodded and pulled out a Swiss pocketknife and chose a flat blade.

She asked, "What's the difference between that and this?"

"The sharp point." He gently dug his knife into the wood along the handle's edge. There was an odd *pop* sound, and, sure enough, the whole thing lifted. She stared at him in surprise.

He said, "Wow, I didn't really expect that."

"Neither did I."

They both stepped back, not knowing how big the opening would be. He lifted the handle, and a big piece of flooring came up. It had been so well hidden by the grains of the wood and having always been under the rugs that nobody had seen it for quite a while, she guessed. She looked down in front of her at the large open space. It was dark and shadowed, but she could see a cement floor. "What is this for?"

He groaned. "Why is nothing ever easy with you?"

"Hey, I found out today people are talking about Penny possibly helping George along on his death."

"I did check, and no autopsy was done."

She looked up at him. "What? Why?"

"Because there was no need. He had a serious heart condition," he said calmly. He bent down, turned on his phone's flashlight, and turned it toward the space. "I thought a basement was in this house?"

"Yes, but I thought it was over there," she said, turning to the wall where the living room pine hutch was.

He looked at it, looked at her, and asked, "Why would there be a basement door back there?"

"I don't know," she said, "but I can't move the hutch to access it."

He walked over and gently pulled the great big pine hutch from the wall. And, sure enough, almost in the same design work as the latch in the floor, was another door.

With the pine hutch out of the way, he opened up the door and found a light switch on the inside. He turned that on, but the light that shone through that space did not reach underneath the floorboards of the living room. He said, "Let's go through the normal door first."

She joined him. Mugs was already sniffing around the new opening. She hoped he was smart enough to not fall in. She called him to her side and motioned at the staircase down to the basement. She stepped inside and said, "I wouldn't have known that hole in the floor was here at all."

"No," he said, frowning. "And I have no idea why it's there. Especially without any stairs over there."

Ahead of her, Mugs ventured down the basement stairs, sniffing as he went. She turned to Mack and said, "It doesn't smell all that fresh." But she headed downward anyway.

A railing ran along one wall, and the wood on the steps looked to have had a lot of use over the years. She made her way down, carefully turning the corner at the bottom.

And let out a cry—one of surprise or pain, even she couldn't tell.

Mack was on her heels. He leaned over her head to see in front of her and laughed. "You could look on this as another gold mine again."

"Or I could look on this as a junkyard," she said with a sigh. The basement was completely stuffed full of furniture. Couches were heaped on top of couches, chairs on top of tables. "How on earth am I supposed to begin to sort through this?"

"I suggest you take photographs and then contact your Scott guy again."

"I can send him some photos," she agreed, "but, yes, after he found the dining room, I should have just tried to have him get in here, but I thought you and I should try first. The guy from Christie's shouldn't be breaking into my basement, right? It was just all happening so fast that I needed a moment to catch my breath."

"Maybe you now have a reason," he said, pointing to something in the far back corner.

He turned on several more lights. There were wooden walls, a wooden ceiling, and a wooden floor.

"I guess this is just storage?"

"It was probably an old rec room for the kids," he said. "But, in the back is a dresser, and it looks awfully familiar."

She peered around his pointing hand and said, "It's hard to see."

"It's got the same scroll markings as your bed set had."

"Really? Because we're missing a tallboy dresser."

"Well, if a dresser that's tall fits that description," he said, "one is right over there." He stepped in front of her and moved a couple chairs off to the side, so he could squeeze in. He led the way until they were at the back, and then, with him almost sitting on top of a table, she squeezed past him to take a look at the dresser.

She cried out in joy, "It is the same, isn't it? That means the set is complete." She turned back and looked up at him in awe. "You know what that means?"

"I'm assuming it means the set is worth a lot more money now that all the pieces are found. But he'll come back. And then, while he's here, have him take a good look at all this."

"He'll tell me to move it so he can really take a good look."

"True enough," Mack said. "So, the only way to handle this is to fill your dining room and your living room again."

She shook her head. "But it's not as simple as that. How could these pieces have been brought down here? Not from the living room or the dining room. Not through that basement door and those basement stairs we just took."

He looked at the wall nearest the living room and said, "Another interesting point is that I don't see that space under the living room floorboards. This area is all under the kitchen."

She turned toward the kitchen and said, "Is that a door over there?"

Mack made his way back to the stairs and, on the left side of the stairs, there appeared to be another door. He moved furniture so he could get that open, and, sure enough, on the other side was a cement floor and cement walls. He turned on a light and said, "This is an old cold room, like an indoor root cellar. But it does lead under the living room." And, sure enough, there was the hole in the ceiling.

"So why did they have a hole in the living room floor and no stairway?" Doreen asked in confusion.

He shrugged. "I don't know." He looked around the area and said, "I see shelves of canning jars, all kinds of old pieces of equipment in here. Looks like your grandmother might have been collecting old kitchen equipment. I think that's a butter churn," he said, pointing to a big wooden stand.

She looked at it and sighed. "Is this more junk then?"

"Everything here appears to be metal or the cheaper

wood stuff, not the antique wood items, so it's like that first basement area was a safe room for the good stuff, and this was for other stuff."

He shone his flashlight around some of the shelves, highlighting where the light didn't reach, and said, "Definitely a lot of interesting things from other eras are here."

"And yet, you don't see a folder or file full of paperwork, do you?"

He said, "Give me a minute." He dug through some of the shelving while she stood back, looking at the room. It was about the length of the house but narrow, maybe twelve feet wide, with shelves all along one side and then one end had a couple big freestanding items, right below where the living room hatch opened up. She just didn't understand why that stairless opening was fully supported and framed. Obviously it had been an opening so someone could either drop things into or hop down through, but there was no ladder.

Finally Mack stepped back and said, "You finally got into your basement."

She laughed at that. "Yes, now all I need is to get a bunch of this stuff upstairs." She looked at some of the furniture and said, "Do you think any of that would have gone up those stairs?"

"Chances are most of what you're seeing will fit in this stairwell," he said. "It's not narrow, and anything with legs might come apart." He pointed to several tables stacked up on the side. "Those have no legs, so let's hope the legs are around here."

She shook her head. "There's got to be like eight tables, just tabletops on top of each other. How on earth will I ever get rid of all of those?"

"I don't know, but we have to sort out some of this. I can do a few trips right now with some of the bigger items, but, if these are antiques, we'll need somebody else to come in and help because we can't lift some of them up and around the corners."

She agreed with him on that. "The door at the top of the stairs isn't all that wide either."

"No." Then he stopped and said, "Hey, another set of stairs is over there, and they look wide."

She peered into the far back of the room. "How could you possibly have seen those?"

"I'm thinking they might come from the garage. That would make more sense, that the items could be unloaded, moved down here, and not go through the living room."

"Nan must have started storing everything down here, and, when she ran out of room, she filled the garage." Doreen raised both hands in frustration. "That's just crazy. At what point did she stop?"

"When she ran out of room, apparently," he said, laughing.

She shook her head. "I can take a few photos of some pieces close by and send them to Scott, but I especially need photos of that dresser. Any chance we can open it and see if the drawers are full or empty?"

Mack squirmed back through everything to reach that corner again. He leaned over at an angle and pulled open the top drawer. "There's stuff in this one," he said. He opened a couple more. "These all have clothes so far, but I don't know what's in the top one." He reached in and pulled out a thick folder.

She cried out, "Please, let that be provenance paperwork."

"Maybe, but why the heck would it be down here where she can't reach it? Give me your phone. Let me take some photos of the dresser itself." He handed the folder to her while accepting her phone in exchange.

She flipped through the paperwork, struggling to understand the mix of old bills, insurance documents, and even letters. Even if the paperwork she was looking for was here, the right receipts wouldn't be easy to find in this unorganized mess. And likely wasn't all of it either. If any of it ...

Mack took several photos of the tallboy and then, from his vantage point, took several of the entire room. Afterward he walked back to the cold room and took photos of a lot of the pieces in there. When he returned, he handed Doreen her phone and said, "Maybe take a few of some of these maker marks on the inside of these chairs and that big hutch over there."

She did as he asked, remembering what Scott had said about how important that was.

"We need to go back upstairs, and I'll close that hatchway before one of your animals finds it," Mack said and proceeded to close the cold room and then led the way back up the stairs, where he closed the trapdoor in the living room floor. "It's very interesting that they had this," he said thoughtfully. "I wonder if that other room sealed itself up. Somehow the wood twisted or whatever, and the door couldn't be opened so they put an opening in here."

"I have no idea," Doreen said. "It feels like WWII, when they hid the Jews from the Nazis, but this is Kelowna, Canada. We didn't have anything like that."

"No, but some of the local history speaks about how things here were still pretty difficult with the Japanese. So, who knows? We could do some looking into the history of the property. I suggest you ask Nan."

"Maybe," she said, "but, for the moment, I'll just set it aside. I have plenty to sort out and have a hard-enough time getting straight answers from Nan." At his curious stare, she said, "Typical Nan stuff, evasive answers. Plus I don't want to give her too many tangents to run off with."

But, having said that, she walked through the living room into the kitchen and straight back to where the garage door was. Mack followed. She opened the door and pointed into the overpacked garage. "Do you really think an access point is in here?"

He stepped forward. "Yes," he said, "big double doors are right here." He pointed where the doors were snug against the wall. "This is a custom modification. And explains why your garage appears to be a little smaller on the inside."

"Interesting," she said. "We'll see where that'll take us, but no way we can get all that furniture out of the basement without coming up this direction, and, for that, we'll have to clean out the garage."

He closed the interior door slowly and in a firm tone said, "And that we'll leave for the weekend. We'll see some garage sales, take a look at what's happening, and then we'll come back. We'll open up that big double door, and we'll start sorting. If there is actual garbage in the garage, then maybe we'll rent a Dumpster."

She just looked at him and said, "Do you know the cost of that?"

"Do you know the cost of what it would be to not have that tallboy go as part of the set?" he asked.

"No, but Scott needs to see it clearly before he can determine that." She frowned. "Do you think we can maneuver it up the stairs?"

"I'm not sure, but it could be damaged that way."

"But it's in the very back of the basement," she complained. "It'll be a pain to get out of there."

"We don't know that," he said. "So, first, let's get food. Then we'll worry about it."

Just as she headed back into the kitchen, her phone rang. Distractedly she answered. "Hi, Nan."

"Hi," Nan said. "Take another look at George."

"George? Why would I take a look at George? He's dead."

"There were rumors he killed someone in Penny's family." And, with that, Nan hung up.

Chapter 20

Wednesday Early Evening…

DOREEN PUT HER phone down on the kitchen table.
"What was that?" Mack asked.

"Nan just said there were rumors George killed someone in Penny's family. We know both her father and brother are dead, her brother from his father's abuse, … leaving her father who maybe George killed?"

"Not that I put any stock into rumors …" He frowned. "I could take a look at the police reports. Although, just because Nan says there are rumors, that doesn't mean anything."

"No," she said. "I hear you. At the same time, it could be something important. Like … maybe George killed the brother, by accident or by design?"

"What difference would it make now?" Mack asked, sighing. "George is dead. It's hardly something we can prosecute. And, even if her father was charged with a crime that maybe he didn't commit, and yet, served time for it, he has also passed away. So no retribution could be made, if any is deemed necessary."

"Penny's father was very abusive," Doreen admitted. "So

I'm not sure any of it makes any difference." She shrugged and smiled. "But what does make a difference is if we can get some food."

He chuckled and said, "It's almost ready. I'll chop up the salad greens."

"Lovely. That means food in a few minutes," she said. "I'm starved." But, she had to admit, her mind felt completely overwhelmed by the time they sat down.

"Outside of hunger," he said quietly, "are you okay?"

She looked at him, wondering. "I feel like I need a vacation," she announced.

He chuckled. "How about a few days of downtime? That might do it."

She nodded. "Since I've arrived here, it's been go, go, go. Just one thing after another."

"And whose fault is that?" he asked, pointing a finger at her. "Slow down and stay out of trouble. It's not all that simple right now for you."

"I know," she said. "I just know something's wrong."

"Something's wrong where?" he asked in exasperation.

She sighed. "With Penny. That's just more pressure on me."

"What are you talking about?"

She walked over to where she'd placed the journal and brought it back.

He looked at it and said, "What's that?"

"It's from George," she said, "and it's odd ramblings. But his last line is very worrisome."

Mack read it and said, "Outside of the fact it shows George was distraught, which we knew, this doesn't really mean anything."

"It might not mean anything, but what I was wondering,

and I guess it's an option now, was what if he *did* kill somebody. And maybe, ... maybe Penny didn't have anything to do with George's death. Maybe he committed suicide."

Mack closed the journal with a snap and said, "Stop. Your mind is overwhelmed. Everything is just too much, and you're making a big deal out of this. George is gone, whether he did it by his own hand or he had help. Obviously I care if he had help, but we can't worry about the fact that he may have done this on his own. He was dying. We already know he had a heart condition. For decades, he was distraught over his missing brother, and, for all you know, things weren't all that great with his marriage. And maybe something there was a final straw. But how much of this is anything that you can control or that you have any right to get involved in?"

She knew he was right, but it was still hard to let go of it.

Chapter 21

Thursday Morning ...

WAKING UP THE next morning, Doreen rolled over and groaned. She couldn't remember the last time her body ached the way it did now. In the back recesses of her mind she remembered reading something about the second day after working out was the worst, and today was certainly the second day after the hard Tuesday she'd spent. But she'd also worked hard on Wednesday, so that didn't bode well for tomorrow either. However, a hot shower might help.

She staggered to her feet, wincing at the pain, and decided maybe instead of a shower, a bath. But that would take a long time, and she wasn't up for soaking. She really wanted coffee and didn't have a clue what to do about the basement. It was time to have a serious talk with Nan.

Doreen opted for standing under the hot shower water for a good ten minutes, letting the heat beat down on her sore shoulders. She washed her hair, rinsed it, and then, after she dried off, she tied it into a braid.

Feeling a bit better, she got dressed, hating the fact that her bedroom was still this chaotic. She would spend a few hours to finish off that dratted closet and then find a way to maybe get another dresser in here from among all that stuff in the garage or in the basement, so she had something to hold her clothes. It was ridiculous, with all the expensive furniture she had just moved out of this place, to realize she now needed practical stuff to store things away in her bedroom. There was the set of shelves she'd emptied. She eyed that one, wondering if she should put it in the back of the closet and maybe use that to put her folded stuff on—or at least her shoes.

Dressed, with the animals looking like they felt as awful as she did—at least Goliath and Mugs—she headed downstairs. There, she found Thaddeus, roosting on his special perch in the living room, almost snoring as he appeared to be in such a deep sleep. "We're all in need of a vacation," she announced.

She walked into the kitchen, put on her morning pot of coffee, and stared out at the backyard. A fine misty haze covered the sky, soaking everything. She groaned. "Today's Thursday, and I work in the garden at Mack's mom's tomorrow. I sure hope this rain has stopped by then," she said. "And I'll never get *my* garden done." As she looked at it now, for all the work that she put into Penny's small bed, Doreen realized just how much it would take to get her huge backyard done.

As she sat with her morning coffee, almost too tired to make breakfast, the file of paperwork that Mack had found at her side for when she had the energy to open it, her phone rang. She looked down and smiled. It was Nan. "I have fresh zucchini bread and bran muffins," Nan announced in a sprightly voice. "If you haven't had breakfast, come on down, and, if you have had breakfast, and you want to wait a little bit, these can wait until teatime."

"I'm still drinking my first cup of coffee," Doreen admitted. "I slept like a log, but I'm not moving very well right now."

"Oh, dear, you're still sore?"

"I worked hard yesterday morning again," she admitted. "So, yes, the answer is, I am still sore."

"Too sore to come down and have a fresh warm bran muffin covered in maybe butter and honey?" Nan coaxed.

Doreen chuckled. "The fact that it means I have to get out of the house almost makes it too much," she said, "but I haven't eaten, and fresh bran muffins sound divine. Then so does zucchini bread."

"It's a pretty crappy-looking day out there. If you want to drive this time, I'd certainly understand."

Doreen had to stop and think about what a difference it would make to her, and then, of course, it hit her. If she drove, she wouldn't normally take Goliath and Thaddeus with her but if she were only going to Nan's she certainly could. But the walk might wake her up. "If we hurry, the walk shouldn't be too bad."

"Well, finish your coffee, dear," Nan said, "although you can have tea here. I don't have coffee."

"I need my coffee," Doreen admitted. "And, well, I do want to talk to you."

"Oh, that sounds serious," Nan said. "Is it to do with Penny?"

"Only if you have any information about Penny's family growing up," she said. "I can't do any research if I don't have better names and a sense of a particular year."

"Well, I gave you a bunch," Nan said. "And not too many people know the details about her brother, just some hushed secret that her father killed him through his abuse. I don't know if he died right away or lived in a coma for a few years and then died or what."

"Her father went to jail for it?"

"Yes. So, in that case, you should be able to get his records off Mack."

She didn't bother saying it was probably public record, and she could look it up. "I need some idea of years though," Doreen said. "Any idea when any of this was?"

"I'll consider asking Maisie and see if anybody else around here knows. If you come soon, while I wait, I can take a look in the breakfast room and see if anybody there has information."

"I've finished my first cup of coffee," Doreen said as she eyed the small pot she'd made and decided to pour herself the second cup. "I added a touch of cream to my coffee so it cools faster, but I'm really not too interested in racing down there until I've had my second cup. I'm not moving very fast at all."

"Oh, my dear, that's why you should come," Nan coaxed.

"I'm coming," she said. "I'll be down there in fifteen to twenty minutes, Nan." She hung up and fed the animals, realizing she hadn't even done that yet, and, while they ate, she finished her coffee.

When everybody was ready, she grabbed a light windbreaker that might keep her dry from the misty rain and called all the animals to her. She walked down the creek and took the corner toward Rosemoor. Nan was sitting outside but under cover to keep dry. Doreen and the animals hopped across on the stepping stones. As she walked onto Nan's patio, she said, "I see those stepping stones are still here.

Nobody gave you a problem about them?"

"Lots of people gave me a problem about them," Nan said complacently. "But I had very valid arguments for keeping them."

She wouldn't say any more, so Doreen shrugged and pulled up her small chair. "I'm glad I brought a sweater," she said. "It's quite cold today with the rain."

"I know," Nan said. She ducked inside and returned with a fresh pot of tea and set it down. "Now the muffins, the second batch, just came out, so these are still hot." She set the little table with fresh muffins, butter, honey, and jam. "And here's some zucchini bread."

Doreen inhaled the aroma, smiling. "I do love muffins," she said. "The zucchini loaf looks great too."

"Any old folks will tell you," Nan said, "we need bran muffins."

Doreen didn't understand for a moment, then chuckled. "I imagine fiber is your best friend these days, isn't it?"

Nan chuckled. "Absolutely. We're supposed to have so many grams a day. It makes you wonder if there's room for anything that tastes decent."

At that, she sat down and poured the tea for both of them. She urged Doreen to pick up a muffin and butter it. "You know they're best when fresh."

Doreen obediently took one, cut it in half, and buttered both sides. Mugs, encouraged by the smell from the table, lifted up onto his back legs and sniffed the table. Nan laughed in delight, but Doreen was not impressed. "Mugs, down, you know better than to beg, and you certainly aren't allowed to jump up like that."

Mugs dropped to the ground and just looked at her sorrowfully.

She shook her head. "Now I can't even give you a piece because you did that," she scolded him. She lifted her gaze to the muffin on her plate and chewed carefully but immediately wondered why Mugs didn't persist with his begging. She looked under the table to see Nan feeding him. "Nan, you can't feed him if I just told him off for begging," she protested.

"Ah," she said, "life's too short for all those rules and regulations. Even Mugs needs to have some freedom too, you know? He's had a pretty stressful month since you got here."

"Wow," Doreen said. "It is over a month now, isn't it?" She tilted her head. "It's certainly a different life."

"Are you sorry that you came?" Nan asked, suddenly serious, her piercing gaze studying Doreen's face.

Doreen shook her head. "No," she said stoutly. "I'm definitely not sorry I came. It's a very different lifestyle, but it feels much more real to me."

"It is definitely real," Nan said. "Just think about it. It's a real life. It's your life. But I think it's a good one for you. You're getting a tremendous amount of satisfaction from your gardening and from your work on the cold cases, plus doing something good for the community with each of those endeavors."

"Something I never thought I could do," Doreen said. "I've always been good at puzzles, but I never really applied it to anything like this."

"If you'd stayed where you were, no way you could have had that opportunity," she said.

"No, very true." She scarfed up the first muffin before realizing it was even gone. Nan chuckled and nudged the plate closer. "I do like to see you eat," she said. "So eat up, eat up. You should be having at least two more."

"One more," Doreen said. "Two more would be too much."

"Then you'll take them home with you. Did you even eat dinner last night? You were so tired, I was worried."

Doreen nodded. "I was pretty tired," she said. "Lots of physical work for several days in a row."

"Plus lots of excitement," she said, "between the antiques and all your cold cases …"

"Speaking of antiques," Doreen said, "I still haven't found the receipts, the provenance, and that would certainly help, but I finally got into the basement."

"Oh, did you? Good," Nan said in delight. "It's such a mess down there."

"It certainly is. What's the best way to get the furniture up and out of there?"

"The garage double doors open up," she said. "I don't even know when those were put in. That house is so full of holes."

"Yes, I noticed," she said. "After the rug was removed, I found the trapdoor in the living room floor."

Nan looked at her nonplussed. "A trapdoor in the living room?"

Doreen slowly put down the muffin she'd held in her hand and said, "Did you not know about that?"

Nan shook her head. "I don't think I've ever seen it. What was in there?"

"It opened up to the cellar side of the basement," she said. "Very odd though."

"Wow," Nan said. "I didn't know. To get the furniture down into the basement, I opened the double doors in the garage. The trouble was, I ran out of room. So we just stacked it the best we could until it was full, and then I started filling the garage."

"I thought the stuff in the garage was mostly garbage," Doreen said.

"Most of it is," Nan said, "I bought an estate lot unseen and found out I'd been taken for a ride as it was all junk. I always intended to get rid of it, but I never got to it."

"And the antiques in the basement, how valuable are they?"

"Not as valuable as the set going to the auction," Nan said. "But they are nice and worth tens of thousands of dollars."

"I don't know which pieces have value and which are just cheap knockoffs."

"Well, if I had my say in the matter," Nan said, "none of them would be. But, of course, like I said, some of them I did get taken in on."

"What about all the small stuff up on the mantel, like the snow globe and the vases?"

"Lots of those pieces cost me quite a pretty penny," Nan admitted. "But I have no idea what anything is worth now." She waved a hand and said, "That's boring. Right now, tell me more about Penny."

"You were supposed to check with some of your friends, so you tell me about Penny," Doreen said in a dry tone.

"We were talking about dangerous plants once," Nan said. "Maybe more than once. Penny was asking about the ones that would affect the heart."

"And, of course, George died of a heart attack supposed-ly."

"Right, so how do we prove Penny killed George?"

"It may not be something we can prove," Doreen said.

EVIDENCE IN THE ECHINACEA

"And maybe it's not something we have any business even trying to prove. We don't know for sure that she killed anyone."

Nan chuckled and said, "But we don't know for sure she didn't either." She took a muffin and put it on her plate. "Her father's name was Randy Foster. Her brother was Anthony."

"And?" Doreen eyed Nan carefully. "How do you know this?" Granted, Doreen had already found this out via her internet search. But she still wondered how Nan had come by this info.

Nan glanced around, as if to make sure no one was listening, and added, "Bridgeman Solomon is a journalist. He's in here with us. He remembered the case well."

Chapter 22

Thursday Midmorning ...

DOREEN STARED AT Nan. "Any chance I can talk to him myself?" she asked cautiously.

Nan's wispy gray hair flew out around her head as she shook it rapidly. "Oh, I don't think so," she said. "He's almost gone."

"What do you mean, he's almost gone?"

Nan's eyes widened. "Dead, dying, six feet under, whatever you want to call it. He's not young, you know."

"How old exactly is he?"

"He's ninety-two. And not likely to see next weekend, according to the gossip."

Doreen groaned. "Is there anything other than gossip going on around this place?"

"Lots of sex. Lots of betting," Nan said with a complacent smile. She hopped up and said, "I almost forgot." She went back inside and came back out and handed Doreen something, more like palmed it to her. "Don't look at that until you're on the way home," she ordered.

Doreen sighed. "Are you trying to give me more money?"

"Pocket it," Nan ordered, her voice turning into a light steel tone. "It's important."

Obediently Doreen slipped the roll into her pocket. "So, if he's dying, it's even more important that I talk to him," she said.

"I did ask him, but he was being taken away to a hospice. There's not really room in any of the other hospices in town, so we are setting one up here," she said with a frown, looking around. "You would think they'd just leave him in his bed then."

"Okay, so he's being moved to another area. Why can't I talk to him?"

"I think it's only friends and family now," Nan said in a somber voice. "That's all they ever allow us on the last few days."

"Even if it's the last few weeks?" Doreen had absolutely no experience with death or dying—outside of dying inside at the betrayal from her husband and then from her own divorce attorney. Now *that* she had way too much experience in.

Nan shook her head. "I don't think so," she said. "I could ask, but I don't think that'll be allowed."

"Can you text him?" Doreen asked hopefully. "I just want to ask him about this case. Maybe he even has case notes," she said brightly.

Nan frowned, pulled her cell phone toward her, and sent off a text. Doreen was amazed at how rapidly her grandmother's fingers moved across the screen. "Nan, you're a pro at this," she said.

"I am," Nan said with great satisfaction. "Of course keeping the bets online have helped. I have to use my phone a lot for that."

Doreen just sighed. "You know you're not supposed to do that anymore, right?"

"What? Put stuff up on the internet? Well, of course not, dear. It's in cloud storage, and it's under a secure password."

Doreen winced. "I meant, not do any betting or run a bookie operation."

"It's not mine. Absolutely no connection from me to that account."

Doreen stared at Nan and shook her head. "You don't really believe that, do you?" she asked slowly.

"What will they do to me if they catch me?" Nan asked with a big grin. "It was really fun to go into the jail cell, and it wouldn't be a bad idea to get locked up for a day or two. It could be fun again."

"What are you talking about?" Doreen said, leaning forward. "That would be terrible."

"Only for you," Nan said, looking at her granddaughter. "That's because you're not ready to experience life yet."

Doreen's jaw dropped. "So being locked up in jail is experiencing life? How does that work?"

"You'll understand when you're older," Nan said. She put her cell phone on the table, lifted the teapot, and poured them each another cup. "I've texted him. We'll see if he gets back to me. He could be sleeping. They administer a lot of those heavy medicating drugs, you know? So basically everybody's in a stupor right up to the end."

"I don't think you should be talking quite so irreverently about death," Doreen said slowly.

Nan looked at her in surprise and then laughed out loud. "Oh, my dear, if I can't, who can? I'm at death's door. Whether it's today or next week or in ten years, you know it'll happen."

Doreen could feel tears gathering at the corner of her eyes. She wiped them away, trying not to let Nan see.

But Nan caught sight of them. "Oh, my dear, please don't be sad when I go."

Doreen gave a half gasp. "How could I not?" she asked. "You know how much I love you, Nan. Please don't die anytime soon."

"No, I figure I'll be around to torment you for at least ten years. Besides, it'll probably take that long to get my money back from some of these gambling idiots who don't have it to gamble with."

"You could let them off the hook," Doreen said. "Imagine the stress if they owe you a decent amount of money."

"We tried playing for toothpicks," she said, "but then everybody got caught stealing toothpicks from the kitchen area. So then we switched to pennies. But that's really not very satisfactory. So we went back to money."

"But pennies are money," Doreen felt compelled to point out.

"Just not enough of it," she said. "When you walk away with baskets of pennies, they're heavy. None of us wanted to take them to the bank to cash them into something, so we were constantly running our own bank, cashing people's dollar bills into pennies so they could come and gamble again."

Everything she said was done in such a commonsense tone of voice that Doreen could only stare at her. When Nan's phone beeped, they both leaned forward to see what the message was. But it was upside down, and Doreen had to wait until Nan read it. "He's awake," she said, "but he's got family with him. And his lawyer."

Doreen just rolled her eyes at that. "Great," she said.

"That'll never get me in there."

"I told you," she said. "They do keep us locked away."

"I just wanted to know more about Penny's family. Does he still have his case files?"

Nan was busy with her fingers on the keypad as she sent yet another text. Finally she got another answer back while Doreen sipped her tea. "He says he does. He'll try to get them to you."

"Really, he would do that?"

Nan held up her phone and shook it. "That's what he says. But don't forget, he's dying. He may not make it through the night."

Doreen felt terrible for thinking only about the case file when this poor man was nearing his last few breaths. "Wow," she said. "Now I don't feel very good about myself. Here I'm more concerned about the information he's taking to the grave than the fact he's actually going to the grave."

"Right," Nan said. "It's a fine balance, especially around here. We tell death jokes as a commonplace occurrence, but it's really a way for people to ease up the uncertainty and fear about where we're all going."

"Understandable," Doreen said. "I noticed a couple churches close by. Do many people attend?"

Nan nodded. "Absolutely," she said, "lots do, and then they head on down to the coffee shop afterward. It's almost like a Sunday outing. Everybody looks forward to it."

"Even you?"

"I've tried most of the churches," she said in a conversational tone. "I just haven't quite found the one that fits."

Doreen knew she should get off the topic, but she couldn't help herself. "Fits what?"

"Me," Nan said brightly. "It's like clothing. You can't

just wear any religion. It's got to be the one that fits inside. It's got to fit you outside as well, but it really has to make you feel good inside."

Nan's phone rang again, and Doreen sat back and thought about her grandmother's church comments because they were excellent words of wisdom. She'd just never had that conversation with Nan before. Nan looked up and said, "He will try to send them over with his nephew. He doesn't want the lawyer to know about them because otherwise he'll make sure it's part of the estate. But, if he hands them off before he dies, then the lawyer can't do anything with them."

"That would be great. Does he know where to send them or should I pick them up?"

Nan was muttering to herself as she answered him back. She looked up and said, "You know what? If I had just called him, it would have been a lot faster."

"Sure, but could he have a phone conversation?" Doreen said. "Or would all the family have gotten upset hearing it?"

"Quite true," Nan said. "So many people are just plain busybodies."

"A lot of people would consider me a busybody," Doreen said in a dry tone. "I keep sticking my nose into other people's business."

"Yes, but you have a purpose, my dear."

Doreen looked over to see Thaddeus waking from his small nap on the table and eyeing her muffin. She broke off a little bit and laid it down in front of him. Instantly Mugs dropped a heavy paw on her knee. She scratched him gently, running her hands down the length of his silky ears. "I don't think you need any more bran muffin," she said to him.

But he stared at it with such a painful intensity that she finally gave in, but, instead of giving him a piece of the bran muffin, she gave him a little dollop of butter. He scoffed it up like it was ice cream. She chuckled. "You know what? I think you'd eat anything."

"Of course he would," Nan said, putting her phone down yet again. "He's a dog. By nature they eat anything."

Doreen smiled and said, "Thanks for being the go-between for me and this friend of yours."

"I'm the go-between for a lot of people in here," Nan said thoughtfully. "Through all their support we got to keep those steps outside my place, and you can bet the gardener is not very happy with me."

"I'm sorry about that," Doreen said, "but it does make my life a lot easier."

"Exactly, and that's what life should be about," she said. They waited a few minutes longer, but there was no further answer from her friend. Finally Doreen said, "I need to head home. I've still got such a mess in the house." Then she sat back down again abruptly. "Do you have a list of what's really valuable in the house, so I don't just give it away in a garage sale for a few pennies?"

"Oh, don't do that," Nan said. "No garage sales until you've had things appraised. I know some junk is in there," she said, her voice rising. "But honestly most of it's worth a lot of money."

"How do I know what is and what isn't?" Doreen asked in frustration. "I thought I had most of the valuable furniture dealt with, but that's only what was in the living room and dining room. Then we found the basement full, and I need to get that garage cleaned out because I'm getting George's tools from Penny. All the workbenches, everything that's hanging up in that garage is coming to my home," she said in delight. "And I'm thrilled because I could probably use a lot of it."

Nan looked at her in surprise and then chuckled. "You know what? That's a really good idea. Most tools aren't hard to handle. I don't do well with a chainsaw," Nan said, reminiscing. "But I can use a circular saw and drills nicely. Never had time to try those air-compressor things, but they always looked fascinating."

Doreen just settled back and watched her Nan again. "I had no idea you knew how to use power tools."

Nan waved a hand at her. "Sweetie, you don't know a whole lot about me in a lot of ways. But, yes, you should get that garage cleaned out so you can get all those tools. A lot of money is in that. More than that, you never know when you'll need something. Although you'll need help moving it all."

"I know," Doreen said. "And I need to get it out of Penny's garage as soon as possible, so do you remember if anything valuable is in the garage? Can we start there?"

"There's car parts, I know that," she said.

"Did you say car parts?" She surely hoped she hadn't because that was something Doreen knew absolutely nothing about.

"Absolutely," she said. "I just don't remember why." And she stared off in the distance, seemingly lost somewhere in her past.

After another long moment, Doreen nudged her. "What about other stuff in there?"

Nan looked at her, blinked a couple times, and said, "In where?"

Doreen held her patience and said, "We were talking about everything in the garage. It's pretty stuffed now."

"It's the reject stuff," she said. "Stuff that I paid too

much for and found out it was fake, stuff I moved out of the living room when I brought in nicer pieces. You can probably still get good money for some of it, but the stuff in the house is by far more valuable. I did do some big lot buys, and some of it I never even unpacked. I remember one. It had all these car parts, and I was so disgusted I just left it there."

"What do you mean?"

"There was a time when I went to auctions a lot. Got some really good deals there too," she said. "And one time everything was all packed up on pallets, and I bought the whole thing dirt cheap. I had it delivered to my garage, and there it sits. I opened up a bunch of it, but it was all these car parts." She shook her head in disgust. "Like what do I want to do with that stuff?"

"Exactly," Doreen said. "And you can bet I don't either."

"Well, maybe ask Mack," Nan said cheerfully. "You might get a few bucks back. I can't remember what I paid for it. Not very much. Otherwise I wouldn't have bought it. But I was hoping to at least find something in there that would earn my money back, but, as I recall, there wasn't anything of value."

"So you're saying that's all just sitting there, still in the pallet in the garage?"

"Absolutely. But you can open the garage double doors without having to move it, *I think*. Once the basement was full, you know, I just didn't worry about it, and I kept filling up the garage."

"I noticed, but it means some stuff in the garage could be valuable," Doreen said and stood. "I'm heading home. I have a lot to sort out." She leaned over, kissed Nan on the cheek, gave her a quick hug, and hopped out across the stepping stones. If there was one thing she wanted to do, it was to get through sorting *something*. And not just a layer. Maybe when she got home, she could get into the garage and figure that out first. If she couldn't work on Penny's case, at least she could work on cleaning up her house. Maybe she'd get Mr. Solomon's files on Penny's family. Doreen grinned, picked up the pace, and called out to the animals, "Let's go, guys. This time maybe we can do something in a big way with some of this stuff."

Chapter 23

Thursday Midmorning...

BACK HOME AGAIN, Doreen stepped through the kitchen door, putting the spare muffins and zucchini bread Nan had given her on the tabletop. She brought out her laptop and sat down to do some research. It was hard to consider cleaning out the garage when all this other way more interesting information was just waiting to be found...

First, she researched Penny's father, then brother, and then Penny and George, hoping something new would show up. Oh, what she wouldn't do for those case files from Bridgeman Solomon. And just because the nephew was supposed to get them to her didn't mean he would or if he could or even when he'd have that opportunity.

After another half an hour, she gave up her latest search of the Foster family on the internet. Without having particular years to match up with certain events, she wasn't sure the library would be too helpful when what she wanted was from years ago. She opened the paperwork file Mack had found in the basement and flipped through it slowly. And found not one receipt for Nan's antiques, yet did see receipts for an expensive handbag, a hot water tank, and even a fur coat. But nothing that Scott was looking for. She closed the file and sighed, her mind returning to the missing case files and how to find out more about Penny and her birth family.

Doreen sat back, thinking about it, and changed her mind, deciding a quick trip to the library would be just the thing. She could spend an hour or two there. She left the house, leaving Mugs barking madly while she was gone. But she did remember Mack's warning and reset the alarm.

At the library, she walked through with a wave to the librarian who gave her a suspicious look. Doreen beamed at her and whispered, "Just looking for a book or two."

But the librarian snorted as if she didn't believe her. Then again, every time Doreen had come here, she got into the microfiche, looking for history on her cold cases. She went back to the same microfiche reader she'd been at before and started pulling up information from way back in the same time frame she'd researched before. *Now Penny was already married. Johnny was there; Penny was about twenty-seven, so maybe ten years earlier than that? That would put her at seventeen.* Wildly guessing, Doreen ran back fifteen years and then slowly worked her way forward. Of course, way back then there wasn't a whole lot of news, and much of it wasn't categorized, so this made for slow reading.

She made it through five years, finding nothing of importance. When she hit the ten-year mark, she found an entry about Penny's brother's and father's case. She read that with renewed interest. Back then, cases went to trial a lot faster, but it still didn't happen within six months. The boy had been abused and tortured all his life and had died from his injuries. It had been an open-and-shut case with the father having a long history of abusive behavior.

Plus, Penny was a witness for the prosecution. Her

mother had passed away when Penny was a child, according to one of the sources. Doreen frowned at that. "I'm sorry, Penny. That must have been a rough childhood. What do you do when you have no mother and your only parent left has fun torturing and hurting his kids?"

Her father was given a ten-year sentence. Ten years for a child's life? How was that fair?

Doreen moved through the years, checking for more tidbits, but this story, although sensational at the time, had died off, and she moved forward. Eleven years after the court case and Randy Foster's subsequent move to prison, she caught another notation, showing he'd earned more time inside for hurting another prisoner. Eventually he had been released. He'd only been out six months before being murdered—shot in an alleyway in the dark. Nobody knew who did it or why. Penny's father hadn't made any friends in jail or outside and was known as a cantankerous and violent man who you didn't cross.

The police assumed it was a drug deal gone bad or a disgruntled cohort on a deal gone bad. Randy Foster had stayed at a halfway house on Bernard Street, free to do as he pleased. His movements weren't tracked back then. Not like today. And even today, those from a more vulnerable lifestyle just seemed to slip under the wire, and nobody knew what happened to them or where they traveled to or from or when.

Doreen kept searching through the years but found nothing more. She printed off the little bit she found and then, knowing she had to leave with a book, she walked through the shelves full of new arrivals. To her delight, she found a release from one of her favorite authors.

Another story about murder and mayhem though. She

looked at the back-cover blurb, and it sounded fascinating. She pulled out her library card and checked herself out before the librarian could say anything. With a smile and a finger wave but absolutely not a word because she didn't want to get shushed for making too much noise, Doreen left the library. She could feel the librarian's gaze boring into her back as she went through the double doors.

But it didn't matter. Doreen had found what there was to find. Unfortunately it wasn't much. As she climbed into her car, she put her hand in her pocket, touching the roll Nan had given her. Inside her vehicle, with the microfiche copies and the library book beside her on the passenger's seat, she pulled out Nan's gift and took a look. And, sure enough, it was money. She unrolled it and gasped. *Five one-hundred dollar bills.* She stared at it, not sure what to do with it.

She pulled out her phone and called Nan. "Nan, why did you give me so much money? I always worry about you not having enough."

"If I didn't have enough," she said complacently, "I would have sold some of the antiques and used that money myself. Besides, that's just my winnings."

At that, Doreen winced. She stared at the money in a horrified fascination. "Then I'm not sure I can even spend it," she said. "Is this illegal money?"

"No, no, no, not on the betting pools," Nan said. "On those scratch-offs. I won a couple of those the other day. They gave me the money at the kiosk, but what will I do with it? Get yourself some groceries, and you should probably pay for somebody to come haul all that crap out of the garage. I feel bad because I should have taken care of that before you arrived. I just didn't want to be bothered. But now I can see what a headache it is for you too. So either use that to pay somebody to take stuff away or to bring in a Dumpster. It'll probably cost you four hundred to dump a load like that."

Doreen gasped. "Seriously?"

"Oh, yes," Nan warned her. "So be very judicial about what you get rid of that way. Sell as much as you can, then give away, and, as the very last effort, see if you can get somebody to do your dump run because that'll only cost you ten dollars or so in a dumping fee," she said. "If you get a Dumpster, it'll be in the hundreds." Then Nan said, "I've got to go out for lawn bowling. I'll talk to you later." And she hung up on her.

Doreen was stunned. Lawn bowling? She hadn't even seen a lawn bowling green anywhere close by. She was tempted to call Nan back and then decided it didn't matter. She tucked the five hundred dollars into her wallet, feeling overwhelmingly wealthy for the first time in a long time. That reminded her of the bowl she had upstairs, full of odds and ends and, of course, money she'd found within Nan's clothes. Doreen needed to finish that job and to make sure she found all there was to find. With that thought, she started up the car and headed home.

Once there, she parked outside the garage and stared at the doors. Before sorting the clothes came checking out the darn furniture … and that meant the garage too. She didn't see a lock at first, but, as she looked at the handles, she found a lock on the second one.

"So maybe the doors aren't stuck or broken, but perhaps we need a key," she muttered. Mugs was jumping up at the door, hearing her voice. She grabbed her library finds and walked up to the front entryway, unlocked it, opened the door, and disarmed the security system. She smiled at Mugs, gave him a quick greeting, and said, "Let's find a key for the garage door, Mugs."

She headed to the catch-all bowl Nan had kept on the kitchen counter. Doreen dumped it on the table with her library stuff and sorted out what looked like five possible keys.

"Doreen, Doreen."

"Yes, Thaddeus, you smart bird. I love you too."

With Goliath, Thaddeus, and Mugs in tow, she walked outside to the garage and tried each.

And, sure enough, the last one went in. She turned it with a triumphant *click* and then pocketed the keys, lifted the handle, and pulled. And just like that, smooth as silk, the door opened up. Then she groaned and slammed it back closed again. She leaned against the door, looked down at the animals, and said, "Mack was right. I should have waited for him."

"Mack was right. Mack was right."

Doreen rolled her eyes. *I'll never live that down.*

Just then one of her neighbors walked by. Doreen smiled and waved. The neighbor gave her and her menagerie a long stare and hurried past. Doreen muttered, "Still haven't made very many friends in town, and, the only woman who's been friendly, I'm wondering if she killed her husband."

With that depressing thought, Doreen locked up the garage doors again and headed into the kitchen. "At least I know I can get into that garage if I need to," she said. The fact that it was completely, overwhelmingly stuffed from floor to ceiling sank her mood even lower.

Cleaning up the garage would entail somebody with muscles, like Mack, to help her move stuff to see what was in there before they could do anything with that space. The problem was, they would also have to put it all back up and away, once they figured out what was there because it couldn't stay outside, and she had nowhere else to put it.

Doreen snagged a file folder from the infamous front closet that held just about anything she might need, and she quickly marked it with the case name Foster Family. She stuffed her papers into it and then sent Mack a text, asking about Penny's father's case, whether it was still considered a cold case.

The response came back a little slower than she had hoped, about twenty minutes later while she was in her bedroom, staring at the mounds of clothing still to be sorted.

Yes, it is. Another text came in saying, **Why?**

Do you have any details on his death?

I can print it off, he wrote. **Not much is here. Shot in the back of the head.**

All details are welcome, she typed.

Okay, will do. I can only give you what I can give you though.

Understood, she wrote. **When are we doing spaghetti? That last dish was awesome, but we still have tons of sauce, and I am craving spaghetti.**

Instead of texting her back, he phoned and chuckled. "Getting hungry?"

"Absolutely," she said. "Today's Thursday. I've got your mom's garden in the morning. I'll be tired afterward and could use a good meal."

"Then tomorrow it is," he said. "I can bring money to pay you for the gardening too."

"Which is even better," she said.

"What have you been up to today?"

She gave him the rundown, leaving out most of the details on Penny's family, and then added, "I got the garage door open too. I didn't realize there was a key for it."

At that, he chuckled and said, "And what did you find inside?"

She groaned. "Just so much. Floor to ceiling. I have no clue. I'm waiting for you."

And then she hung up.

Chapter 24

Friday Early Morning ...

WHEN DOREEN WOKE the next morning, she was grateful to find more spring to her step, and her muscles had calmed down. Instead of every movement jarring up her back and feeling the ripples all the way down her shoulders to her sore wrists, she could move and shift quite a bit easier. She took a shower to loosen up a little more, and then, with a look at her still-full bedroom and a heavy sigh, she headed downstairs. She'd gotten a lot done last night but had run out of enthusiasm and had gone to bed early. Now today, she had to work at Millicent's garden and then try to get a handle on her bedroom again before she could relax as Mack arrived to cook pasta. Her stomach growled at the thought of more real food. She patted it gently. "Don't you worry. We'll get fed properly again tonight."

On that note, she walked into the kitchen, Mugs at her heels, Goliath stretched out full-length on top of the table where he knew he wasn't allowed, and Thaddeus walking up and down, pacing behind the cat, as if trying to tell him off for doing what he was doing. She turned off the alarms, opened the back door, and propped it ajar, letting Mugs out to the backyard. Seeing freedom, Goliath took off too. Even Thaddeus flew out to the railing. She was surprised he made it. The last couple times he had tried, he'd ended up crashing into the lower part of the railing and then falling to the porch.

With all the pets outside, she put on coffee and stepped out into the morning sun to join them. "It's a beautiful day," she said to Mugs. He was wandering through the echinacea bush. She didn't understand why that patch appealed to him, but, as she watched, he dumped his chubby body into the middle of the plants, knocking them sideways. "Mugs, get out of there," she said. He just looked at her and rolled over onto his back. She raced down the steps, calling to him. Finally he got up and ran toward her, as if this was a game and he just hadn't understood they were playing.

She groaned and headed to the echinacea to see how bad the damage was. A couple stalks had been broken. It appeared he hadn't damaged too many of the plants. A lot of them were gathered together, probably sixty. They were too crowded, but the clump was a good-size collection. It would be a beautiful display whenever the plants came into flower. It made her remember Penny's echinacea bush and the mess right beside the fence—a lot of old ashes and bits and pieces all around the plants. She should have suggested to Penny that she transplant them. Replant them somewhere else in the backyard. While she was thinking about it, she figured, what the hell, and she texted Penny and mentioned her thoughts. Penny sent back a text with a single question mark.

She sighed and called her. "I don't know why," she said, when Penny answered, "but I'm looking at my echinacea, and the echinacea plants by your corner fence came to mind.

You really should move them into the backyard garden, into one of those places where I took out some plants," she said. "The current location is terrible."

"I put that there to help fill a spot George used to bury garbage in. I put in a whole pile of potting soil and put those plants there just to clean it up a bit," Penny said, laughing. "Now you want me to move them?"

"They don't get enough sun, and the soil is really poor, and such a lovely plant will give the rest of your garden a lot of bright color," Doreen argued. "If you plant them along the empty patches of the back wall, I'm sure the echinacea would do much better."

"Let me put it this way," Penny said. "If you want to come and move it, then do so. I don't have any intention of moving it, and I can't afford to pay you to move it."

"Fine," Doreen said, laughing. "I'll think about it, see how much it bugs me."

"You do that," Penny said, chuckling. "Feel free any time. I'm sure anybody looking at the house won't even notice."

"Have you got showings lined up yet?"

"Gosh, no," Penny said. "The listing hasn't even gone live. They did take all the pictures, but I haven't seen any of them. They're supposed to send them to me when they've got the listing ready."

"You'd think they'd have been on it a little faster."

"Apparently it also involves the real estate board, who gets sent everything that gets posted, but it's not like Kelowna has its own posting service. It's all out of Vancouver, so they take in all the Vancouver listings and then everybody else at the same time. They did say they thought it would go live on Saturday."

"So, if I move that bed of echinacea," Doreen said, "it should be today."

"Yeah," she said, "but it's really not that big a deal, is it?"

"No, it'll just look better," Doreen said. "I'm over at Millicent's working on her garden today. I'll see how I feel afterward."

"Good enough. I'll be gone most of the day anyway. A girlfriend and I are going up to Vernon for the day."

"Okay, good. I was thinking I might pick up a few things out of your garage while I'm there."

"Great. Bring your car, load it up, move the plants, and carry on," Penny said, then hung up.

"Sounds good to me," Doreen said to the animals. "I should have been taking stuff back every time, but I walked to Penny's, so it's not like I could carry much." And she could hardly take away stuff she might need for Penny's project, like the wheelbarrow. She herself could use a new one. She had one, but it was pretty ancient. The tire was more flat than full of air. It was frustrating in a way. But first food—for her and her family—then to Millicent's, and afterward Doreen would drive over to Penny's and take a look. In her mind Doreen didn't think moving the echinacea would be that big a deal, but she also knew it could very easily become a big deal, depending on the ground at that site. It was also hard to imagine why George would have dumped all his burned garbage into that pile, and what could he possibly want to burn anyway that the city wouldn't pick up as is, in the weekly trash run?

On that note, Doreen heard the coffeepot beep that it was done dripping. She grabbed a cup and then grabbed George's journal and sat outside, letting the animals wander.

She flipped through the beginning of the journal and

read an awful lot of dark thoughts. Maybe George hadn't been all that healthy mentally throughout the years. A lot of thoughts were about his missing brother, worrying that maybe it was George's fault and that his own actions had led to somebody terrorizing his brother. That appeared to be George's main theme. But Doreen didn't understand how that could possibly be. George, so far, didn't explain who was involved or what actions he could possibly have taken that would have affected somebody else.

He did make a notation. *Helped at the church bazaar. Surely I'm building brownie points to help offset the negative points.* She frowned at that, turned down the corner of that journal page, so she could refer back to it, and read on.

She found so much more of the same, as if trying to counteract a bad deed. He did mention Penny many times but always in a good light. The journal seemed to be spottier in the last five years. There were a couple dated entries but not many. Nothing was consistent.

Checking her watch, she was running out of time. She needed to get to Millicent's before nine a.m., so she could get the work done before noon, particularly if she wanted to get to Penny's. And, of course, Doreen had yet more stuff to take to Wendy's.

She felt like her life was crazy busy all the time, yet she knew she needed to get stuff off her plate so she could properly tackle the garage and the basement with her full focus. Resolved, she went inside and had toast and peanut butter, and then filled her travel mug and walked with the animals toward Millicent's. The journal was always in the back of her mind. George appeared to be a strongly religious man who had loved his brother dearly. So many of his entries were about how his heart ached for what could have happened to Johnny. It didn't appear George believed at any time that Johnny could have walked away. George was sure his brother would have contacted him if he could have.

As she walked into Millicent's back garden, she held the gate open long enough for Goliath to come racing through. Thaddeus had walked the whole way and looked weary. She scooped him up into her arms and perched him on one of the rocks near where she would be working. And then, grabbing her gloves, hoping Millicent wouldn't be disturbed by her gardening, Doreen went to work weeding the backyard. She needed to spend time in the front yard too, but she'd spend an hour here and an hour there, and hopefully that would be enough to keep everything from getting any rougher looking.

By the time she was done in the back, her muscles were aching again. She moved the wheelbarrow around to the front, and there she found Millicent having a cup of tea. She was surprised at that because normally Millicent was friendly and enjoyed talking with her. But Millicent looked at Doreen in surprise and said, "My goodness, have you been in the back this whole time?"

Doreen smiled. "Just for the last hour."

Millicent nodded. "I came out front this morning, for whatever reason. I just wanted to sit out here today." She held up her carafe with her tea and said, "And I've probably been sitting here the whole time you've been out back."

Doreen chuckled. "Doesn't matter," she said. "I'm just weeding your garden." She moved to the front bed that was prominently displayed from the street side and cleaned up the weeds encroaching along the edge. With that cleaned up, she moved to the next set of garden beds.

"You do work hard, don't you?" Millicent said in admiration. "It's nice to see somebody just get out there, work, and not fuss about it."

"Can't afford to fuss," Doreen said. "These weeds are waiting for that opportunity to jump up, and, when you're busy talking, they grow into ten weeds."

"Isn't that the truth?" Millicent said. She sounded tired.

Doreen cast her a sideways look, checking her color. "Are you okay?" she asked casually.

"I'm fine," Millicent said. "Just a little tired. There's been enough excitement in this town to last me a lifetime. I don't know how you young ones can handle it."

"Sorry," Doreen said. "I didn't want to create such chaos."

"I'm not sure you had a choice, my dear. And I'm certainly grateful to you for bringing out all these nasty specimens, these vipers in our bosom here. If you find any more," she said, "I hope you purge them as well."

"I'm working on one right now," Doreen said. "I'm just not sure if it's a wild goose chase."

"Oh my." Millicent looked at her in surprise. "Another one already?"

Doreen winced at that. "Well, it started from the last one …"

"Well, you probably don't want to talk about it yet."

"Exactly," Doreen said, chuckling. She stared at the lamb's quarters. "You do have a lot of this weed, don't you?"

"I do," Millicent said. "I know you can eat those, but I never really took a fancy to them."

"True enough. You can eat dandelions too," Doreen said with a chuckle. "That doesn't mean it's my favorite salad green."

"An amazing amount of stuff in a normal garden is dangerous," Millicent said. "And nobody ever seems to know."

"That's because, most of the time, it's not dangerous, unless you take an awful lot of it or you make a heavy distillation."

"Oh, yes," she said. "I don't know how many years ago it was—quite a few though—that there was a discussion about some of the more dangerous plants. I think I have foxglove in the backyard."

"You do," Doreen said cheerfully. "But you know? In the right hands, that's a modern miracle medicine. In the wrong hands, of course, it can cause all kinds of trouble."

"Isn't that the truth? But then some of the most common plants are that way too."

Doreen nodded and said, "Yes, exactly, like the hydrangea."

"Really?" Millicent asked. "I heard somebody say that to me one time. We were doing a little ladies' club a while back, people coming together with their gardening ideas. I can't remember who it was who brought up poisonous plants. It might even have been Nan."

Chapter 25

Friday Midmorning ...

THAT MADE DOREEN do a double take; then she chuckled. "Oh, I wouldn't be at all surprised. Nan does have a wide and varied grasp of many subjects."

"I think she said she had quite a few different plants, almost like a garden of death." Just then Millicent clapped her hands. "That's what it was. There had been a documentary on the Garden of Death out of England. It was fascinating. We talked about it for quite a while."

Doreen had certainly heard of the garden. "I can't imagine a garden where you have to suit up and be so careful that you don't end up accidentally killing yourself by going to work each day."

"It sounded fascinating though," Millicent said. "Just imagine the information you could find there."

"True enough," Doreen said. But, in her mind, all she could think about were the opportunities to cause harm.

"Of course, with the change in modern medicine and forensics," she said, "our forensics are doing much better at catching poisoners."

"I don't know," Doreen said. "Some of the oldies but

goodies are still the best bet. Some of them dissolve in your bloodstream very quickly. A couple drugs are like that too."

"That's fascinating," Millicent said. "I wonder why the police don't take courses on stuff like that."

"Not sure it's for the police as much as it's for the coroners," Doreen said. "Coroners and pathologists, I guess. And I imagine they do keep up with these drugs."

"As long as nobody is poisoning anybody around here, we're all good." There was an awkward silence, and she said, "Nobody is, are they?"

Doreen looked at her, startled, her hands full of weeds. "Nobody is what?"

"Poisoning anybody?"

She understood the question; she just didn't understand why Millicent was asking her. "As far as I know," Doreen said carefully, "no."

Millicent sat back with a sigh of relief. "That's good," she said. "I know poison is considered a woman's trick, but I think, in this day and age, anybody can get away with it."

"They might try," Doreen said, "but that doesn't mean it's always successful."

"No," Millicent said. "A gunshot to the head is much better."

Doreen chuckled. "Speaking of that, I didn't realize Penny's father had been murdered, and it's still a cold case. It's sad that her father and her brother-in-law were both cold cases."

"At least her brother wasn't," Millicent said. "They knew who caused his death, and he paid for it."

"Her father, Randy, yes," Doreen said. "I've learned a lot about her family over this last case."

"Of course you have," Millicent said. "You do all kinds

of research to find out this stuff, don't you?"

Doreen nodded. But the actual fact was she'd found this out *after* they had discovered what had happened to Johnny. "The thing is, one can never really understand what went on so long ago because it's hard to get enough information. You know with these cold cases, some of the files are pretty darn small. Doesn't give me a whole lot to go on."

"I imagine that's true," Millicent said. "We didn't have computers. We didn't have the internet. We didn't have emails. We didn't have the forensics like we do now. There was no DNA testing." She just shook her head. "That's depressing. People got away with all kinds of bad things back then."

"They did," Doreen said, yet a smile took over her face. "But that doesn't mean they're continuing to do so."

"Not with you around," Millicent said. "I'm really happy you're here cleaning up the town."

"Well, not everyone is," Doreen said. "When you think about it, it's been a rough month."

"Not for you, I hope," she said. "For everyone else, yes. It's just amazing how many cases you've closed."

At that, Doreen didn't say anything. What she really wanted to know was that none of the thoughts in her mind were correct when it came to Penny. The last thing Doreen wanted was to consider that her friend was responsible for her husband's death. And yet, that whole idea wouldn't leave her alone.

She finished up the weeding and then slowly straightened. "I'm a little over time, but I started a tad late. It's eleven-twenty now," she said, rotating her shoulders and loosening out her arms. "I'll take these weeds to the backyard and put away the wheelbarrow. If you want me to work on any particular area next week, just let me know."

"I will," Millicent said. "You go on home now. You've done lots of work, and it looks wonderful." So much admiration filled Millicent's voice that Doreen believed the sentiment was heartfelt.

She felt pretty good by the time she loaded up the wheelbarrow to take out back, with Thaddeus riding on top of the pile of weeds. Millicent was one of few people who still had a compost bin. Thaddeus was now on her shoulder, so Doreen dumped the weeds, and then she called the other two, and they headed home via the creek. It was nice to get that much work done. Now her day was more or less her own, if anything in that house of Nan's was *her own*. It was such a nightmare. Still, with the living room and dining room and her bedroom cleaned out, that was something.

She hadn't heard back from Scott Rosten on the tallboy she'd found in the basement. Once home she made herself a fresh pot of coffee and emailed him again. In the subject line she wrote *I didn't hear from you about this.*

When her phone rang twenty minutes later she didn't think anything of it. She'd been having coffee and writing out a grocery list. It was a very excited Scott. "I didn't get the original email. Is that really what I think it is?"

"I think so," she said. "It's in the basement."

"Oh my," he said. "You sent me a couple other pictures, and it looks like the furniture is stacked almost from floor to ceiling."

"The garage is full too," she said, "but that dresser looked to be part of the same set."

"We definitely should have a look," Scott said. "And it is Friday again."

"I know, and you were just here on Tuesday. I should

EVIDENCE IN THE ECHINACEA

have contacted you before you left town, but I couldn't even get into the basement at first."

He chuckled. "That's all right. We've still got people unpacking and assessing your pieces. It's not like this is a done deal yet."

"No," she said, "but, if having this piece helps, well …"

"If it's part of the same set, it would be an amazing find," he said, "and that would just help cement you getting the maximum price possible."

"Which, you know," she said, "I really need."

He chuckled. "So it's noon on Friday. I don't think I can get there until tomorrow morning, maybe tomorrow afternoon."

She crowed in delight. "Can you come that fast?"

"I think we should," he said. "I want to know if that's the last piece, so it won't be a long visit, but hopefully we can take a few minutes and see what else you might have."

"In order to do that, I must empty out some of the garage, so we can move some of the pieces up from the basement."

She tried to explain the layout of where everything was jumbled together, and he just kept exclaiming, "That's crazy. The more pieces I can see clearly, the easier it'll be for me to let you know what has any value and what doesn't."

"Right," Doreen said. "That's what I was thinking. I do have somebody helping me in the morning. Maybe we can at least get a path for you or some of this stuff cleaned out."

"Okay. I'll confirm my arrival time, but I should be able to come in around noon tomorrow."

She hung up and sent Mack a text. **Scott can come back tomorrow at noon, but he needs access to the basement stuff.**

The response that came back made her laugh. **Sounds like we might need more than just me to move furniture then. We should probably haul everything out of that garage, so we can open up the stairs. Not sure I can do that on my own.**

She frowned. **Is there anybody I can hire?**

Let me think about it, and that was it.

She opened the living room door to the basement and headed down there. She turned on the light and studied the rest of the room. An awful lot of furniture was here, and, if Scott was coming, he needed to see everything he could possibly see. So, giving up all thoughts of working in her bedroom upstairs, she laboriously brought up chair after chair into the living room. She sat them all in a row and then brought up two different coffee tables. At least she had a corner cleared out within the basement. Outside of the tallboy, she didn't think anything here was of any value, but she didn't know why Nan had stored all this here in the first place.

Doreen almost had a path cleared to the dresser when her phone rang. It was Scott again.

"Okay, I've confirmed tomorrow," he said.

"Great. I can almost get the dresser out now. I moved up ten different pieces and put them in the living room."

"Send me as many pictures as you can," he said, "of as many different items. At least it'll give me an idea if we should go digging deeper."

"Okay, I can do that." When she hung up, she took pictures of as many different pieces as she could. She did the same with all the pieces she had taken to the living room and then walked out to the garage, unlocked the doors, opened it up, and took pictures from there.

When she was done, she went inside, downloaded all the images, and sent them in a zip file to Scott. Then she sat here in the kitchen, wondering what else she should do next. The basement and garage projects were pretty much out of her hands until she could get somebody to help her carry some of the bigger pieces. And then she remembered Penny's place.

Doreen made a sandwich, called Penny, got no answer, and thought, *Perfect timing.* She didn't want to bring Mugs with her because she could get more stuff into her car that way, and that was what she needed to do. But, in order to do that, she had to get some stuff out of her house first.

She went upstairs and grabbed the three new bags full of clothing she had sorted out for Wendy and the one box for Goodwill. She carried everything down in several trips, loaded the car, and, leaving the animals at home, made a drop-off at Goodwill and, after a short stop and with a fast wave to Wendy, headed to Penny's place.

There Penny's garage door had been left open. Doreen loved seeing the inside of that garage and all the tools. Also this was a nice reminder that Kelowna was a safe-enough place where you could leave thousands of dollars' worth of expensive tools on display, and yet, they were still there hours later.

But first Doreen had to do something to make herself feel better. She walked around the fence to the crappy corner and saw the echinacea still struggling. She'd removed a piece of it, and it was doing much better out in the new front bed, but still a good chunk of ten to twenty echinacea plants needed to be moved to a better spot. She walked around the backyard garden, found a spot that looked good, raked back the mulch, and then dug out a big hole to transplant the echinacea here.

Then she meticulously broke up the echinacea clump into smaller groupings. With great effort, she lifted each into the wheelbarrow and moved it all to the hole she had just dug. She replanted it and turned on the hose to give it a really good soaking, then moved more dirt in and around to help pack it down around the transplants.

Although Penny may have put a lot of topsoil on when she had planted the echinacea at George's dumping spot, the poor soil all around had taken its toll, and the echinacea itself did not have a decent root system. She walked back to the hole where the echinacea had been and looked in. Sure enough, all kinds of pieces of metal and other junk were in there. Why wouldn't they have at least cleaned it out before they tried to plant on top of it?

Doreen bent down to a piece of plastic, pulled it up to see something laminated on one side of it. She looked at it and then dug more to see if there were other bits and pieces. She found several pieces of the same laminated card, but they didn't make a lot of sense. She pocketed all the pieces she could find, then grabbed her shovel, grabbing whatever dirt was nearby to fill the hole where the echinacea had been.

When she was satisfied, she moved the wheelbarrow back into the garage, and leaned it up against a wall. There, she stopped and looked at all the tools, wondering where to start.

Chapter 26

Friday Noon ...

THE IDEA OF accepting George's workshop for her own was a great idea in theory, but the execution ...

Her small car was a hatchback. She reversed it up to the large open garage and parked. Then opened the hatchback. She started with the first pegboard, carefully removed all the hammers and screwdrivers and all the hooks. The actual wallboard itself was nailed in, but, with the hammer, she popped it off the wall, and, with the first piece down, she put the tools from this pegboard in the front seat on the footwell and put the wallboard itself in the back of the car. The pegboard pieces were about four feet across and fit in easily enough. Then she went on to the next one and the next one, and, within half an hour, she had one wall empty.

She then opened up all the doors to her car, emptied all the tools from the back wall into her floorboards or on the seats. Mostly there were saws and hand saws, a wrench set, and some other things, like pry bars. It was quite a collection of tools. Many she didn't know what to call them.

Doreen took everything off the remaining side wall and loaded that all up too. She stood in amazement, realizing all the garage walls were now clean, and everything had fit in her tiny car. The pegboards were in the back of her car, and, although the hatch may not close properly, she didn't have far to go. The passenger seat and the back seats were completely full too. She had filled the rear well with several circular saws, what looked like a jigsaw, a bunch of other tools, and several small tool boxes.

She wished she could get the three workbenches, but that would take a trip with a truck. One bench was small, and two large ones were in the back. Each had drawers. She cleaned off as much as she could of the actual workbenches and then rocked a couple of them to the side, wondering how hard they would be to move. If she could empty the drawers and lay them in her car, she would just need help to get the actual workbenches home. And, of course, she had absolutely no place to put any of this stuff. She groaned when thinking about it, and then pulled out her phone and called Mack. "I'm not sure when you're off duty, but any chance I could get you to come to Penny's place and help me load up these three workbenches?"

"Already?" he asked in surprise.

"Yes," she said. "There's some urgency. Penny hasn't had any viewings yet, but they're likely to start this weekend. I've got all the pegboards off and all the tools loaded, but there's three workbenches and a couple tool chests. And I definitely need a truck to move them."

"I'm on my way out in a few minutes," he said. "If you're still there, I can come by."

"I'll stay here and wait, and thank you," she cried out happily.

She walked back to the first drawer, where she had seen the journal, and pulled it out. As she did so, something from the back fell to the floor. She reached down to find a small black book that was clearly from a long time ago. Opening it, she gasped when she saw the dates. Just as she started to read it, she heard a vehicle, knowing it would be Penny. Doreen pocketed the book and collected the tools in the drawer, but then thought she could probably fit the drawer on top of the pegboards. She moved the drawer to her car and grabbed the other two from the same workbench. By the time Penny came out here, Doreen smiled and said, "Two more drawers to load up, and then it's just the big stuff."

Penny shook her head in astonishment. "I had no idea you would take all this stuff. Look at how big the garage is now." She just smiled in delight and said, "It's huge. That'll definitely help to sell the house."

"I hope so," Doreen said, "because now I have to figure out where to put all this stuff at my place."

Penny looked at Doreen's car and laughed. "Oh, my goodness, that's so true," she said. "You've still got toolboxes and workbenches, but that's it, right?"

Doreen nodded. "Mack has his truck, so he'll come and give me a hand."

"That's quite a friendship you have there, isn't it?"

"A friendly business relationship," Doreen corrected with a chuckle. "He's been very helpful to me."

"Sure," Penny said with a knowing smile. "But I imagine you've been helpful to his career too."

"I hope so," Doreen said. She motioned at the walls of the garage and said, "You probably don't have to fill in any of those holes, but you know? Maybe even a good brushing of the walls would clean it up a bit."

"It's a garage," Penny said with a wave of her hand. "If anybody wants to clean it up, they can fix it themselves."

"That's probably a good attitude," Doreen said.

Penny unloaded more groceries. "I have company coming tonight."

"Mack said he'd be here in a few minutes," Doreen rushed to say. "So can you give me maybe another half an hour?"

"That's good timing then." And, with that, Penny disappeared inside. She stopped at the open door to the garage and grinned. "Thank you," she said to Doreen.

Doreen nodded and smiled. "Actually thank you." She turned around at the sound of another vehicle, and, sure enough, there was Mack. He backed his truck up to the side of her car, hopped out, took a look at her car, and raised an eyebrow.

She shrugged. "I didn't want to leave anything behind, just in case," she said.

"I didn't think it was possible to get this cleaned out that fast."

"Because George had it all hanging up so neat and orderly," she said, "it took nothing to remove the tools, and there weren't as many as I thought because he had them spread out."

He nodded. "So what have we got, three workbenches?"

She nodded at the two in the back and said, "I haven't pulled the drawers out of those yet. I've got the drawers out of this one." She motioned to the back of her car. Then she added, "The big tool chests are coming too."

Mack picked up the workbench, hefted it, and said, "Okay, this one's not bad," and he walked it to his truck. He put it on the side and headed for the other two. He lifted the next and frowned. "This one is heavier."

"I have room for at least another drawer," she said,

pointing to the hatch of her car.

He pulled out a drawer and said, "Well, this is very heavy." He placed it in her hatchback and then grabbed the last drawer and put it there too. "We'll put the other two drawers from the other bench inside my cab."

She grabbed the drawers, noting what looked like files and all kinds of stuff inside that she had no clue what to do with, and carried that to the front of Mack's cab. Part of her worried she was becoming Nan and grabbing stuff she had absolutely no need for. Another part of her worried she was just being cheap or thought she could sell this stuff. But, with the three workbenches now empty, she grabbed the end of one, and, with Mack's help, they lifted it up into the back of his truck's bed. He turned it on its side, took the smaller one, and laid it on the side inside, nesting them. Then he grabbed the third one and put it on top.

She stared at that in delight. "Wow," she said, "I didn't think that was possible."

"Those weren't the problem." He wheeled the tool chest toward the box. "This piece will be the problem."

She looked at it and frowned. "We could take out the drawers maybe?"

He shook his head, and, while she watched, he lifted off the top half of the toolbox and set it on the ground.

"I had no idea it came apart," she said in delight.

"Not really apart," he said, "but this bottom piece will be very heavy. It should be wheeled up via a ramp. We can't do that." But Mack was a huge man. He reached around from the back and, moving carefully, lifted the entire tool chest up onto his tailgate. And then he wedged it in close enough up to the benches that nothing would go anywhere. He made it all look so effortless. Then he lifted the top piece too. With the smaller ones up and tucked into corners he nodded. "Knew it would fit."

She looked at the garage and said, "It's almost completely empty. That's unbelievable." There was a broom in the corner. She grabbed it and swept up the empty room, so Penny wouldn't have to do it. But there was no dustpan. With everything in a corner, she knocked on the inside door.

Penny stepped out and looked at the empty room. "Wow," she said.

Doreen pointed at the dust pile and said, "I swept it up, but I don't have a dustpan or a place to put the garbage."

Penny nodded. "No problem," she said. "I'll clean that up." She turned and looked around the garage. "This is big enough for two cars, maybe even three."

"It's a big garage," Mack said. "It looks huge now. That should be a big selling point for you." He secured the tailgate, gave the top bench a shake, and said, "Good thing we're not going far."

Doreen walked over to her car, waved at Penny, hopped into the driver's seat, and then slowly pulled out. With all the tools lying everywhere in her moving car, there was an incessant clinking and rattling of steel on steel. But she drove carefully to her place and then parked off as far on the right side of her driveway as she could. She had absolutely no idea what she was supposed to do with the stuff Mack was bringing.

He backed into her driveway and stopped a good twenty feet away from the garage doors. He hopped out and said, "Did you really think about this?"

"I really didn't," she confessed. "Wouldn't be so bad, but the garage ..."

He nodded and said, "Let's take a look at the garage."

She went inside the house and opened the doors for the animals, who all raced out to say hi to Mack. He bent down to scrub Mugs's ear, when Thaddeus jumped up onto his shoulder. Chuckling, he gave Thaddeus several moments of cuddles too. Goliath just sat there and stared up at him. Mack went down on one knee and reached to pet Goliath, but Thaddeus bit him on the ear. "Ow," he said.

Doreen chuckled as she came back out of the house with the garage key in her hand. "That means Thaddeus doesn't think you've given him enough attention."

"Well, it's not exactly making me eager to give him more," Mack snapped.

With a smile, Doreen unlocked the garage door and opened it. Mack stared at the contents and groaned. "How will you put any of George's shop stuff in there?" he asked.

She shrugged. "On a good note, I did contact Scott, and he is excited about the tallboy down below, at least he'll get to see it tomorrow," she said.

Mack nodded. "That's great, but we have to get to that door first."

"The weather looks to be decent for the next day and a half, and, if we could have Scott at least look at whatever is here, we could possibly get in a dump trip or hire somebody to take this stuff to the dump or maybe even get one of those Dumpsters." Although she winced at that.

"That'll cost you a few hundred dollars," he warned.

She nodded and said, "I know. I do have the money, if needed, but, if I can get away without one, I'd like to."

Mack walked forward into the garage and said, "Some of this is just junk." He carefully pulled out a table missing a leg, and the table looked like cheap pine with a big scratch on the top. He moved that outside off to the grassy spot alongside the driveway, and Doreen pulled out several chairs that looked like they went with it, but they were in bad shape too.

She shook her head. "Nan did say a lot of junk was in here."

"Let's get as much of the *junk* out and see what's left," he emphasized after a sigh.

She helped him move out a dozen pieces, and they were now a good ten feet in.

"It's going better than I thought," he said, "but I don't understand what this is."

Doreen looked over at the pallet and groaned. "Nan said she bought this lot sight unseen and then got really upset when it was just car parts."

He sighed. "We should take a look at it to see if it's got any value. But let's get the rest of this busted-ass furniture out of here."

"And, if anything is good or decent," she said, "I'm a little short on furniture inside now."

He chuckled at that. "Serves you right for getting rid of it all," he said.

"And I'd get rid of all this too if I could."

They moved out several more pieces. A table crumpled as soon as they put it down on its legs. Mack looked at it and asked, "Did you get a sledgehammer from Penny's house?"

Doreen nodded and pulled one out of the front footwell of her car. She dragged it back toward him.

He just laughed, picked it up, and tapped a couple of the table legs from the junk furniture pile, and it all just collapsed. Within minutes, he had a small pile of expensive kindling. "That'll make it a little easier to haul out of here." Then he went back into the garage and brought out several more pieces.

She got into the rhythm of things, hauling them out, and, if they were busted already or scratched up, he just destroyed them, further adding it to the pile of junk. Very quickly they were down to having almost a cleaned-out garage.

She stood in the middle of the room. "Just like that, I now know how Penny feels. This space is huge."

He nodded. "Still a lot of stuff is on the walls." He pointed to a bunch of hanging tools and some stuff leaning against the back wall. He looked over at the pallet again and said, "The question is, what will we do with this?"

Chapter 27

Friday Afternoon ...

"I HAVE NO idea," Doreen said. The large pallet was still wrapped in clear plastic. She opened up one of the boxes and pulled out some sort of silver pipe. "Nan said it was all car parts, so I don't know what that means."

Mack looked at that piece she held and whistled. "That's not exactly a car part," he said. "That's a stovepipe for a Harley."

"Stovepipe? How does this hook onto a stove?"

She watched him as he turned it around in his hand and squatted in front of the box. "Okay, so this could be worth some decent money."

"Seriously?"

He nodded. "But you need somebody who knows what they're talking about." He opened a couple more boxes and then said, "I have a buddy who collects and restores old cars and bikes. Let me talk to him." He pulled out his phone and walked out to the driveway.

She busied herself opening the rest of the boxes, but, to her, it was all unrecognizable. The pallet itself was a good four feet by four feet and at least another four feet high.

She turned to find a couple spindles from something and another chair behind it that she dragged out to the junk pile in the grass. She looked around at a collection of brooms and just more junk and said, "What do I do with the rest of this stuff?" She moved something leaning up against the wall, and she realized it was a massive mirror. She cried out softly as she turned it around. Something about it made her think it didn't belong in the junk pile. She stared at it for a long moment, and then she took a picture of it and sent it to Scott. She moved it safely in the back of the garage with a blanket over it until everything was cleaned out but the pallet.

Dusty, tired, but absolutely thrilled to have her garage back and to know the stuff outside was literally garbage, she turned around to find Mack once more buried in the pallet of boxes. "What did your friend say?"

"He's on his way," Mack mumbled as he pulled out more pieces.

She stepped forward and said, "Did you say he's coming right now?"

He looked up at her and nodded. "He is coming right now. And his brother. One handles the bikes, and the other restores cars, so, with any luck, they'll be able to tell us what this is."

"That would be lovely." She shoved her hands in her pockets as she waited, and her fingers came into contact with the laminate stuff she had found at Penny's. She pulled out the pieces and held them in her hand, trying to put them together. She looked down and frowned. Pieced together they looked like a nurse's badge. The metal clip was still attached to one of the pieces. She laid them down on the garage steps. It wasn't a complete badge, and it had been chewed up and blackened in places, but a name was here. *Nancy Cousins.* She took a picture of the pieces together.

Mack walked over and asked, "What have you got there?"

She pointed at the pieces. "Apparently George used to burn garbage behind his house, and he always dumped it where the echinacea plants originally were. Penny was trying to make the corner look better, but the plants weren't doing so well, and, when I dug them up to transplant them, I found a bunch of these laminate pieces."

"The plastic is partially melted, and some of it's quite black," he said, "but it looks like an ID tag for a hospital."

She nodded. "But I don't know how or why," she said.

Mack frowned and said, "I know that name." He stared off in the distance. "I'll check on it. Don't you lose those."

"Do you want them?"

He thought about it and nodded. "Put them in a bag for me, will ya?"

She could hear vehicles parking out front. She looked out into the driveway to see a couple very rough-looking guys.

Mack grinned and said, "That's the brothers."

"Are you sure you should have called them?" she asked doubtfully.

"They're good guys," he said. "Go put that stuff in a bag please, and then come on out. I'll introduce you." He walked out and shook hands with both men. A lot of shoulder slapping was going on as he brought them over to the pallet, pulled out his pocketknife while she watched, and he cut off the rest of the plastic.

She went inside and bagged up the laminate pieces Mack needed. When she came back out again with the bag in her pocket, she found the men exclaiming over the boxes. She stood off to the side and asked, "Is anything there of value?"

The two brothers looked at her, one coming over with his hand outstretched, and said, "You must be Doreen."

She grinned and shook his hand. "What gave me away?"

"How about that big bird on your shoulder? And this handsome fella." He bent to greet Mugs, who seemed delighted to see the man.

She chuckled. "I forget Thaddeus is there most of the time."

"He was on my shoulder not long ago," Mack said cheerfully, "until he pecked me because I wasn't giving him enough attention."

The men just laughed. She looked at the boxes on the pallet and asked them, "Do you know what any of this stuff is?"

"We certainly do," one of the brothers said. "And, if you're interested in selling the whole lot of it, we would be interested in buying it."

She stared at them in surprise. "Wow, okay. That's not what I expected."

One nodded. "They're all parts, original pieces from what we can tell, but a bit of a mismatch, like they're from a parts shop or something going under, where everything was sold off in lots. It does happen on a regular basis," he said, "but, in this case, you've got some decent inventory here."

"The question then becomes," she said, "what's it worth and what would you pay me for it?"

"And, of course, you're wondering if those are two different things, right?"

She laughed. "Well, I admit I'm a little on the broke side, so, if we can do a solid deal, that would be nice."

"We're prepared to give you a fair deal," the taller one said. "What happens is, when we restore bikes, we're always looking for original parts, and sometimes we scour the countryside for them. All of these parts here don't belong on the same type vehicle. So we always need the right parts for each vehicle we work on."

"Ah," she said. She walked over, and they had all the boxes open and laid out in the garage. She shook her head. "None of that looks special to me."

"Don't feel bad," one brother said. "It doesn't look like a lot to most people. But we can probably do a few thousand dollars, if you're interested."

The other brother said, "Absolutely. That's about the right amount."

Doreen looked to Mack, who shrugged before looking over at the brothers. "What do you mean by a few thousand dollars?" he asked.

The two brothers looked at each other and said, "Top dollar would be three thousand, and we'll take it right now off your hands."

Mack raised an eyebrow.

"Don't suppose you can do a dump run as part of the deal, can you?" Doreen asked craftily.

Mack laughed. The men looked at her in surprise. She pointed to the pile of stuff in the grassy area and said, "I have no way to get rid of all that busted-up material."

They took a look and said, "We can take that too. We'll throw it in the back of our truck, put all this stuff inside the truck, and we're good to go."

She beamed. "So three thousand dollars and a dump run. It sounds good to me."

They all shook hands. One of the brothers pulled out a

roll of one-hundred-dollar bills and counted off Doreen's three thousand. When done, Mack threw an arm around her shoulder, hugged her, and whispered in her ear, "Tricky bit to add to the deal but nicely done."

The brothers were already loading the individual boxes into their truck. They had one of those big cab things and it just seemed to absorb the boxes.

She beamed up at Mack. "Hey, once we can get rid of the garbage and the car parts, we can unload your truck and my car into my garage, and we can open the doors to the basement. Maybe move some of that up here."

He groaned and rolled his eyes at that. "I was happily forgetting the basement."

She smiled.

"But, if that's where the money is," he said, "I can't forget about that."

"Well, before that," she said, "let's get rid of all this and the outside stuff."

He nodded. "That's my marching order then," he said. "How about you put on coffee? I'll give the guys a hand loading up everything, and maybe we can get them to give me a hand unloading those workbenches and the tool chests. I'm not looking forward to unloading that sucker."

When she had the coffee on, she stepped out to see all the junk had been loaded, her garage was empty, and the men were cheerfully helping Mack unload the toolboxes and the workbenches. They placed everything neatly, almost identical to the way it had been in George's garage, and then she popped the trunk on her car and started unloading the drawers.

With the drawers in place, the men stood back and said, "Wow, you got yourself a nice little workshop."

She smiled and brought out the pegboards and said, "Not yet but, once I get these hung, then maybe yes. I've got all the tools to hang, and I took pictures to see how it all should be set up."

One brother grabbed a pegboard and said, "We can have these hung in no time. I've even got nails in the truck."

Doreen said, "I've got a hammer. If you can do that, I'm about to pour coffee. I'll bring out a couple cups." And that was what she did. She poured coffee for everyone and brought them out with sugar and cream for the men. She'd chosen the best of the mugs but they were still chipped. The men didn't seem to mind. It took only fifteen minutes, and all the pegboards were hung, with the workbenches below. She stared in amazement. And then she took the tools from the back seat of her car and hung them up. Using the pictures off her phone, all three men stayed long enough to get everything hung until her car was empty. She turned, looked at the guys, and smiled. "Thank you so much," she said. "I had absolutely no idea how I would get all that done."

They shook their heads, and one said, "That's a hell of a deal you got here today. Thousands of dollars' worth of tools are here."

"I know," she said. "Unfortunately tens of thousands of dollars' worth of renos have to be done on Nan's house, so I'll learn how to use some of these tools myself. Not to mention the gardening that has to be done here too."

"Whenever you get ready to hire people to do stuff you can't do, let us know," said one of the brothers. "We have a pretty good network of tradesmen." They tossed back their coffees, handed her their empty cups, shook Mack's hand again, and took off.

Doreen stood there, holding the empty cups and staring at her garage. She looked back at Mack and said, "How the hell did we do that? We went from a garage full of junk to an absolutely fantastic workspace."

He shook his head and said, "Only you. You're the only person I know who could possibly make this happen so fast. Now get into your car, turn it around, and park it inside your garage. It's a much safer way to come in and out every day."

She grinned, hopped into her vehicle, and parked right in the middle of her newly repurposed garage. As she got out, she cried out, "Look. It fits."

He nodded. "It does now." He walked to her car and placed the garage opener that she hadn't seen before on her visor. "Now you can get in and out using this. And to open the door from the inside use the control on the wall beside the light switch." He pointed it out to her.

She beamed and tried it out. "Perfect."

"Except... we have to get some of the furniture out from the basement. There's a lot to move so we might want to get a start on it now. Especially as I don't have to go back to work today."

She groaned, got in her vehicle, opened the garage door and backed it out, and parked it where it had been before. "I think I might need more coffee before we start that."

Chapter 28

Friday Dinnertime ...

I NSIDE, DOREEN PUT on a second pot of coffee. Mack stood behind her and said, "I don't know if you're anxious to get out there and work on that right now, but it is past dinnertime."

She looked at him in surprise. "What time is it?"

He tapped his watch. "It's after six. If we're doing pasta, we still won't be eating until six-thirty or a quarter to seven."

She nodded. "Food then. It should still give us an hour, maybe two hours to haul some of that basement stuff upstairs before I give out completely."

"I noticed you already put some stuff in the living room. Is that for Scott to check over?"

She nodded. "And, so far, it seems to be a bit of a mismatch. I took out what I could, but I can't reach the dresser. It's still in the far back corner."

"I remember that," he said. He pulled out a big pasta pot, filled it with water, and turned it on to boil with a lid on it, then brought out the sauce she had frozen and put it into a pot to warm up.

She looked at him and asked, "Are we having the same

thing as last time?"

"Yep. We need a bit more sauce," he said, "so I'll extend it while the water for the pasta is heating up."

With everything set, he said, "I want to go take a look at what you've pulled out so far."

He walked into the living room, and she stood there, saying, "See? It's just chairs and coffee tables at this point."

He opened the living room door to the basement and disappeared. He came back a few minutes later, bringing up an odd-shaped high-backed winged chair. She looked at it and frowned. "That's odd, isn't it?"

"I've seen them before," he said. "But I don't know if there are more of them. Nan seems to have a group of individual items down there. Hopefully, by the time we get them all out, we'll know what belongs with what, so we can keep like things with like. We need to open up those big doors in the garage too. I can start on that end."

She led the way through the kitchen into the garage, crying out in joy again as she walked into the big open space. She hit the lights, walked over to the double doors, and opened them wide.

Mack stood behind her and whistled. "Now that's a nice set of wide stairs."

She nodded. "That really helps, doesn't it?"

He went down the stairs from the garage side and turned on the lights in the basement, and now they could see the full extent of all the furniture down here. He groaned, motioned at one end of a table, and asked, "Can you lift that up?"

She grabbed it, and together they lifted up a large dining room table, which they upended onto its legs and set it in one corner of the garage. Six trips later, Doreen wiped her forehead and said, "Maybe we should check the pasta pot."

He grinned and nodded. "And you need a break."

She rolled her eyes. "I tell you, since I arrived at Nan's, I've done more physical work than I have in a lifetime."

At that, he burst out laughing. "It's probably good for you," he said.

They trooped into the kitchen. Mack stirred the sauce, added more tomato, some garlic, and she wasn't sure what all else, but it looked like various herbs, and then he added oil and salt to the big pot. He said, "We still have another ten minutes before this thing is boiling. We can do three more trips."

Privately she thought they'd have time for one more trip, but she was willing to give him a chance.

They walked back into the basement, and he said, "Okay, what's next?"

She looked around and said, "A couple really big mirrors are here as well."

Carefully Mack picked up one and carried it up. She picked up a much smaller one and carried it to the garage and then said, "You know what? It's foolish for you to carry stuff that I can take care of. Why don't you carry the bigger stuff because I can do the rest on my own."

He nodded, went back down, and grabbed a matching pot chair to the one they'd seen earlier. As she stood here in the basement, she pointed out a couch. "Looks like it matches the chairs."

He nodded. "Looks like it."

Instead of three trips, they ended up doing five trips before dinnertime. As she carried up yet another mirror, Mack disappeared into the kitchen. Grateful, she followed him to see him adding the pasta to the big pot. "So, do we get to eat soon?"

"A few minutes yet," he said. "Let's take another look in the basement."

The garage was half full by now, with everything well spaced out instead of being stacked on top of each other. Mack and Doreen returned to the basement again.

He looked at a few of the bigger pieces and said, "If we get those up into the garage, that'll give us access to some of these on the side here."

It took several attempts to lift her end of the couch. Then she had to back up the stairs, so he carried the bulk of the weight. They stopped halfway, and then gamely she grabbed her end and lifted it up two more stairs. She shook her head at him. "I'm sorry. This is just really heavy."

"Take your time," he said. "Every step you take, the closer we are to getting it into the garage."

She sighed, bent down, gripped it again.

"Lift with your knees," he warned, "not your back."

She lifted using her quads and found it much easier. She got to the top and backed up slowly through the doors as Mack came up the stairs behind her. When they set it down, she said, "This couch is quite pretty."

"Do you like it?" he asked. "It'd be a bitch to get into the living room, but if that's what you would like there …"

"Not until I hear what Scott has to say," she said.

At that, he chuckled. "Still after the money, are you?" he teased.

"I'm okay with modern furniture that's worth a fraction of what Scott took out of here," she said, "and I don't want anything worth big money with the animals to ruin it."

"Good point," he said, disappearing into the kitchen. He came back out a few moments later while she was still resting and said, "Noodles aren't quite there. Let's get another bit done, then we can eat."

She headed down herself, relieved to see the basement was at least half empty now. "We can probably get another four or five pieces into the garage," she said, "if they're not too big. Maybe we can sort these out here so they're not stacked, and Scott can take a walk through here too."

"Yep, it's a good idea," he said. "Let's see if there's any more of that set."

She pointed out two end tables and said, "I think those belong, if you look at the bases of the feet."

He nodded, grabbed both of them, handed them to her, and said, "You can take those. And a big coffee table is there. I'll grab that." And he carried it up, putting it in front of the couch and the two pot chairs.

She just smiled. "Did Nan really buy all this stuff thinking about me down the road? It just boggles the mind."

"It also means she had an inkling you would need it," he said with a sideways look at her.

"She never really met my ex, but I think she understood from our conversations that I wasn't happy."

"Did she know he was very wealthy?"

"Yes, she did, but she also knew I was on a budget and couldn't spend money on what I wanted."

"And yet, you still had five thousand dollar outfits."

"Yes, but he would instruct me to buy them so as not to feel embarrassed by me at certain events," she said. "But when I gave fifty dollars to an animal charity, he chastised me pretty heavily."

"Wow, what a nice guy," Mack said.

"I know," she admitted. "I argued a couple times, and I did have some spending money I gave them, but it was still nothing compared to the amount he was spending on luxury items."

Finally Mack went back in, checked the spaghetti, returned to the garage, and said, "The water is back up to boil. It's almost done."

She nodded and looked around the garage. "There's a little room here but not a whole lot," she said. Motioning him into the basement again, she noted, "But a fair bit of room is here now." She lifted a couple chairs off another dining room table and set them up so they looked like they were seated at the table and pulled the table toward her so she could set up the remaining chairs on the other side.

"We still have to get the dresser out," Mack said. "That's really not a piece you want to leave down here."

"No," she said. She pointed out a couple big hutches too. "I wonder if they're of any value."

"I don't know," he said, "but I can't even begin to lift those alone. You should also be checking the drawers. Knowing Nan, I wouldn't be at all surprised if they were full. Come on. Let's go eat. We can take another look afterward."

They headed back up, and Doreen was grateful to see him drain the pasta. She cleared off the kitchen table and set two place settings, and very soon he walked over with two plates heaped with pasta and sauce. She looked at it with a happy sigh. "I was dreaming about this pasta ever since you made it the first time," she said.

"You could have used up the sauce anytime," he said.

She shook her head. "Not only did I not know how to warm it up," she said, "I also didn't know how to cook the pasta properly."

He nodded. "Well, then that's my gain tonight." He complained good-naturedly, "I could certainly use a good meal. I feel like you've put my muscles to heavy use today."

She nodded. "So what's with this person on that ID card?" she asked, and he frowned at her.

"I don't know for sure," he said, "but it's a cold case."

Lowering her fork, she said, "Seriously?"

He nodded, his face grim. "But you can't say anything on that until I get a chance to tap into the database and see."

She nodded. "That wouldn't bode well for George if it was cut up and buried in his garden."

"Cut up, burnt, and buried in the garden," he corrected. "But again we don't know anything yet."

She willingly put it out of her mind, for now, and tackled her spaghetti.

Chapter 29

Friday Evening ...

DOREEN STOOD AT the garage door and waved as Mack reversed out of her driveway and headed home. It was past nine. Daylight was well over. He was exhausted, and so was she. But they had the garage full, but not overly so, and most of the furniture still in the basement was set up so they could at least see each piece. She'd taken as many photos as she could, and, in fact, it was probably way too many and would be more of a headache to sort through.

She locked up the external garage doors, happy to see someone had allowed for them to be locked from the inside as well as the outside of the garage. She headed into her house through her kitchen access door. She grinned at the accessibility. As she stepped inside, she locked the side door to her kitchen area and set the alarms in the front and back. She was way too tired to do anything else.

Even her animals were dragging. Goliath had been too worn out by his day to run up the stairs past her, like he usually did to claim his preferred sleeping spot.

Upstairs, she took a look at her bedroom and groaned. "Now if only I had all those willing hands I had today to give me a hand with this stuff." She couldn't believe the stunning amount of work that had gone into accomplishing so much today. It was an incredible feeling to have her garage completely cleared of junk and now stocked the way it needed to be. Granted, it was full of furniture, but that was just temporarily. She didn't know what she would do with all that furniture yet, but she hoped Scott would take a big portion of it off her hands, but he only would if it was high-end stuff. Another antiques dealer locally may be able to help out with what Scott didn't take, and she should probably give Fen another phone call at that point. But, for the moment, she was absolutely thrilled and exhausted.

She looked at her closet and thought, *Why the hell is this project taking so long?* Because she did some, and then she stopped, and then she did some, and then she stopped. It was too late tonight to tackle any of it, but she knew that would be her next big project. She would take everything out of that closet, lay it all on her bed, still a pallet on the floor, and not be able to go to bed until she had it sorted. Especially since she knew more money was to be found there. Somehow, as her pockets had been filled in other ways, and as the antique furniture issue arose, she'd let the treasure hunt in the clothing slide. But she couldn't let that happen forever. Her bedroom was a nightmare. She'd feel so much better when she finally got it organized.

As much as she'd been living here for the last month plus, she hadn't fully moved in. Her clothes were still half lying inside her suitcases, for crying out loud. They needed to be put away. But into what? She had seen some shelves and dressers in the basement that she might use. If they were in decent shape, not antiques, then she'd be more than happy to have a piece or two up here to work with.

She needed something, that was for sure. Most of her clothes weren't hanging pieces, and she needed something for all the leggings and T-shirts and her underwear too. Most of that sat in boxes at the moment. With a shake of her head, she had a shower, lay down in bed, and crashed. But it was a disruptive sleep. She tossed and turned, woke up, groaned because it was just midnight, and then rolled over again.

When she heard something drop downstairs, she bolted upright. Mugs, who'd been sound asleep, jumped to his feet, growled, and raced from the room. Thaddeus, who'd taken to sleeping on the corner of the window ledge—and she couldn't imagine it was terribly comfortable, but she hadn't given him any new roost after taking away the big bed— flapped to the floor and cried, "Intruder, intruder."

She hated to even think of it. *Not again.* She pulled on a pair of leggings over her panties and a sweater over her camisole and quickly slipped on her tennis shoes, then crept downstairs with her phone in her hand. Mugs raced around the living room and headed for the garage door. She stared at the garage door and groaned. Because, of course, the alarm wasn't wired on that side of the house. The kitchen door to the garage had not been accessible before, and the outside door to the garage had been wedged shut too.

With that thought in mind, she worried somebody was after the antiques but had no clue who it could be. And who would even know what she and Mack had done today, except for the two mechanic brothers, and they hadn't been here when she and Mack had hauled a bunch of the antiques up from the basement, unloading them in the garage or her living room.

As she stood in the kitchen, wondering what to do, she thought she saw a shadow at the back door. She frowned and waited. But she saw or heard nothing else. Making a quick decision, she disarmed the security system, and, with Mugs on a leash beside her and Goliath now weaving between her legs, she stepped out on the deck. As soon as the door opened, she saw a shadow run through the backyard to the creek. She unhooked Mugs and cried out, "Go get him."

Mugs ran, and so did Doreen. She had no clue who her intruder was, but she'd be damned if she would let him get away with this. She ran to the pathway heading north and saw the dark figure fighting off Mugs. She called out, "Mugs, let loose." He turned toward her, and the intruder bolted over a fence into somebody's yard. It wasn't high but the bushes around it were dense. Mugs barked at the base of the fence, and Doreen knew, by the time she made it over the fence, if that was even possible, the intruder would be gone.

She swore under her breath and then grinned. She was actually swearing. Not that that was a good thing, but it was definitely a sign of her loosening some from her husband's strict rules. She didn't really want to be somebody who swore all the time, but it was nice to know she could and not be terrified of doing it. She knew that sounded foolish too. But she was working on those issues.

She checked her phone and saw it was only one-thirty in the morning. Back at her house, she walked around to the garage to figure out what was going on. The outside garage door, the little one, looked like it had been opened. Weird. She opened it and stepped inside, turned on the light and could see that a couple of the chairs they had so carefully laid out had been disturbed. Somebody had come in here and either had looked at the pieces or had moved them to get to another piece. Frowning, she checked out several of the items, wondering what was going on.

And then she got an inkling of an idea as to who her intruder was. She matched the smaller shape she'd seen first off to the people she knew. ... She stood for a long moment, wondering about the past few minutes, and then carefully closed up everything and headed back to bed. She was pretty sure her intruder wouldn't break in again.

Chapter 30

Saturday Morning ...

THE NEXT MORNING, she woke after a surprising amount of sleep, had a quick shower, and thought about what she would do next. Mack contacted her at eight a.m. and said, "Garage sales are generally early, so when do you want to go?"

"The sooner, the better. I'd like to be back relatively quickly."

"Okay," he said in surprise. "Do you still want to go?"

She nodded. "Yes, I still want to go. Besides, there aren't very many, are there?"

"I've picked five from the list I found this morning," he said. "Chances are two or three of them will have absolutely nothing, but the others might have something of interest."

"Perfect," she said.

"You sound distracted. Are you okay?" he asked sharply.

She frowned. "Yes. We'll talk about it when you get here. Oh, and, by the way, did you look up that woman's name?"

"I did," he said, his voice suddenly quiet. "We'll talk about it when I get there." And he hung up.

She could hardly be pissed off at him when that was exactly what she had said to him, but, at the same time, it was irritating.

Downstairs, she grabbed a piece of toast, made herself a cup of coffee, wondering if Mack would need one too. At the thought of leaving, she worried that she didn't have a lock on the exterior side door into the garage, nor was there a working lock on the rear kitchen door. It looked to be damaged. She tried to lock it, but it didn't take too much jiggling to make it pop open again. Not liking that at all but having little choice, she propped a kitchen chair under it and then went into the garage and did the same thing. She didn't know if it would keep anyone out, but it gave her some peace of mind.

Mack arrived within a few minutes, but he remained on the porch. She offered him a coffee. He shook his head and said, "Why don't you just bring yours in a travel mug. I'll drive."

And that was what she did, hopping up into his truck. They headed out to the first garage sale. As they parked outside the house, she was amazed to see a good half-dozen people wandering through tables set up outside. She'd never been to a garage sale before, so she was curious to see how this worked.

Mack headed for the tools, and she wandered up and down the tables but didn't see anything of interest. She found everything from Tupperware to odd plates to baby clothes to toys. She smiled when she got to the pet toys, but they'd been thoroughly chewed, and who knew what kinds of diseases they might have. She walked back over to Mack, who was waiting for her. He looked at her with a raised eyebrow. She just shrugged, and he nodded.

He said, "Okay, on to number two."

They hopped back into the truck, and Doreen said, "Are they all like that?"

"Like what?"

"Like people's stuff that they don't want and they're just trying to get rid of?"

He chuckled. "Absolutely they're all like that, but sometimes there are estate sales, where somebody's passed away, and it's left to somebody in the family to empty out the house."

"Oh," she said. "That might be a little rougher. Or better," she added.

"Exactly," he said. "Come on. You'll have a better idea by the time we get through all five."

The second one was very much the same as the first; the third one was different in that it had a lot of high-end dishes and plates and cutlery and pots and pans and stuff. She was itching to buy a bunch, but she really had no idea what she could use or when. Mack, on the other hand, was looking at a huge cast-iron frying pan with a lid.

She studied it and said, "I'm not even sure I could lift that sucker."

He chuckled. "But it's really good for cooking on a fire, and it's good in the oven too." He finally bought it for five bucks. He appeared to be very pleased. He was still crowing about the price when he got into the truck, saying, "That's a steal." He looked over at her. "You didn't see anything you wanted?"

"I did," she said, "but I don't want to fill the house I'm still trying to empty."

"Actually that's very insightful," he said, "because one of the best things you can probably do, once you get the furniture sorted out, is go through all of Nan's cupboards and get rid of stuff. Not just pick and choose but do every corner. That'll help you to make it yours. It'll also let you see any damage on the property that needs to be fixed and help you to move in fully. I'm not trying to move Nan out but just have you acknowledge there'll be a lot of her stuff that you don't want."

Privately she thought that was a wonderful idea.

At the fourth place, Doreen stopped in front of several beautiful blankets. She looked at the price. Mack was at her shoulder, and he asked, "Do you like them?"

"I'm not sure what the winter will be like here, but I like to sit outside in the evening, and I want something to wrap around my shoulders." He helped her shake out a couple of them, and the woman who owned the residence said, "I'm looking for twenty dollars for each of those."

Mack nodded and said, "We don't have that much. How about thirty for two?"

Doreen gasped, wondering if that would fly.

The woman frowned and then said with a shrug, "Sure, why not."

He paid her the thirty and carried the blankets, while Doreen kept wandering around. She was absolutely over the moon. The blankets were cuddly and soft; one was large, one was smaller, and they were gentle colors of a baby blue and a baby green. As far as she was concerned, this made garage sales completely worthwhile. She wandered up and down the rest of it but didn't see anything else she wanted. When they got back into the truck, she grabbed the blankets and pulled them onto her lap. "These are beautiful," she said, "and I do have the money to pay for them."

"I know you do," he said, "because I haven't paid you

for the gardening yet."

At that, she burst out laughing.

He grinned. "One more and then we'll head home."

"Good," she said, "because, even though we got a lot done yesterday, so we're well ahead out of the game, there's still more to do."

"I wanted to take a look in that basement again," Mack said. "I'm pretty sure a couple more pieces matched up. The more we can get to match, the better chance you'll have of selling the pieces."

She nodded. The last garage sale didn't offer anything she was interested in. As they pulled up into her driveway, she hopped out happily with her beautiful blankets in her arms and said, "Coffee?"

"Absolutely," Mack said. They went inside, and he stopped in front of the chairs gathered in the living room. "Two of these chairs belong with the dining room tables we've put out in the garage. I'll just move them."

She heard him and smiled. "Thank you."

He came back a moment later, a frown on his face as he looked to the kitchen door to the garage. "Explain."

She winced. "I had an intruder last night."

"What?" His eyebrows shot up to his hairline. "And you didn't let me know immediately?" he roared.

"Well, I chased him down to the creek and up about ten houses," she confessed. "But, when he went over the fence and disappeared into one of the backyards, I didn't think I could catch him."

He just clawed his hands into his hair, looking like he wanted to pull his hair out in frustration.

She explained. "I think I know who it was, and maybe I know why, but I don't have all the answers. So I'll do a little more digging before I tell you my theory."

His glare deepened.

She tried to glare back. Only his was better. "Besides, do you have some information for me on that nurse's ID?"

He reached into his back pocket, pulled out several pieces of paper, and unfolded them. "She went missing a good thirty-odd years ago," he said. "Her body was never found, and there were absolutely no suspects."

Doreen snatched the pieces of paper from his hand and studied them. "She worked at a clinic on Bernard." She nodded slowly. "Wow, interesting." She sat at the kitchen table, opened her laptop, and brought up the address of the clinic. It wasn't there any longer and was now a pretty rough area of town.

"Because we never found a body," he said, "we don't know for sure that she's even dead, but we assume so."

"So no family or friends had any contact afterward? She just disappeared off the face of the earth?"

"Essentially, yes. She finished her shift at five o'clock that day. She walked home, but nobody saw anything, and she didn't arrive home."

"Wow," she said. "I wonder what went wrong." She stared off in the distance, her mind trying to fit the pieces together, but they weren't fitting. She looked at Mack and asked, "What about Penny's father?"

"It's on the other sheet. Also a strange one. Shot dead in the head on a street. A back alley actually. Again nobody knows anything."

"And we don't know about the nurse, if she was shot either?"

"No, since no body was found." He pulled out a kitchen chair and sat down beside her. "Are you thinking it's the same person?"

She nodded. "I am. I just don't know the motive behind it. Well, I know the motive behind one. I'm not sure about the motive behind the other."

"Okay, that's getting interesting," he said. "You seem to have a handle on cold cases nobody else does, so how the devil do you link these two?"

"Because Randy Foster was at that halfway house down on Bernard," she said. "I wouldn't be at all surprised if he and the nurse worked together, or if she wasn't involved in some way."

"You're saying she might have killed Penny's father?" he asked in confusion. "That doesn't mean it's the same person then, because, if she committed suicide, we would have found her body."

"No, that's not what I mean." She shook her head and looked toward the garage. "Some stuff I still have to go through in my head, but I haven't had a chance yet. I've been a little busy."

He thrummed his fingers on the kitchen table and said, "You're not making sense. You know that, right?"

"I am," she said, "and it will make sense, but ..." She tilted her head at him and said, "Look. Can you give me an hour? Just an hour to sit down, map out some of the stuff in my head, and I'll present my ideas to you. But I don't want you hovering over my shoulder while I do it."

He just stared at her.

"I know. I know. You're the official. I'm nobody. *We don't do this on assumptions. We need evidence.*"

He bolted to his feet, gave a curt nod, and said, "One hour." And he went back to the living room to start moving furniture.

She grabbed the little black book she hadn't had a chance to look at thoroughly and started reading it with a notepad beside her, jotting down notes. She was formulating a pretty strong case, but she didn't understand why the book had been left behind, although it had been jammed in the back of the drawer, so maybe it had been lost for decades. And she had the larger journal George had kept as well. That one showed an unraveling state of mind. She flipped to the last page where he'd written that cryptic message, wrote it down again, and sat back, looking at the pieces. On her laptop, she brought up the picture of where the nurse had worked and wondered what could possibly be the connection. If Penny's father had died immediately from a gunshot wound, then nobody would have needed the nurse's help.

And then ... Doreen knew what it was all about. She sat back and said, "It hasn't been an hour, but do you want to come in?"

He was at her side, glaring at her, his anger vivid.

While he'd been busy moving furniture from the basement to the living room, he'd obviously been getting angrier and angrier.

"I don't have all the answers," she said. "All I have is a working theory. Which means it's an assumption, not evidence," she underlined heavily with her tone. His frown deepened. She rolled her eyes at him. "Open mind, please."

He nodded, sat with a *thud*, and said, "Go for it."

"Penny's father was very abusive. He beat up the family after his wife died, took out his temper on the kids. His son ended up dead. Father did jail time. We know all that, right?"

Mack nodded.

"Penny moved on, married George, probably told

EVIDENCE IN THE ECHINACEA

George, or maybe he already knew about her terrible history and was likely very protective. Then her father gets out of jail and moves to a halfway house in Kelowna because that's close to where Penny lives."

Mack settled back, crossed his arms, and said in a low voice, "Go on."

"I couldn't figure out why the nurse was involved," Doreen said, "but, if you think about it, Penny's father was dangerous. He's only been in jail ten years plus whatever he earned for bad behavior. When he's released, it's not like he's infirm now. It's not like he's elderly. Chances are he's one badass angry male. And he comes to Kelowna to see Penny, who wants nothing to do with him. But what if they could knock him out? They could then kill him."

"Whoa, whoa, whoa," Mack said. "Who is *they*, and how will they knock him out?"

"With the nurse's help," she said.

"No reason for the nurse to help."

"I don't know how that fits in yet," Doreen admitted. "But the theory is, they needed the nurse's help for some reason. Father was in a halfway house, and somehow they got him alone out in the alleyway, and they shot him."

"That's a really big jump right there."

"Let me continue," she said. "Whether this is Penny and George, just George, somebody else in their circle of friends, I don't know. Father is gone. Brother is gone. Penny is married. Soon afterward poor Johnny disappears, and maybe George starts a journal to deal with his feelings. I know that's not a very manly thing to do in some circles, but, ... over the years, maybe there is an unraveling sense of guilt that George has done something terrible, and it's because of him that Johnny went missing."

Mack looked at her, looked at the journal she held, and snatched it from her hand. He flipped through a few pages and said, "Wow."

She nodded. "You can see as you read from the beginning to the end how there's definitely a sense of guilt. George never writes down what he did that was wrong, but … it's clear how he felt. He was afraid his actions may have been behind Johnny's disappearance. As if through some karmic rebalancing. Or as if fate had stepped in and said, *You know you killed so-and-so, so we killed so-and-so in revenge.*"

Mack frowned. "So you think George had something to do with Penny's father's death. Then Johnny gets killed, and George blames himself, and what happens at the end?"

She said, "Honestly, I think George commits suicide because it just got to the point where he was unraveling, and, whether Penny was having an affair or not, as some have speculated, I can't say because I don't know about that. There had to have been some sort of trigger, and it could have just been the passage of time, the accumulation of all that guilt of George's. It could have been mental illness run amok, but George ended up killing himself."

"So then Penny had nothing to do with any of this, and your suspicions were completely wrong?" he asked for clarity. "Because, although suicide is frowned upon in many sectors of society, it's not against the law in Canada. It was decriminalized in '72. And, of course, Penny wouldn't be charged."

"No, I no longer think Penny had anything to do with George's death."

Mack settled back with a sigh. "If George did have something to do with her father's death, we can't prosecute a dead man anyway, so that would mean any murder case would never be closed."

"Well, we're back to that *theory versus evidence* problem again," she said. "I need evidence to make my theory stand."

"I still don't understand how the nurse comes into play."

"I don't either," she admitted. "But she has to. Somehow she has to."

"In what way though?"

"Because that ID card," she said, "was buried right there on George's property. On Penny's property. That is the one piece of evidence we can't argue with. It connects George and, therefore Penny, to the nurse."

Chapter 31

Saturday Morning...

MACK JUST STARED at her, as if his mind was trying to wrap around it. "We have to actually *prove* this. You know that," he said with an attempt at a lighter tone.

"We could talk to Penny."

"She might not even know what George did, if your theory is correct."

"I know," she said. "It's quite possible she doesn't know anything about it. I was worried maybe she had killed George, but, at this point, I think George committed suicide. So maybe let sleeping dogs lie."

He shook his head. "I hear you, but, if we can clear up either of these cold cases, there are families who want to know what happened to their loved ones."

"I know," she said softly. "And Penny, of course, is the only family member left as far as Randy is concerned."

"You don't know anything about the nurse's family."

"Oh, I didn't even think of that," she said. She frowned, looking down at the data sheet. "I do need to understand the nurse thing." She tapped it in confusion. "I keep trying to fit that piece back in."

"Evidence is like that. Some of it fits, and some of it doesn't. Usually we're lucky if we can get eighty percent of it to make any sense."

"Just keep lifting rocks," she said, "and see what nastiness crawls out."

He chuckled at that. "What time is Scott coming?"

"Noon to early afternoon," she said. "I'd like to get the rest of this reorganized and try to match up whatever pieces we can."

"Which I think is a good idea. But you won't let this Penny thing go, will you?"

"We should talk to Penny," she said. "I'm just not sure how to make that happen nicely."

"Nicely?"

She slid a look at him. "I'm pretty sure she was my intruder last night."

He stared at her. "Not if she jumped over a fence, she wasn't."

She frowned at that and nodded. "No, that's a good point." *A very good point.* She sat back and remembered her surprise as the intruder jumped the fence. She sat up straight suddenly. "There were two of them," she cried out. "Because, when I came around the corner of my fence, somebody much bigger jumped over that neighbor's fence. And I didn't realize it at first, but you're right. It was someone else. The hoodie was also darker."

"So now you've got Penny and an accomplice?"

And then she knew who that was too. She nodded, then groaned. "I don't know why, and I don't know how, but it's Penny and Steve."

He raised both hands in frustration. "Okay, now I really don't understand."

"We need Penny to explain it," she said slowly.

"It's hardly like you can go up to her and say, 'Hey, so, did George commit suicide, and did he kill your father, and were you the one who broke into my garage last night?'"

"Right."

"And why would Penny even care about getting into your garage?"

She lifted both books and said, "You've seen this one, but you haven't seen this one."

He looked at her and asked, "Where was that?"

"When I pulled out one of the workbench drawers, it fell to the ground. I pocketed it and didn't get a chance to really look at it until this morning."

He started at the beginning of the little black book and said, "This is from a long time ago."

"I know, and I haven't had a chance to really figure it all out."

He sat back and flipped through the pages, reading every entry. When he got to one, he lifted his gaze and said, "He did kill her father."

"Well, it doesn't specifically say so, but it does say, *Problem solved.*"

He nodded and kept reading.

"You're right though. All the puzzle pieces don't make a whole lot of sense."

"But it does, since it mentions a Nancy here," he said slowly. "George talks about meeting with her." Mack looked up at Doreen. "This definitely connects George to Nancy."

"But why? Was she a victim of Penny's father's? Was she a victim of George's?"

Mack flipped through it all and said, "This is almost a confession."

"I think George wrote it just afterward, just after he had killed someone, and then hung onto it all these years, and it's the part that bothered him. And maybe he lost the book, and that terrified him, thinking somebody would find it. Because, in the other book, he does talk about needing to find something." She held up the journal. "We just don't know what. The older one was jammed in the back of the workbench drawer. Why he kept the nurse's ID, I don't know. Maybe as a reminder of what he'd done? But then, as to why he burned it, well, that's yet another mystery."

"Have you checked through all of George's drawers?"

She shook her head. "I haven't had time."

He stood up and said, "No time like the present."

He removed the chair at the kitchen door and stepped outside. She went first to the drawers where she had found the two books and said, "This is where both of them were." She pulled them out, and pieces of paper, yellowed and old, were in there. At the bottom was one folded up. "It's the death certificate for Penny's father." She laid it down so Mack could see it.

"Cause of death, a single gunshot to the head," Mack read. "It's not out of line that George and Penny would have this. Randy was Penny's father."

And then she picked up another piece of paper, glanced at it, and handed it over. This was a faded purchase record of a weapon.

Mack whistled. "This is a handwritten note—and no names are on it—saying a purchase was made for a revolver," he said. "Even the number on it is hard to read. It's been fading out for so many years."

She nodded and picked up another piece of paper. "I can't really see what this is either."

"No, but it's got Nancy's name on it," Mack said, frowning. He placed it on top of the other paperwork and said, "Why would he have left all this in this drawer?"

"Maybe because he wanted to be caught, to be punished. Maybe he wanted to confess," she said. "He was very religious. This had to eat away at him."

"But then why wouldn't Penny have cleaned it out?"

"I don't think she knew any of this stuff was here. She said this wasn't her world. She never went into the garage, never had anything to do with George's tools."

"So what's this Steve guy got to do with that?"

"They're old friends. And, for all I know, he knew."

"So, what then? They both came back last night looking for it?"

"If he happened to stop by her place and realized the garage was empty, he might very well have told her about the books and the papers. Then they came here after them."

Mack looked at her and sighed. "Some of this makes a crazy kind of sense, but none of it's conclusive."

"I know," she said, "and that's why we need Penny."

Just then her phone rang.

"Doreen," Penny said, "I hope you got everything home okay. A couple documents I need apparently were stored in one of those drawers I wasn't aware of. Do you mind if I come and check the drawers for it?"

"Oh, my goodness, of course not, Penny. Come on by," Doreen said, staring at Mack. "I'm working in the garage myself. We got it all set up again, but I've been moving furniture out of the basement, so I haven't had a chance to go through any of the drawers yet."

"If you don't mind, I'll come now then," Penny said fretfully. "I wouldn't want that stuff to get into the wrong hands. People would get the wrong idea."

And she hung up, leaving Doreen to stare at Mack. "She's coming here for this stuff right now."

Chapter 32

Saturday Late Morning ...

DOREEN LOOKED AT Mack as she put away her phone. "What do we do?

"That's very curious timing on Penny's part," he said, studying the papers.

Doreen nodded. "She also sounded almost desperate."

"I wouldn't be at all surprised."

She straightened up, collecting the paperwork. "Here. You take it."

He accepted the stack. "What will you do?"

She winced. "I want to record the conversation."

"Which you're not allowed to do unless you tell somebody you're recording," he said.

"If you use it as evidence maybe," she said, "but that doesn't mean I can't record. It's not illegal if I don't do anything with the recording."

"True. ... Besides, if the kitchen door is open, and I'm in the kitchen, I should be able to hear," he said. "Then I'll be a witness."

She nodded. "You know what? That might not be a bad idea. You want to go move your truck then?"

He eyed her for a split second, then hopped into his truck, and parked it out of sight. He was barely back inside when Penny barreled around the side of the house, coming from the creek.

When she saw the garage full of furniture, she cried out, "Oh, my goodness."

"Like I said, Nan has been filling the basement for a long time," Doreen said, placing her phone on the workbench, the video on. "How are you? You sounded quite upset on the phone."

Penny nodded. "I'm looking for a book. It was George's. He used to jot his thoughts down sometimes," she said. "I didn't want people to find it and think he'd gone off his rocker."

Doreen motioned at all the drawers. "I just pulled out the drawers. We moved the benches here, and I stuck the drawers back in again. But why didn't you check before you told me that I could take it all?"

"I thought it was in the house," Penny said. "Steve was over last night, and, when he saw everything was gone, he asked if I had taken those books out. I didn't realize what he meant until he explained George's journals were here."

"He knew about George keeping journals?"

She nodded. "Steve is an old friend," she said. "We've known him since we were first married. Maybe even before that. Then there is not much from that time frame I care to remember."

Something about that struck Doreen as odd. "I did hear through the grapevine you had a pretty rough childhood."

"I'd hoped that old gossip had died down," she muttered. "There's rough, and then there's hellish," she said. "Mine was hellish. But, at the end of the day, I stand here all alone with no family except my two daughters, and that's why I'm trying to sell the house—to get closer to the people I love."

"Sorry about that." Doreen nodded. "Hey, take a look and see if you can find what you're looking for."

Penny nodded and began her search.

"Was there anything in the books?" Then Doreen said, "You know what? Maybe that's part of the stuff I took inside." She ran inside, pocketed the small book, and brought the big one back out. "Is this it?"

Penny's face lit up. "Oh my, yes, it is." She snatched it from Doreen's hands, flipped through it, and then clutched it to her chest. "I should have just burned it," she said.

"So nobody would know?"

Penny nodded and then stopped and said, "Know what?"

Doreen leaned against the workbench. "That he committed suicide. That he took one of those lovely plants in your back garden and made himself a strong tea and probably did it consecutively for a few days. I don't know. It depends on which plant he used," she said, her head tilted to the side. "But he did commit suicide, didn't he?"

Penny gasped, and tears filled her eyes. Clutching the book against her chest, she nodded. "I didn't want people to figure that out," she said. "Everybody loved George, and they would look at his memory so differently. Then there's his church," she cried out. "I don't want any of that to get out to the public."

"It's not for me to make public," Doreen said. "As long as nobody killed him, then that's on George himself."

"Exactly," Penny said. She wiped the tears from her eyes. "He really was a good man. He did a lot for me."

"I know," Doreen said, her voice gentle. "And I'm very sorry. I know more than I would like."

Penny froze and stared at her in horror. "What are you saying?" she cried out. "What do you know?"

"I know he killed your father," she said slowly. "I'm sorry about that too. If ever a man deserved killing, it was him."

Penny's jaw worked, but nothing came out. And then she burst into tears. "You have to understand," she said, "when my father contacted me after getting out of jail, I went to pieces. I'd been to hell and back already, but to know he was out and in my life again, I just couldn't handle it. George never told me any details. But he came home one night and just said, 'It's finished.' His tone was so hard, so cold, and just so flat, I knew. I didn't know how, but I knew what he'd done. The next morning, George woke up as if absolutely nothing had happened. And I was so damn grateful for him. I just held him close all night because of what he'd done for me. My father was a really bad man," she whispered. "I was abused sexually, physically, mentally, emotionally all my life after my mother passed. But what he did to my brother," she said, shaking her head, "that was just as terrible, if not worse."

"Is that why you killed him?" Doreen asked, her voice so very soft and gentle. "Is that why you killed your brother? To put him out of his misery because of what your father was doing to him?"

"If he was dead, my father couldn't hurt him anymore," Penny cried out in pain. "My brother suffered so much. He would never have a normal life. He was one step away from being completely mentally incapable. He had brain damage, physical damage, he was emotionally just a wreck. I should have stopped it long before I did," she said, slumping to the floor, her arms wrapped around her knees. She rocked back and forth. "It was a mercy killing of the highest order. At least as long as he was dead, my father couldn't torture him anymore."

"But he found out, didn't he?"

Penny nodded. "Yes, he guessed. He didn't have any proof. But the night my brother died, my father turned on me in the worst way possible, trying to get me to confess, but later that evening I escaped. I crept out to the road, and a neighbor picked me up and took me to the hospital. And that's what started the police investigation. They came to the house, found my brother, accused my father, and he finally went to jail and was out of my life for so long. But when he was released from prison ..." She shook her head. "He told me that he knew what I'd done, and he was back to take it out on me for killing his only son. I told George everything," she said, crying, her body shaking from the horrors of everything she'd kept close to her chest for so long. "And I know George took care of it. You have to understand. George would never let anyone hurt me anymore. I spent the first eighteen years of my life in terror. Once my father was gone, I could finally relax."

"But it bothered George, didn't it? What he'd done? He was afraid what had happened to Johnny was God's retribution—or karma or fate or whatever you want to call it—that somehow George's actions led to Johnny's murder."

Penny dried her eyes as much as she could, but the tears seemed to be pouring in a river down her face. She nodded. "It didn't matter what I said to him. It didn't matter how many times that I told George that it wasn't his fault. He believed firmly he'd brought about Johnny's death. And he found it so terrible to bear."

Doreen couldn't believe it, but, at the same time, she'd already known this much. She crouched in front of Penny and wrapped her arms around her, holding her close. "I'm so sorry. George's actions did not have anything to do with Johnny."

"I know, but George had worked so hard trying to find Johnny to absolve his conscience, and George never did get an answer. And I think, somewhere along the line, he finally gave up. But then that asshole came back into our life," she said. "And that's what triggered his suicide."

"What triggered George's suicide?"

"Hornby," Penny said. "Allen approached George, saying he knew what George had done. And that he was to blame for Johnny's death. George went to pieces, and then he went really quiet again. It was that quiet period that terrified me. Hornby wanted money to keep silent. We didn't have much money, but George paid him. He didn't tell me what Hornby had done until I got a letter after his death, telling me that George had paid Hornby ten grand to keep quiet and to leave. But Hornby came back, and George knew it would never end. And that's when he killed himself. It was just the final straw." She took a huge gulping sigh. "I'm sorry," Penny added, quietly sniffing. "I'm so sorry."

"And that's when you shot Hornby?"

"Not right away," she said. "But I couldn't forget what he'd done to George. ... I was selling my house, and I was moving, and I was losing everything. And Hornby was out here tormenting all these people, bringing up so much nastiness. Then when I realized what he'd done to Johnny ... You hadn't proven it yet, but I knew. Oh, I knew," she said, "and I took the same gun George had hung on to all those years, and I shot Hornby. From the side of the road at the intersection. I just looked at him, and I fired. I knew where he'd be. I'd seen him at the grocery store. And I drove ahead, and I waited. And it was dark out, and I just shot him. Believe me. Nobody was more surprised than I was when I hit him. I didn't kill him, and that's a shame," she whispered. "That man needed to die."

"Which, of course, he hasn't, but he will go to jail for having killed Johnny."

Penny nodded. "And for that I'm grateful. I'm just so damn sad George never learned the truth before he died."

"Maybe you'll get a chance to tell him yourself one day."

Penny sighed and said, "My God, it's been such a long lifetime."

"And you don't get to quit now," Doreen said in alarm. "What about your girls?"

"For them to find out their father was a murderer? And that I tried to kill somebody too? Or helped put my brother out of his misery?" She shook her head. "They're better off not knowing."

"Stop," Doreen said. "You might get a few years. I don't know how the police would handle this, but you'll still have a life afterward, and you'll still have your daughters. You're not that old. You still have decades ahead of you."

Penny just sagged in place as she looked up at Doreen and said, "It feels so much better to have said all that. Yet, at the same time, a part of me really hates you for having done this."

"And yet, you're the one who asked me to look into Johnny's death."

"I know," she said, "but then Hornby said he'd told you that I had killed my husband. I didn't know what to do. I didn't kill George. Please, you gotta believe me." She clutched at Doreen's shirt and whispered, "Please, tell me you believe me."

"I believe you," Doreen said gently. And she did. The ramblings of a tormented mind hadn't left room for doubt. She helped Penny to her feet and said, "I'll have to phone the cops. You know that, right?" She looked at Penny for a long moment, then seeing the resignation in Penny's eyes turned toward the kitchen, but a blow smashed down hard on the side of her head, hit the top of her shoulder, and bounced off again. She crumpled to the floor, crying out. In the background, she could hear Mugs barking and howling.

Penny screamed.

Doreen twisted to see Thaddeus on top of Penny's head, pulling at her hair and pecking at her nose and going for her eyes. Goliath crawled up her back as she hunched over, trying to get away from Thaddeus, and Mugs busily chewed on her ankle. And suddenly the din just got way worse as Mack barreled through the kitchen door into the garage. He brushed all the animals away, turned Penny around, and pinned her up against the nearest wall, her hands behind her back. He turned to Doreen. "Are you okay?"

She groaned and said, "I don't know what she hit me with, but it hurts, dammit." She put a hand to her skull and found blood. She looked at Penny and asked, "Why?"

"Why?" Penny said, her tone irate, no longer any sign of the teary-eyed woman. "Why? Because, if you weren't alive, nobody would know, and this would all go away. And I'd be able to go home and to finally have a few years with my daughters," she cried out. "All I had to do was get rid of you."

"When did you decide that?" Doreen asked.

Penny looked at her and said, "Just now, when I realized

you were the only credible person who still knew anything. And, once you told the world, I'd go to jail for having shot Hornby."

Doreen slowly made her way to stand on her feet. "What about your brother? What about for killing your brother?"

Penny just glared at her. "You don't know anything about that," she snapped.

Doreen tilted her head, looked at her, and said, "You did kill him. So now we know George killed your father. You killed your brother and shot Hornby, and George killed that nurse, which I don't understand."

Penny looked over at Mack and then at Doreen and said, "What nurse?"

Doreen mentioned the name and said, "We found the ID tag in the ground. Actually it was in that echinacea bed at the fence. All the pieces of the ID tag were burnt, as if George had tried to destroy them."

Penny looked at her, and her face crumpled again. "He didn't mean to. He said she was a friend. And he'd been telling her about my father, and she came up with all kinds of solutions for how to kill him. But, after George had done the deed, as soon as the body showed up, the nurse wanted to talk and to tell authorities it was him. She worried about being an accomplice. Thought this would clear her of any wrongdoing. George followed her home one night and just snapped her neck."

"Just like that?" Mack said. "You go from killing one person to killing two?"

"He had to," Penny said. "Don't you understand? He had no choice."

"And you knew about that too?"

Penny nodded. "He told me that same morning."

"What did he do with her body?"

"She's in the lake. Wrapped in old wire fencing, with some big rocks tied around her ankles and her neck and her waist. He didn't want to take any chances. He said he took her out in a small boat and dumped her in."

"And we've never seen any sign of her in all this time?" Doreen asked incredulously. "That doesn't sound normal."

Penny just shrugged. "Who knows? Probably a whole pile of unidentified bodies are coming up from that lake." Doreen looked over at Mack and said, "Are there?"

Mack shrugged. "I don't know about that. I'll look into it."

"Did her body ever surface?" Doreen asked.

"I don't think so," Penny said, "but it wasn't her real name anyway. She was a runaway. She took a different name entirely."

"But she went to nursing school and all the rest. How did she do that under a fake name?"

"Things were much easier back then," Penny said. "Besides, I'm not sure she really was a nurse. George had helped her do something way back when. That's why he thought maybe she could help him this time. But then he didn't trust her."

"Holy crap," Doreen said as she leaned against the workbench. "Is that all you guys think about, killing people?"

"All I wanted was to have a nice peaceful life," Penny cried out.

"And yet, you killed your brother."

"To save him," she whispered. "I killed him to save him."

Unbeknownst to Doreen, Mack had already called the

cops, and they arrived a few minutes later. Mack led Penny to them and explained some of what was going on. The cops looked from an obviously injured Doreen to Penny and asked, "Did you attack Doreen?"

She stared at them defiantly. "She was going to tell everybody. I couldn't let her do that."

The men just sighed and moved her into the back of the cruiser. Mack told them, "I'll be in later. There's a ton of paperwork to do. You have no idea how many cold cases are about to close."

One of the men, Arnold, looked at Doreen, gave her a mock salute, and said, "No, but we're starting to understand," and they took off.

Mack turned to Doreen and said, "Let's get your head checked out."

From her point of view, Mack was growing two heads and turning blurry. "I think I'm better, but I'm getting a hell of a headache."

As she sat in Mack's truck, and he drove her to the ER, Nan called.

"Seriously, Penny attacked you?"

"Hi, Nan. How did you hear the gossip so fast?"

"Arnold's mom had called him at work about something else. He said he was taking Penny into the station and would call her back when he wasn't so busy. After that, it was just easy to figure out."

"I don't know how easy it would be to figure out from that little tidbit, but, yes, she attacked me. I'm heading to the ER to get my head checked, but I'm fine."

"Is Mack taking you?"

"Yes, Mack is taking me."

"Perfect," Nan said. "I'll just up those bets a little bit

more on that relationship thing. You take care of yourself now. Bye." Nan chortled before ringing off.

Doreen put her phone away and said, "Nan is betting on us having a relationship. She thinks the fact that you're taking me to the hospital helps her odds."

"It probably does," he said. "Unless, of course, you want me to dispute that and put a siren on top of my truck and take you in officially."

She looked over at him and grinned. "Can you do that?"

"Absolutely I can do that. But it'll make your head worse."

She groaned at that. "How about we don't?"

"Sounds good to me," he said. "Why don't you just sit there and relax?"

"I can't. I'm still trying to figure out how many cold cases we have involved here. Because we've got Penny's father, and we've got the nurse. But we also have the nurse as a runaway child, and we have to figure out who the hell she really was, and we have the Hornby shooting."

He said, "Not bad, not bad. One of these days, you might make a decent police officer."

She turned to him in outrage. "One of these days?"

He was still laughing as they pulled into the emergency entrance. After parking, he helped her out of the truck.

She stood in the sunshine for a long moment and smiled up at Mack. "You know what? Life's not too bad today."

"You solved an awful lot of cases," he said, "and, even better, you found out that sometimes you're not always right."

"You mean, the fact that Penny didn't kill George?"

"Right, that was just Hornby spreading vicious gossip." Mack led her toward the building. "Let's hope Penny feels like talking when she's at the station," he said, "because we need more details."

"I don't know how interested she's likely to be by the time she gets there."

"If we keep George's role in this to a minimum, it might help," he said. "That seems to be what she was really concerned about."

"I think you're right there," she said. "I guess love really does have no boundaries."

"Exactly," he said with a chuckle. He grabbed her hand and said, "We can carry on with the garage full of furniture as soon as you're all fixed up."

"Sounds good to me."

And he led her through the emergency room doors once again.

Epilogue

Saturday Early Afternoon ...

DOREEN STAYED AT the hospital for several hours, and, by the time she was released, she saw Mack walking back up the front entranceway to the ER. "Did they call you to tell you that I was done?" she asked as his fingers gently pushed her hair back to check out her stitches.

He nodded. "I did ask them to tell me."

"I'm feeling much better. Hopefully Scott will be there when I get home."

"I'm sorry I was detained. I had planned to be here earlier, but, while I was at the office dealing with Penny, something else popped up. We have another case that just came in with footprints, very strange footprints that's giving us a connection to a case from ten years ago."

"Oh, interesting." Doreen perked up.

He shook his head. "No, no, no, it's not a cold case."

"But it is ten years old," she said. "So it's a cold case."

"Nope. Not now it isn't," he said. "It's got nothing to do with you."

She rolled her eyes and said, "Fine, I could use a break. I don't plan on solving footprints in the ferns."

He froze. "Have you heard of the case?"

She tossed a look at him. "What case?"

"A young girl was kidnapped from her bedroom," he said. "And all they left were footprints. Footprints in the ferns outside the house."

Her jaw dropped. "Seriously?"

"Seriously," he said.

She chuckled and then reached up to her head and moaned. "How about you tell me all about it later. I can't wait to figure out why there are footprints in the ferns. But not now."

The truth of matter was, by the time she woke up from a nap, she found herself laying on her bed, the animals curled up all around her, as if understanding how badly hurt she was, and she realized she'd be happy to just have a few days with no case to contemplate. Sure, it was her own fault, and she'd be the first to admit it, but, when things came to a crunch, they seemed to always come to a crunch on her.

Mack was right. She kept getting hurt. She had to figure out how to do these cold cases and close these files without the same ending. The trouble was, when she talked about putting people away for life, not one of the suspects wanted to just walk that path happily. They all tried at the very end to grab that last hope for a bit of freedom. She understood that in theory, but it sucked in real life.

Groaning slightly, she rolled over, spent the next few minutes cuddling the animals, telling them how much she loved them and loved having them in her life. Then her gaze caught sight of the time. It was after two p.m. already, and, as far as she knew, it was still Saturday, which meant Scott should have been here already or would be at any moment. She took a deep breath and slowly sat up. The room spun a little, but it wasn't too bad. At least her head didn't start to boom.

She walked into the bathroom and almost cried out in surprise at her face. She had blood along her temple and something on her cheek, which she scrubbed at. It looked like some sort of medication or iodine. She filled the sink with warm water and, using a washcloth, gently cleaned her hair and face as much as she could.

Somewhat presentable, if she ignored the couple stitches sticking out of her scalp, she changed her shirt to something that didn't go over her head and hopefully wouldn't get more blood on it. Her jeans were covered too. She stripped out of those and put on leggings. Barefoot, she padded downstairs gingerly, then through the kitchen to the laundry room, and loaded up the washing machine, trying to remove any sign of her rough morning. Then, moving carefully, she wandered the first floor. She didn't remember Mack leaving, but presumed he had, as the alarms were set on the doors again. She pulled out her phone and sent him a text, thanking him.

Instead of texting her back, he called. "How are you feeling?" he asked.

"Better," she said. "I'm up. I'm downstairs, and I'll put on a pot of tea."

"What, no coffee?" he asked humorously.

"Nope, not today. My head is aching already. Don't think coffee would improve that."

"I don't think headaches and caffeine have anything to do with each other," he said. "This has more to do with the pry bar you left on the workbench."

"Is that what she hit me with?" she whispered, aghast. "I knew I should have found a place for that damn thing."

"Are you okay to keep all the tools now, after what happened?"

"Absolutely," she said. "It wasn't the tools' fault. Besides, I'll use the tools."

He chuckled. "I guess if I need something, I know who to borrow from."

"Anytime. I don't even know what half of them are called."

"I know," he said. "The irony wasn't lost on me."

"But to think she used one of my own tools …"

"I think she thought it was still hers. And George up in heaven was probably rooting her on."

"I wonder," she said. "From his journal entries, it seemed like he was very much saddened by everything that came to pass."

"You've been asleep for a couple hours," he said, "so don't freak out when you look outside and see cop cars."

"Why are cop cars here?" she asked in an ominous tone of voice.

"Because they have to go through the garage and take forensic evidence. There's your blood and the attempted murder weapon, etcetera."

She groaned and said, "How long before the media finds out?"

"Hopefully not until after Scott leaves," he said. "Any word from him?"

She glanced down at her phone as a beep and a text came in. "I think it's him texting me now. I'll call you back."

She checked the text, and, sure enough, it was Scott. She walked out to the garage and asked the officer, "How much longer will you guys be here?"

Arnold just waved at her and said, "We're almost done.

Why?"

"Because I have an antiques dealer coming to look at this stuff," she said, pointing around the garage. "I need him to have access."

"Not a problem," Arnold said. "How are you feeling?"

"Like somebody hit me over the head with a pry bar." She groaned and glanced around. "And, by the way, where is that?"

"It's got to go in for evidence."

She sighed. "I don't really need it for anything, so whatever." She caught the grin that flashed on his face, but he immediately schooled his features into looking sorry for her. She smiled at him. "I know," she said. "I'm not badly hurt. Besides, it's worth it. An awful lot of people will get some closure now."

"We didn't even know we needed to find closure for some of these," Arnold said with half a snort. "What the hell did we do without your help before?"

She thought she heard a really heavy note of sarcasm in there, but she hoped he didn't mean it because she wasn't feeling well enough to deal with it. "Just so long as you realize I'm not trying to do this."

At that, he burst out laughing.

She glared at him, her hands on her hips. "I don't deliberately walk into dangerous situations, you know."

"Absolutely you do," Arnold said. "And you keep doing it time and time again. On the other hand, the community thanks you. Not one of us would have thought Penny had ever committed murder or even attempted a murder."

"What about George?"

Arnold shook his head. "He was the biggest teddy bear anybody ever knew."

"Which is, of course, why he did what he did," she said gently. "He was trying to protect Penny."

"But the nurse?"

"Once you go down that path," Doreen said, "I guess every other murder gets easier. And, in this case, once again, George was trying to protect Penny. Because the nurse would likely blackmail George or confess and create all kinds of problems."

"So then why didn't George go after Hornby?" Arnold asked. "Just so many unanswered questions."

"George didn't go after Hornby because, I think by then, he was completely wracked with guilt. He knew he was dying, and he was trying to make good so that he could go to heaven," she said quietly. "And knowing he had done so many wrongs, he spent the rest of his life trying to do so many rights. And, when it was about trying to save Penny, it was justified in his mind, but he didn't have any reason to kill off Hornby."

"And yet, Penny had absolutely no problem with it?"

"Well, she blamed Hornby for George's death," she said. "After Hornby had blackmailed George, he got serious about committing suicide."

"Any idea what he used?"

"There are a lot of plants in their garden," she said, "many of them lethal."

Arnold stopped, looked at her garden, and she nodded. "Absolutely. I have a lot of lethal things in my garden too. But so do you, and you don't even know it." She chuckled at the look on his face. She waved her arm at the furniture. "I just need to make sure the appraiser can take a look at this furniture." Arnold looked at the furniture, and she shook her head. "You know as much as I do. For all I know, none of this is worth anything, and it's just great junk. But, until I know, I don't want anything damaged." Thankfully the officers were already packing up their equipment and loading their vehicles. She smiled and waved as they took off, muttering, "I don't have a death wish, you know?"

They hadn't been gone more than a couple minutes as she stood here, her face up in the sun, before Scott drove up in a rental vehicle. He hopped out and said, "Now that's what I like to see, somebody doing nothing but enjoying the day."

She didn't dare tell him about what her morning had been like. "Nice to see you again."

"I hope it's for all the right reasons," he said, rubbing his hands together.

"I don't know," she said. "We emptied the garage of junk and hauled that away, and then we moved up as much as we could from the basement into the garage, but the basement is still full too."

He stepped forward, his gaze going to the set of coffee tables and two pot chairs. His eyebrows rose, and he said, "Well, this isn't quite the same quality or value as the set we already took, but this set will fetch a very nice penny."

She winced. "Could you be a little more specific?"

He chuckled. "I have to go over all the pieces to be sure …" He walked around, counting. "This is, what, one, two, three, four, five pieces here. Two, four, five, six pieces," he corrected himself. "Maybe forty thousand at the end of the day?"

She just stared at him.

He said, "I know that's not as much as you would have liked …"

"It's a lot more than I had thought to get," she corrected.

"So selling this set is an absolute yes."

He nodded. "Good." He took some photos and made some notes. "What else have you got?" He wandered around and said, "This dining room table is easily seventeen thousand. The fact that you have six chairs and original covers on them," he said, "yeah, absolutely. Do you want to sell it?"

"Let me just tell you right now that anything here that you want, you can have if you can sell it for a decent price," she said. "I know some very high-end furniture would easily cost seventeen thousand, but I'm not living at that level anymore. So, if you can get seventeen for this set, please do it."

"Oh, that's what you'll get. We'll probably be able to sell it for twenty-three or twenty-four. Maybe higher."

And, at that, she just wandered behind him as he went through piece by piece by piece. He turned, looked at her with a happy smile, and said, "Well, over one hundred thousand dollars' worth is sitting here in this garage."

"How much?" she whispered.

He said, "One hundred thousand. It depends on what we can do. These are cherry, specially made, and that maker's mark says they were done for a special occasion. I'll find out how and why and for whom, but just the fact that you have all the chairs in the set ... The set almost always had six or eight. You've got six."

"And I can't guarantee that there aren't more in the house or in the basement," she said.

"Good."

After that, she wandered around in a daze as he finished up the garage. Before going down to the basement, she took him inside to the living room and the dining room where she'd stacked up more. He pointed out the two that went with the set.

"Perfect," he said. "We'll take those two as well." He looked at the others, shrugged, and said, "I really don't know what these are, or these, unless we can find a few more pieces of it in your basement maybe."

He took some photos, and, just as she was leading them to the basement, she got a text. She looked at it, and it was Mack. She called him and said, "Hey, Scott's here. We're going through the stuff in the garage and the house, about to take him into the basement."

"Does it look good?"

"No," she said, "it looks freaking fantastic. And I still want to know more about the footprints."

He groaned.

"You know what? I'll just go to the library and waste hours and hours looking this stuff up."

"I'll give you what was released to the press," he said, "but that's it. The child was never found."

"Really? No body?"

"None."

"Then send what you can to me," she said, "and then I'll give you the further details from here, but I've got to go." She hung up on him, and, with Scott's quizzical face, she smiled and said, "Just a case I'm helping the police out on."

She led the way down the stairs to the basement, where the rest of the furniture was stored. Scott stopped halfway down and exclaimed in amazement. She pointed to the far back corner where the tallboy was. "I can't guarantee it's what you're looking for," she said cautiously, "but it may be the same piece that belongs with the set you took out of here."

He beelined for it and stood back several feet, studying it

for a long moment. Then he turned happily and looked at her and said, "And you remember how we checked?"

"I wondered if it might have secret drawers," she admitted. "But I didn't want to try to open them and break something."

Now that they were standing right in front of it, he reached around to the back and said, "I looked it up, and this one is right here." He pushed something on the far back, and, instead of a small drawer, a long, skinny drawer opened from the side.

She cried out as he lifted up a long strand of pearls. She held her hand out for them and stared in amazement. "These are real, aren't they?"

"That, my dear, is not my field," he said, "but they sure look good to me."

"And here is a small note too."

Of course it was in the same feminine handwriting—presumably her great-great-grandmother's. It was a note about when she got the pearls. It was a gift from her husband on the birth of her first son.

Doreen smiled and said, "I'm so grateful you found these drawers. I haven't even had a chance to see what's in the big drawers. We worked all of yesterday and this morning to try to get access to the pieces down here."

Scott looked around and nodded. "I can't believe your grandmother had so much furniture stored away."

"Neither can I." Doreen motioned at the dresser and asked, "Is there a second drawer?"

"There definitely is." He reached around and popped open a similar drawer along the other side.

Doreen smiled when he pulled out a long velvet bag. She held out her hand, amazed to see the dark green velvet. She opened up the end and carefully emptied the contents into her hands. It looked to be a long jeweled necklace. She whispered, "It can't be real. Surely the jewels can't be real."

Scott lifted the strand of green stones and said, "This is a gorgeous emerald necklace."

She looked down at the rest still in her hand. A bracelet and two earrings. She wanted to cry for joy for that connection to her ancestors—more pieces of her family's history. There was also a crumpled piece of paper. She held it up and read it. "For the birth of our first daughter."

He smiled and said, "You don't see gifts like that anymore. Now a wife is likely to get flowers for the birth of a child, but certainly not gems like this."

Doreen smiled, gently placed everything in the velvet bag, and wasn't sure she could sell any of these, no matter the money it might bring her in return. These were part of her family's history, an emotional and happy memory from her family.

Something now very dear to her heart.

This concludes Book 5 of Lovely Lethal Gardens: Evidence in the Echinacea.

Read about Footprints in the Ferns: Lovely Lethal Gardens, Book 6

Lovely Lethal Gardens: Footprints in the Ferns (Book #6)

A new cozy mystery series from USA Today best-selling author Dale Mayer. Follow gardener and amateur sleuth Doreen Montgomery—and her amusing and mostly lovable cat, dog, and parrot—as they catch murderers and solve crimes in lovely Kelowna, British Columbia.

Riches to rags. ... Controlling to chaos. ... But murder ... not this time!

One night 10 years ago, 8-year-old Crystal, vanished from her bed in her parents' house, the only clue a footprint in the flowerbed below the girl's window.

Now that footprint's reappeared, this time at the scene of another crime, and Doreen is under strict orders not to stick her nose into Corporal Mack Moreau's new investigation.

But while Mack is busy with the new case, Doreen figures it can't hurt if she just takes a quick look at the old one. Her house is empty, her antiques removed, and she has time on her hands. She's finished working on Penny's garden and needs a new project to keep her busy – and allow her to avoid the heavy work waiting in her own garden. And with the help of her assistants, Thaddeus the parrot, Goliath the Maine Coon, and Mugs the Basset, soon Doreen is busy navigating the world of pawn shops and blackmail as she looks for clues as to what happened to the girl stolen from her bedroom so many years ago.

Surely, it's not her fault when her case butts up against the new one – is it?

Book 6 is available now!
To find out more visit Dale Mayer's website.
https://geni.us/DMFootprintsUniversal

Author's Note

Thank you for reading Evidence in the Echinacea: Lovely Lethal Gardens, Book 5! If you enjoyed the book, please take a moment and leave a short review.

Dear reader,

I love to hear from readers, and you can contact me at my website: www.dalemayer.com or at my Facebook author page. To be informed of new releases and special offers, sign up for my newsletter or follow me on BookBub. And if you are interested in joining Dale Mayer's Reader Group, here is the Facebook sign up page.
http://geni.us/DaleMayerFBGroup

Cheers,
Dale Mayer

About the Author

Dale Mayer is a *USA Today* best-selling author, best known for her SEALs military romances, her Psychic Visions series, and her Lovely Lethal Garden cozy series. Her contemporary romances are raw and full of passion and emotion (Broken But ... Mending, Hathaway House series). Her thrillers will keep you guessing (Kate Morgan, By Death series), and her romantic comedies will keep you giggling (*It's a Dog's Life*, a stand-alone novella; and the Broken Protocols series, starring Charming Marvin, the cat).

Dale honors the stories that come to her—and some of them are crazy, break all the rules and cross multiple genres!

To go with her fiction, she also writes nonfiction in many different fields, with books available on résumé writing, companion gardening, and the US mortgage system. All her books are available in print and ebook format.

Connect with Dale Mayer Online

Dale's Website – www.dalemayer.com
Twitter – @DaleMayer
Facebook Page – geni.us/DaleMayerFBFanPage
Facebook Group – geni.us/DaleMayerFBGroup
BookBub – geni.us/DaleMayerBookbub
Instagram – geni.us/DaleMayerInstagram
Goodreads – geni.us/DaleMayerGoodreads
Newsletter – geni.us/DaleNews

Also by Dale Mayer

Published Adult Books:

The K9 Files
Ethan, Book 1
Pierce, Book 2
Zane, Book 3
Blaze, Book 4
Lucas, Book 5
Parker, Book 6
Carter, Book 7

Lovely Lethal Gardens
Arsenic in the Azaleas, Book 1
Bones in the Begonias, Book 2
Corpse in the Carnations, Book 3
Daggers in the Dahlias, Book 4
Evidence in the Echinacea, Book 5
Footprints in the Ferns, Book 6

Psychic Vision Series
Tuesday's Child
Hide 'n Go Seek
Maddy's Floor
Garden of Sorrow
Knock Knock...
Rare Find

Eyes to the Soul
Now You See Her
Shattered
Into the Abyss
Seeds of Malice
Eye of the Falcon
Itsy-Bitsy Spider
Unmasked
Deep Beneath
Psychic Visions Books 1–3
Psychic Visions Books 4–6
Psychic Visions Books 7–9

By Death Series
Touched by Death
Haunted by Death
Chilled by Death
By Death Books 1–3

Broken Protocols – Romantic Comedy Series
Cat's Meow
Cat's Pajamas
Cat's Cradle
Cat's Claus
Broken Protocols 1-4

Broken and... Mending
Skin
Scars
Scales (of Justice)
Broken but... Mending 1-3

Glory

Genesis
Tori
Celeste
Glory Trilogy

Biker Blues

Morgan: Biker Blues, Volume 1
Cash: Biker Blues, Volume 2

SEALs of Honor

Mason: SEALs of Honor, Book 1
Hawk: SEALs of Honor, Book 2
Dane: SEALs of Honor, Book 3
Swede: SEALs of Honor, Book 4
Shadow: SEALs of Honor, Book 5
Cooper: SEALs of Honor, Book 6
Markus: SEALs of Honor, Book 7
Evan: SEALs of Honor, Book 8
Mason's Wish: SEALs of Honor, Book 9
Chase: SEALs of Honor, Book 10
Brett: SEALs of Honor, Book 11
Devlin: SEALs of Honor, Book 12
Easton: SEALs of Honor, Book 13
Ryder: SEALs of Honor, Book 14
Macklin: SEALs of Honor, Book 15
Corey: SEALs of Honor, Book 16
Warrick: SEALs of Honor, Book 17
Tanner: SEALs of Honor, Book 18
Jackson: SEALs of Honor, Book 19
Kanen: SEALs of Honor, Book 20
Nelson: SEALs of Honor, Book 21

SEALs of Honor, Books 1–3
SEALs of Honor, Books 4–6
SEALs of Honor, Books 7–10
SEALs of Honor, Books 11–13
SEALs of Honor, Books 14–16
SEALs of Honor, Books 17–19

Heroes for Hire

Levi's Legend: Heroes for Hire, Book 1
Stone's Surrender: Heroes for Hire, Book 2
Merk's Mistake: Heroes for Hire, Book 3
Rhodes's Reward: Heroes for Hire, Book 4
Flynn's Firecracker: Heroes for Hire, Book 5
Logan's Light: Heroes for Hire, Book 6
Harrison's Heart: Heroes for Hire, Book 7
Saul's Sweetheart: Heroes for Hire, Book 8
Dakota's Delight: Heroes for Hire, Book 9
Michael's Mercy (Part of Sleeper SEAL Series)
Tyson's Treasure: Heroes for Hire, Book 10
Jace's Jewel: Heroes for Hire, Book 11
Rory's Rose: Heroes for Hire, Book 12
Brandon's Bliss: Heroes for Hire, Book 13
Liam's Lily: Heroes for Hire, Book 14
North's Nikki: Heroes for Hire, Book 15
Anders's Angel: Heroes for Hire, Book 16
Reyes's Raina: Heroes for Hire, Book 17
Dezi's Diamond: Heroes for Hire, Book 18
Vince's Vixen: Heroes for Hire, Book 19
Heroes for Hire, Books 1–3
Heroes for Hire, Books 4–6
Heroes for Hire, Books 7–9
Heroes for Hire, Books 10–12

Heroes for Hire, Books 13–15

SEALs of Steel
Badger: SEALs of Steel, Book 1
Erick: SEALs of Steel, Book 2
Cade: SEALs of Steel, Book 3
Talon: SEALs of Steel, Book 4
Laszlo: SEALs of Steel, Book 5
Geir: SEALs of Steel, Book 6
Jager: SEALs of Steel, Book 7
The Final Reveal: SEALs of Steel, Book 8
SEALs of Steel, Books 1–4
SEALs of Steel, Books 5–8
SEALs of Steel, Books 1–8

Collections
Dare to Be You...
Dare to Love...
Dare to be Strong...
RomanceX3

Standalone Novellas
It's a Dog's Life
Riana's Revenge
Second Chances

Published Young Adult Books:

Family Blood Ties Series
Vampire in Denial
Vampire in Distress
Vampire in Design

Vampire in Deceit
Vampire in Defiance
Vampire in Conflict
Vampire in Chaos
Vampire in Crisis
Vampire in Control
Vampire in Charge
Family Blood Ties Set 1–3
Family Blood Ties Set 1–5
Family Blood Ties Set 4–6
Family Blood Ties Set 7–9
Sian's Solution, A Family Blood Ties Series Prequel
    Novelette

Design series
Dangerous Designs
Deadly Designs
Darkest Designs
Design Series Trilogy

Standalone
In Cassie's Corner
Gem Stone (a Gemma Stone Mystery)
Time Thieves

Published Non-Fiction Books:

Career Essentials
Career Essentials: The Résumé
Career Essentials: The Cover Letter
Career Essentials: The Interview
Career Essentials: 3 in 1

Made in the USA
Monee, IL
27 October 2023